Closer

By

Heleyne Hammersley

Print ISBN 978-1-912175-67-3

Also By Heleyne Hammersley

Forgotten

Fracture

PRAISE FOR
HELEYNE HAMMERSLEY

Before you know it the slow starter becomes a roller coaster hurtling towards the climax in a whirlwind of events.'

Caroline Vincent – Bits About Books

'A really enjoyable, page-turning read.'

B.A. Steadman – Author

'This book is a great suspense novel, which will make you question your own belief of events.'

Alexina Golding – Bookstormer

'You could say that reading this book is like going on a rollercoaster ride in that there are lots of twists, turns and stomach churning moments.'

Amanda Oughton – Ginger Book Geek

In memory of my mum, Elaine.

1975

*I*t's stuffy down here. Not just hot, but a damp heat like being smothered by a bed sheet fresh out of the washing machine. Except it doesn't smell as nice. It's musty and earthy like old potatoes. The darkness is absolute, and Tracy feels as though she's breathing it in, coating her lungs with blackness each time she inhales. And then, she turns the corner. It's just like her friends described; five feet in complete darkness, a sharp bend, and then, there is, quite literally, a light at the end of the tunnel.

She eases her upper body around into the next section, pushing forward with her forearms against the sandy floor, trying to get her hips through. Her lower back scrapes against the brick ceiling so she dips it further, cramps in her thighs making her cry out. There's nobody to hear her, though. Back in the quarry, which feels like it might be a hundred miles above her, she knows her friends are long gone. She wouldn't have attempted this with them all standing there ready to jeer and call her "fatty" and "lardy bum." She'll prove them all wrong, though.

She tries to back up, but that makes the pain in her back and thighs even worse. If she could just ease herself further forward, she could lie flat and wriggle like a worm, but there seems to be no give in her buttocks or in the bricks that line the tunnel. She's stuck.

The humiliation makes her start to weep, silently at first, but soon, the soft whimpers become drawn-out wails of fear and frustration. It's too late for any of her friends to come back tonight. It'll be dark soon, and the light will disappear, leaving her back in the darkness.

On the surface, the heat builds towards yet another summer storm, and it starts to rain.

CHAPTER 1

2015

'Shit, shit, shit,' Kate muttered as she pushed the pool car up to the speed limit. 'How did they miss her yesterday? What time did they call off the search?'

'When it got dark,' Hollis said in a strangled voice that was a complete contrast with his customary deep tone. He had one arm braced against the dashboard, and the other was wrapped around his seatbelt. 'Must've been about half nine. Can we slow down just a bit, please?'

Kate eased up on the accelerator, and Hollis let go of his seatbelt. 'Look, we don't even know if it's her yet?'

Kate snorted at his misplaced optimism. 'Course it's fucking *her*. What other girls have been reported missing?'

'Even if it is,' Hollis said, 'there's nothing we can do about it now. Let's just get there and see what's what.'

Kate wanted to scream at him. How could he be so calm when a seven-year-old girl was probably floating face down in a filthy pond? Sometimes, life just wasn't fair.

It was just before half past seven when they pulled up at the rusted iron gates that marked the entrance to the quarry. When Kate had lived in Thorpe, the gates had been padlocked shut, but the fence on either side had been riddled with holes and gaps the kids on the estate exploited at every opportunity. Kate had never been interested in playing there; she believed her dad's horror stories of quicksand and black sludge from the steel works that could burn off your skin with a single touch. It hadn't deterred some of her friends, though, who had come back with stories of fantastic finds such as a complete dog skeleton wrapped in carpet or a stack of dirty magazines under a bush.

Now, the rusty metal gates hung open, sagging on their hinges. The chain that held them closed was scarred silver where it had been cut open to allow access to the ambulance Kate could see parked on a patch of high ground. The process of filling in the huge hole in the ground had begun before she'd left, but she hadn't been expecting the final result. Instead of level, flat ground, the whole area was a mass of hummocks and small grassed-over mounds, the grass brown and patchy like the remnants of hair on a balding scalp. She abandoned the car at the gates and set off on foot, Hollis trailing in her wake, and stopped at the blue-and-white tape to flash her warrant card at the PCSO on guard duty.

'How bad is it?' she asked.

He shrugged. 'Didn't look. I don't think I could face her parents if I'd seen the body. I took their initial statements yesterday, and they were in bits. God knows what they'll be like today. The mother was trying to stay optimistic, but the stepdad looked like he was already expecting the worst.'

'You're Rigby? You were at the house yesterday and had a look around.' Kate had read his preliminary report and was surprised the young and inexperienced PCSO of her imagination turned out to be a man of about her own age. He stood smartly to attention, and she could see the bristles of a closely shaved head poking out from beneath his perfectly placed uniform cap.

'Give me a ring,' she said, handing him her card. 'I'd like to have a chat about yesterday.'

'Not much to tell. Me and Tatton responded to the call, did everything by the book,' Rigby said. 'Tatton's FLO trained, so she stayed with them. I ended up joining one of the search teams. I wish I'd bothered to have a look over here, though. Obvious place for a lost kiddie, really.'

It was, Kate thought, *really obvious. So why hadn't Search and Rescue found her yesterday? Or any of the police search teams?*

'All the same, I'd appreciate a chat,' Kate said, heading through the gates. If this was the body of Aleah Reese, Kate wanted as much background as possible, and Rigby should be able to at least give her some impression of the parents.

DCI Raymond was standing next to the forensics van, already clad in protective overalls and nitrile gloves. He was remonstrating with one of the technicians, and Kate could tell from his body language he was determined to make his point. As though sensing the presence of his junior officers, he swung around and caught her with the full force of his frown. 'About bloody time. What kept you? Christ, this is a fucking mess.'

'What's wrong?' Kate asked, reaching into the back of the van for a plastic packet containing overalls and bootees. She checked the size, far too big for her, and passed it back to Hollis, before turning and looking for something smaller. Raymond looked like he was about to burst out of his overalls. He was a big man, and with his huge frame tightly encased in white and his customary flushed complexion, he looked like a retired weightlifter who had quickly gone to seed. His eyes were widely spaced, giving him an innocent, almost childlike look, but the expression on his face was exactly the opposite.

'Him. That's what's wrong.'

He pointed to the ambulance which had been parked about thirty yards away from the van, mindful of the crime scene. The back doors of the ambulance were open, and an elderly man sat on the step, a blanket around his shoulders and a Jack Russell terrier curled up at his feet. The bottoms of his trousers and his shoes were wet, and he was trembling despite the warmth of the morning. He was staring at the ground, seemingly oblivious to the activity around him.

'He didn't?'

'Yes, he bloody did,' Raymond confirmed. 'I thought everybody watched bloody *Silent Witness* or *CSI* these days. You don't mess with the body!'

'He might have thought she was still alive. Have you spoken to him?' Kate asked.

'Don't trust myself,' Raymond said. 'I might want to wring his neck if I get anywhere near him.'

She heard Hollis behind her stifle a snort of laughter at Raymond's outburst, trying to cover it with a cough. She didn't know the DCI very well, but her colleagues had given her a clear impression he was a man who liked the sound of his own voice and believed the louder it was, the more likely he was to get things done.

'Let's go and talk to the dog walker,' she said, turning away from the DCI and making a cutthroat gesture of warning to Hollis.

Please don't let him have handled her, Kate thought to herself as she approached the man in the back of the ambulance. If he'd just pulled her out and left her, there might be something left for the SOCOs to find, but if he'd tried to resuscitate her, the contamination would make their job extremely difficult.

'Detective Inspector Fletcher,' she said, holding out her hand. 'Are you the one who found the body?'

The old man looked at her hand then up at her face as though he wasn't sure what would be an appropriate response. He leaned over to pat his dog who rolled onto her back inviting more attention.

'Bessy found her,' he said, ignoring Kate's outstretched hand. 'We don't usually come up to the pond because she likes the water, and if she gets in, I have a job getting her out. You never know what's in it over here, so I try to keep her away.'

He scratched the dog's stomach.

'I let her off the lead this morning, though. It was early, and there wasn't anybody else around, so I thought she'd be fine and stay with me. She ran off when we got to the top here and started barking. She's not really a yappy dog, are you, Bess? So, I came up to see what was up. Then, I saw her. Rang 999 and asked for an ambulance and you lot.'

'Did you touch the body, Mr…?' Hollis asked.

'Garrett. Jack Garrett. I'm sorry. I know I should have left her, but I had to know if she was still alive. I called Bess away, and when she wouldn't come back, I waded in a bit and grabbed her, and then, I caught the sleeve of the… you know…' He waved a hand in the general direction of the pond. 'I pulled her out as gently as I could and just left her on the edge of the water. I didn't touch her after that.'

'Right,' Kate said. 'That's been very helpful, Mr Garrett. We'll need to take a swab to get your DNA, just for elimination purposes. I know you thought you were doing the right thing.' She tried to sound sincere, hoping he wouldn't hear the irritation in her voice. Too many investigations were messed up by well-meaning members of the public. Raymond was right: there were enough police shows on television nowadays; you'd think people would know.

Bess sat up and gave a cautionary woof, and Kate turned to see a huge, bald man approaching the ambulance. He strode across the grass, as though on a parade ground, and his khaki jumper and camouflage trousers added to the effect.

'Ken Fowler, Search and Rescue. And before you ask, I've been cleared to be here. The PCSO on guard let me through. I met him briefly, yesterday,' the giant said, extending his arm further so Kate could shake his hand. 'I just heard you've found the missing girl.'

No thanks to you lot, Kate thought. *They may be volunteers, but you'd think with all that training and with us directing them… How the hell had they missed her yesterday?*

'Dog walker phoned it in,' she said. 'Would've thought that somebody from your team would have spotted her yesterday. Assuming somebody checked the pond and didn't just phone it in so he could get away for an early tea.'

'It was checked.'

Something about Fowler's size made Kate instinctively want to trust him. He looked safe and reliable in his work boots and practical trousers. She put his age at about sixty.

'You can vouch for your team? Somebody definitely looked at this pond?'

Fowler nodded, keeping his eyes fixed on Kate; a challenge. He had the slightly squashed looking features of somebody who had done some boxing in his youth, and his upright posture and straightforward manner suggested ex-forces.

'Who did the search? Specifically, who looked in this pond and didn't see a dead girl?'

He frowned. 'I did. She wasn't here last night.'

'Right,' Kate nodded. 'And you're absolutely sure? You checked before the search was called off for the day?'

'I checked over here yesterday afternoon and last night sometime between nine and ten. She wasn't there.'

Kate considered apologising for her belligerent manner, but Fowler didn't look offended; he looked like he'd been expecting her to challenge him. Either he was a convincing liar or the girl had been dumped in the pond overnight, sometime between the end of the search and Garrett's unpleasant discovery.

'You came here twice?'

Fowler shrugged. 'It seemed an obvious place to look. I went around the whole area twice in case she hadn't been here the first time but had decided to hide out later on. I didn't miss her. She wasn't here.'

'The team's ready,' Hollis said from behind her. He'd wriggled into his overalls and was snapping latex gloves on. 'You might want to get kitted up.'

She opened her plastic package and turned towards the pond, feeling Fowler's eyes on her back as she grappled with overalls and gloves. *Strange man*, she thought. *Very intense*. She pulled on the protective suit and forced her sweating hands into gloves before covering her hair with the hood and heading back to the pond. The area had been cordoned off with blue-and-white tape, and stepping plates had been laid in place to form a path to the edge of the pond where the body lay. Kate approached, glancing at the water. What she saw didn't compute in her brain for a few seconds; it wasn't as deep as she'd been imagining. She could clearly see the muddy bottom, barely three inches below the surface, and there was little vegetation surrounding the edges, as though the soil was too contaminated to allow anything to take root. The water was flat-calm, mirror-like, but it bore no reflection of the horror of the girl's death. Instead, it showed a moving image of lazily drifting clouds.

This wasn't an accidental drowning, Kate was sure. The girl had either been held under the water until she drowned, or the body was dumped here after her death. She turned her attention to the body to confirm her impressions; this was clearly a crime scene. Kate had no doubt this was Aleah Reese. She was lying on her front, facing away from Kate; her hair was darkened by the water, but it was obviously blonde, and the jeans and hoodie matched those described by Jackie Reese in the statement Kate had read the day before.

This was the part Kate hated. The watching and waiting. She had to let the SOCOs do their job, but it always took forever, and she could have no part in the examination of the girl's body. Their first job was to study the body *in situ*. Kate watched as photographs and measurements were taken, including the depth of the pond at the point where the body had lain in the mud. Raymond watched each part of the operation with hawk-like focus – he wouldn't allow anybody to miss anything – until it was time for the recovery. One of the SOCOs knelt on the ground near the dead girl, put out a gloved hand, and gently turned her over onto her back.

'Oh, shit,' Hollis said from behind her, as the face from the photo Jackie Reese had sent them yesterday came into view. 'It is her, then.'

Kate closed her eyes, imagining having to break the news to Jackie and Craig Reese.

'Shit,' Hollis said again. 'What the hell…?'

The girl's hands were tied in front of her with bright yellow cord.

CHAPTER 2

2015

'Here drink this, love.' Craig Reese placed a steaming cup of black coffee on the table in front of his wife. 'Can I get you some toast or something? You need to keep your strength up.'

Jackie shook her head. 'I'm not hungry.'

Craig sat down at the opposite side of the table, feeling useless. She didn't want him here; she barely seemed to have noticed him since Aleah went missing, and he knew she blamed him for not keeping a closer eye on her daughter. He also knew if he eventually told her the truth, she wouldn't want anything to do with him.

The woman he'd married was nowhere to be seen in the person who sat across the table. Jackie looked much smaller than she had yesterday, her tiny frame swamped by her fluffy, white dressing gown – a birthday present Aleah had helped him to pick out. He'd tried to persuade the girl that white was impractical and would get dirty too quickly, but she'd insisted, telling him it would make her mum look like an angel. This morning, it made her look like a melting snowman, her features sunken and blurred by lack of sleep.

'Where did you go last night?' she asked, taking a swig of coffee. She wouldn't look directly at him, her eyes flitted from the table-top to the door as though she was expecting her daughter to walk in and demand a bowl of cornflakes. Her lack of focus made lying easier.

'I couldn't settle, so I went out looking for Aleah. Just wandered around the estate for a bit. No sign, though.'

Jackie nodded, accepting his explanation. 'Anybody else about?'

'Saw a police car; they'd obviously had somebody out all night, just in case.'

Another nod.

'Time is it?' Jackie asked.

Reese tapped the screen of his phone. 'Just after eight. The policewoman from yesterday's here. Time to start looking again.'

Jackie sighed heavily, close to tears. 'She's not coming back, is she, Craig? She'd have been here by now, if she'd just run off. Somebody's taken her.'

Reese reached across the table and covered one of Jackie's hands with his own. This time, she didn't pull away, allowing him to comfort her as she sobbed quietly. He hoped she wouldn't feel the tell-tale trembling as he kept his arms wrapped tightly around her. Jackie could never know he'd lied to her. He'd rung his dad the previous evening and explained the situation, and his dad had sworn to keep his mouth shut. As long as nobody else had seen him and put two and two together, he'd be fine. His story made sense, so why would anybody even think to question it?

Kate pushed the car door open and stepped out of the air-conditioned chill into the late-morning humidity, sweat prickling the skin of her face within seconds. She scanned the street looking for changes. The houses were much as she remembered though. Regimented, red brick made from clay hewn from the quarry she'd visited earlier; it was like the houses and walls belonged to the earth and might one day return to it. There was one huge alteration to the skyline. One which Kate had been expecting but one that shocked her much more than the grassed-over hump which had once been the biggest clay quarry in Europe. The pit had gone. The winding gear that had dominated the view from her bedroom window had been demolished. Where it once stood was an absence like the gap of a missing tooth in a familiar smile.

Kate knew it had closed down; they'd all closed down years ago. "Unproductive" or "not profitable;" the ideas of economics condemning generations to the realities of unemployment. She was glad she'd been long gone by then – she hadn't had to witness the decline of the place first-hand.

Hollis led the way through a rusting, wrought-iron gate, which left flecks of black paint on her damp hands as she closed it behind them, and up a steeply stepped garden path to the back door. It opened before they had a chance to knock.

'Detective Inspector Kate Fletcher,' Kate said, stepping forward. 'This is DC Dan Hollis.'

The police officer who had opened the door smiled at her as though she was salvation. 'I'm PC Tatton, the FLO. Have you found her?'

Kate nodded and put a finger to her lips to prevent Tatton from asking anything else. The woman's face quickly transformed from an expression of excited optimism to sorrow as she realised the implication of what Kate had just said and done. Tatton led them through to the kitchen where Jackie Reese was sitting at the table and Craig was hovering near the sink, both studying the screens of their mobile phones.

Kate immediately found them an unlikely couple. Reese looked like an overgrown student in his baggy hoodie and skinny jeans, and she could see he was a few years younger than his wife. The flesh around his wide, blue eyes was barely bothered by wrinkles and his dark hair was thick and unruly. His high cheekbones and slightly flushed cheeks gave him a slightly androgynous look she knew a lot of women would find attractive. She wondered what he'd seen in Jackie, who looked thin and haggard, almost skeletal, as she sat hunched across the table, dark eyes deeply set in her worn face and grey roots just starting to show in the parting of her dyed black hair.

'Mrs Reese?' Kate said, trying to get Jackie's attention. 'I'm Detective Inspector Fletcher, and this is Detective Constable Hollis. We need to ask you a few more questions about Aleah.'

Jackie finally looked up. 'You've found her, haven't you? They wouldn't have sent you two if it wasn't serious. You've got some news.'

Kate nodded. 'We think we've found your daughter, Mrs Reese. I'm sorry, it's not good news.'

Jackie leapt up from the table. 'God, I don't know what I was thinking. No manners, that's me. Can I get you a cup of tea? Coffee? There's bread, if you want some toast, or eggs or something.'

Hollis gestured to Reese to go to his wife and try to get her to sit down again, but as Reese tried to put his arms around her, to guide her back to the chair, she slapped him away.

'Not now, Craig, I'm busy. Do you take sugar?' She smiled at Kate, nearly convincing, but her eyes were frightened and bright with unshed tears.

'Jackie,' he begged. 'Come and sit down. We need to hear what they have to say.'

She collapsed into his arms, the sudden surge of energy spent as abruptly as it had appeared. He hauled her back into her seat where she sat, staring at the table-top, refusing to acknowledge the presence of the two detectives.

'Mrs Reese,' Kate started again. 'Does Aleah ever play over the road, where the quarry used to be?'

'She's not allowed over there,' Jackie said, without looking up. 'She knows that. It's not safe. I told you, she's a good girl; she wouldn't just go off for no reason.'

'Has she ever said anything about playing there?'

'She does go wandering off sometimes,' Reese said. 'One of the neighbours told me our Aleah had been over there with one of her friends. I think it was that Bailey lass.'

Jackie smiled. 'That'll be it, then. It's one of her friends, trying to get her into trouble.'

'Do either of you go over there at all?' Kate asked.

Jackie shook her head.

'How about you?'

Reese looked confused as though he had been asked a complicated question and wasn't sure of the correct answer. 'I sometimes use it as a shortcut,' he said eventually. 'It's a quick way over to my dad's. Saves going up through the village.'

'Mr Reese,' Kate said. 'Have a seat.' She pointed to the chair next to Jackie and then sat down opposite them both.

'We've found the body of a girl in the pond on the old quarry site. She fits Aleah's description.'

Reese grabbed his wife's hand and looked at her as though waiting for her to respond before he dared to say anything.

'Our Aleah's a good swimmer,' Jackie said. 'It can't be her. She's been swimming since she was eight months old. I took her to the baths. Made sure she wasn't frightened of water. It's important they learn young.'

Kate could hear she was babbling, delaying the inevitable. 'It might not have been an accident, I'm sorry,' she said. 'The pond's too shallow to swim in.'

Jackie Reese began to wail as she took in the implications of the words "not an accident." A high-pitched keening came from between her clenched teeth, and she started to rock backwards and forwards.

'Is it her?' Reese asked. 'Is it our Aleah?'

Kate nodded. 'We think so. We'll need formal identification though.'

'So, you're not sure?'

'As I said, we'll need somebody in the family to formally identify her.'

Jackie was shaking her head, refusing to accept anything the two detectives were saying. Reese tried to keep hold of her hand, but she pushed him away.

'This is your fucking fault!' she yelled. 'You were supposed to be a dad to her, to look after her, and what do you do? Nothing. Fuck all! Letting her roam the streets, when there's all sorts out there. And you know it. That's why you went back out last night to look for her. Guilty conscience.'

'Please sit down, Mr Reese,' Kate said. 'DC Hollis and I would like to ask you a few questions, if you don't mind. It might help us to establish a timeline. You told the PCSO who first interviewed you Aleah had gone out to play. Did she often play out in the street?' Kate asked.

Reese reddened, and Kate mentally filed away his inability to meet her eyes and the way his index finger started to drum on the table-top. It could mean nothing, but it was different from his demeanour a few seconds ago.

'I told her to go out,' Reese said, dredging the words up from somewhere deep inside himself. 'If I'd just let her stay in and watch CBBC, she'd still be here. I just needed a break from those bloody stupid cartoons.'

Kate noticed his wife had removed her hand from his fist. He obviously wasn't the only one who thought he was to blame.

'What time was this?' Hollis asked.

'About half past eleven. I thought she'd just go in the garden and play on her trampoline, but when I came in here to get a cuppa, she wasn't there. I looked in the front garden and then went out onto the street. There was no sign of her. I rang a couple of her friends. Nothing.'

'The friends would be Evie Moran and Lucie Bailey?' Hollis asked, reading the names from his notes taken from the initial statement Reese had given the day before.

Reese nodded. 'I rang both their mams. Both girls were at home, and they hadn't seen Aleah.'

'What about neighbours? The people next door?'

Reese shook his head. 'Next door is in Whitby, and there was no answer on the other side. They're new. Only moved in a few weeks ago.'

'So, who else did you ring?' Hollis prompted.

'Mrs Moran, Mrs Bailey, Jackie's mum, and my dad,' Reese counted on his fingers as he listed names. 'And then Jackie.'

Hollis consulted his notes. 'PCSO Rigby, who took your initial statement doesn't mention you rang your father. Did you tell him that?'

'I don't know. I must have. Or maybe I missed Dad off the list. I don't know. I was in a right state.' Another defensive blush.

'What about Aleah's father? Could she have gone to visit him?' Hollis asked.

Reese shook his head. 'Jackie never hears from him. Hasn't done for years.'

'Useless waste of space,' Mrs Reese interjected. 'Buggered off up to Scotland somewhere when our Aleah was a baby and not so much as a birthday card since. Never sent a penny for her. We don't talk about him. As far as she's concerned, Craig's her dad.'

Tatton placed two cups of tea in front of the parents and raised her eyebrows enquiringly at Kate and Hollis. Kate shook her head before Hollis could respond, and the woman retreated, trying to be unobtrusive as she leaned back against the sink. Kate felt for her. It was a crappy job being with the family when somebody had gone missing, and it usually only got worse when they were found. Tatton would be up to her neck in the investigation while trying to support the family.

'Right,' Kate said. 'We'll need names and phone numbers for Aleah's friends' parents and for your family. While DC Hollis gets those from you, would you mind if I had a look at Aleah's bedroom?' Kate stood up, allowing the parents no room to refuse her request.

'What for?' Mrs Reese asked. 'There's no point.'

'I know,' Kate said gently. 'But there might be something in her room which might give us a new lead. A picture, a book, something that seems familiar to you but might stand out to me.'

The woman stared at Kate for a few seconds as though deciding whether to grant her an audience with minor royalty, and then saw the wisdom in letting a fresh pair of eyes have a look around.

'Last door off the landing. Don't touch anything, and don't make a mess. I want it just like she left it.' Her voice cracked on the last word, and she started to sob as the enormity of her daughter's absence washed over her again.

From the directions, Kate knew which room would be Aleah's – the small one at the front of the house. The layout of the Reeses' home was exactly like the one she'd grown up in. Out of the kitchen, down the hallway towards the front door, stairs on the right, sitting room on the left. She counted them as she climbed, knowing there would be twelve, just like in her dad's house.

At the top of the stairs, the toilet had been knocked through to the bathroom instead of being the two separate, claustrophobic spaces Kate remembered. Back bedroom next, exactly where her own had been, then the main front bedroom, and finally, the "box" room. The smallest one in the house, the room Kate's sister, Karen, had occupied until they'd moved further south when Kate was sixteen and Karen was fourteen.

There was nothing on the door to show it was a little girl's room. No poster, no little porcelain plaque like the one an auntie had bought for Kate which announced the door was the entrance to "Kathryn's Room;" Aleah's bedroom door was just like the others. But inside was clearly a girly place. A single bed occupied the length of one wall, neatly made with a *Frozen* duvet cover. Above the bed were posters of Justin Bieber and a boy band Kate didn't recognise. A bedside table held a night light and a pile of books – Jaqueline Wilson, Enid Blyton, and Beatrix Potter. Nothing unusual.

Kate stepped over to the desk which was littered with pencils, crayons and papers covered in drawings. Picking up the top one, she recognised Aleah's mother sitting at the kitchen table smoking an oversized electronic cigarette. Another was the view from the bedroom window. Underneath were a series of pencil sketches on smaller pieces of paper, street scenes and faces, some of which were quite sophisticated for a seven-year-old. She turned one over. A betting slip. A quick flick through the others revealed all the pencil sketches had been drawn on the back of betting slips from the bookmakers in the village. Kate slipped her phone out of her pocket and took photographs of the pictures and of the reverse side of one to record the address and phone number of the bookies. A quick glance in the small chest of drawers added nothing of interest to her search, so she headed back across the landing.

Hollis had finished collecting the information they needed when Kate returned to the kitchen. He was standing at the sink with PC Tatton, drinking a cup of coffee and discussing a mutual friend in hushed tones. The Reeses were still at the table, mugs of tea forgotten as they sat in identical poses of grief, elbows on the table and heads in hands.

Mrs Reese looked up accusingly as Kate pushed open the door. 'You didn't touch anything, did you?'

Reese's hands jerked out from under his chin, and he knocked one of the mugs, sending a river of tea across the table. His wife didn't seem to notice as she stared back down at the table-top.

'Mrs Reese,' Kate said. 'It's important we establish all the facts surrounding Aleah's disappearance. Can you tell me where you work?

'I… er… what do you want to know that for?'

'Just routine,' Kate reassured her.

'At the doctor's surgery. I'm a receptionist.'

Kate nodded. 'And you, Mr Reese?'

Craig Reese shifted in his seat as though it had suddenly grown too hot to sit on. 'I'm not working at the minute. I got laid off when the tyre place in Doncaster shut. Can't find anything else.'

'So, neither of you have ever worked in the bookmakers on Main Street?'

Both parents shook their heads.

'Only, I noticed a lot of Aleah's drawings were done on the back of blank betting slips.'

Mrs Reese jumped to her feet, grief replaced by a blazing anger. 'Craig, you bloody bastard! You said you'd stop.'

She began slapping him round the head, and he raised his hands to protect himself.

'They're not mine, Jackie. Bob gave them to her. I told him once she likes to draw, and he gave them to me in the pub. Said he had a spare pad with an old phone number on it, and she could have them.'

'Fucker,' his wife hissed and stormed out of the kitchen.

'They're all blank,' Reese yelled after her. 'You can check.'

Kate nodded to Hollis. Time to go.

'I think we need to give you some time,' Hollis said, turning to rinse his coffee cup in the sink. 'We have everything we need for now. Please let PC Tatton know if there's anything else you think of that might help us. Or if there's anything you need to know. Somebody will contact you about the identification.'

Reese nodded and slumped back in his chair.

As the FLO followed them to the door, Kate turned to her. 'You missed the betting slips, Tatton.'

She looked startled. 'What?'

'When you looked upstairs. Thought you'd have spotted them.'

'I didn't look. Rigby took a statement and did a preliminary search before he rang it in. He didn't mention it to me. I took on the FLO role. I'm trained.'

'You're doing a good job,' Kate said. 'Keep them calm. Give them somebody to talk to, to yell at if necessary. And listen to them. Let me know if either one of them says anything that doesn't tally with their story. Anything at all.'

'Well, that was interesting,' Hollis said as he slammed the car door closed and stuck the key in the ignition. He'd obviously decided it would be safer if he drove after Kate's performance earlier.

'In what way?'

'Craig Reese seemed very uncomfortable.'

'A lot of people feel uncomfortable around us, and he's just been told his stepdaughter is dead.' Kate said. 'What were you getting from him?'

Hollis frowned, thinking. 'He's not telling us the truth about something. I'm not suggesting he did anything to the kid, but his story of where he was when she went missing seems to make him a bit fidgety.'

He jiggled the front seat, trying to get enough room for his long legs. Kate watched, trying not to smile. In the close confines of the car, he was all elbows and knees, reminding her of a marsh-wiggle from one of the Narnia books she'd read as a child. The carefully styled blond hair and soft hazel eyes didn't quite fit with the image, though.

'So, what do you propose?'

'I think we need to check again with everybody he said he rang; uniforms doing the door-to-door can check to see if anybody remembers him knocking at the other houses on the street. We need to check times and find out exactly what he said.'

Kate grinned. 'Couldn't agree more. Let's have a look at that list.'

Hollis passed her the notebook, flipped open to the appropriate page. It was a short list. Two family members and two friends of the missing girl.

'Shouldn't take long,' Kate said. 'The two friends live up near the shops. Then, we can head up the village to call in on Reese's dad.'

Hollis laughed and pulled away from the kerb. 'You got a map in your head?' he asked with a grin.

'No,' Kate said. 'I know the area.'

'Really?' Hollis looked like she'd just told him that she had webbed feet. 'I thought you were from Cumbria.'

'I've been up there for twenty years. But I was born here. In fact, I was born over there.' She pointed to a house on the corner of a cul-de-sac. 'Never thought I'd come back, though,' she muttered to herself.

CHAPTER 3

1984

'Kathy! Kathryn! You're going to be late. And give your sister a shout.'

Kathy spat toothpaste into the sink and stuck her head under the tap to get a mouthful of water. She didn't care if she was late. She didn't care if she didn't go at all. School was crap. It wasn't the lessons, or even the teachers, they were okay. It was the other stuff. Ever since the strike, school had been more of an ordeal than an education. She couldn't make anybody there understand. It wasn't her dad's fault; it wasn't his decision.

'Come *on*, Kathy!'

A quick swipe of a towel around her mouth and she left the bathroom.

'Oy, Kaz, you lazy git!' she yelled in the direction of her sister's bedroom door.

Karen poked her head round the jamb, hair still sleep-ruffled, and mouthed "fuck off" at her older sister.

'You coming to school?' Kathy asked.

Karen shook her head. 'Got period pain.'

'Again? You had period pain last week.'

Karen shrugged and closed the bedroom door. Kathy grabbed her school bag from the foot of her bed and raced downstairs, narrowly missing crashing into her father who was standing in the sitting room doorway, scowling.

'Where's your sister?'

'Poorly.'

'What now? Headache? Flu? Yellow fever?'

'Period pain.'

Kathy knew that "women's troubles" were the one thing guaranteed to ensure her father asked no questions; she and her sister exploited his embarrassment whenever the opportunity arose. He had done his best with "the girl stuff" after their mother had died, but he'd had to summon his sister to explain the facts of life, and she was of the "curse" generation. It had taken a few months for Kathy to fully understand what was really happening to her body – with a lot of input from her friends. She didn't want Karen to have the same experience she'd had, so she'd been thorough in the information she'd given to her little sister.

Her father grunted, but she could see he wasn't convinced. This was the third time in two weeks Karen had decided to skip school, and Kathy was beginning to wonder if she was being bullied by some of her supposed "friends." They were an unlikely bunch of thirteen- and fourteen-year-olds from different backgrounds – Karen was the only one whose father worked at the pit, and Kathy knew how much trouble that could cause.

Deciding not to get involved, for now, she slung her schoolbag over her shoulder and went to open the back door.

'Breakfast, Kathy?' her dad asked, pointing to the kitchen table where he'd laid out a mug of tea and a slice of toast with jam.

'Not hungry. I'll get something at school.'

His expression softened. 'You have to eat, love,' he said, and she felt a tug of guilt. He was genuinely worried. 'It's a long time 'til your dinner break.'

'Longer than you can imagine,' Kathy mumbled, closing the door behind her.

She knew her dad was doing his best, and she was old enough to realise it wasn't easy raising two girls on his own. His sister had offered to move in and help out after Mum had died, but her dad wouldn't accept her help. Sometimes, Kathy wished he had, though. It would have been good to have another woman around, especially when Karen was growing up and asking questions. She'd only been six when their mother had died and hadn't really understood what was happening, so nine-year-old Kathy had been the one to explain cancer and death, even though she was struggling to come to terms with the unfairness of having her mother snatched from her at such a young age. And now, she saw herself as a surrogate mother to her younger sister, despite there being only three years between them.

There was a bit of sniggering and muttering when she got on the school bus, but not as much as usual. Kathy risked a glance towards the back seat and noticed Sharon Carter was absent from her customary corner by the window. Her friends were doing the usual nudging and whispering, but it was all a bit half-hearted without their glorious leader. Kathy ignored them and sat in the first vacant seat she could see, close to the front and near where the conductor normally stood. Being close to an adult usually stopped the other girls from bothering her in the morning, and this bus ride promised to be a bit more tolerable due to Sharon's absence.

Kathy hopped off the bus as soon as it pulled up outside the school gates and ran inside to put her books in her locker. If she could get to her form room a few minutes before registration, she might manage a peaceful morning; the other kids only tended to bother her in the fifteen minutes or so before school, and then, lessons gave her a reprieve until break. She saw the corridors were fairly empty, and there was nobody lurking in ambush in the fifth-year area; hardly anybody seemed to even look at her as she fumbled in the pocket of her blazer for the key.

Bending slightly, she opened the door of her locker, intending to dump the books for her afternoon lessons inside, but there was a piece of paper on top of the books she'd left there the day before – a sheet of lined A4 folded in half so it would still be thin enough to fit through the gap between the top of the door and the metal locker housing. It was common to pass notes in this way, Kathy had done it lots of times before, but recently, she hadn't been the recipient of any invitations or bits of juicy gossip. All the notes she'd received were malicious, threatening, or insulting. Sighing, she opened this latest one.

It was even worse than she'd been expecting.

CHAPTER 4

2015

It was past 10pm when Kate pushed open the door to her flat. She and Hollis hadn't found out anything useful from the Reeses' neighbours, and they'd not been able to find George Reese either at his home or in any of the pubs and clubs in Thorpe. A quick call to Jackie Reese's mum revealed she was on her way to be with her daughter and had nothing to say to the "fucking useless" police. They'd decided to call it a day after that.

They'd dropped the pool car back at Doncaster Central, and Kate had driven her Mini back to her "executive apartment" just off Town Field. The flat was a bit more expensive than she'd intended when she'd moved back to the area, but as soon as she'd seen the views, she had decided it was worth it to have the sense of space and openness in the middle of a large town.

It was totally different from the house she'd shared with Garry in Kendal – a new build in a tiny cul-de-sac on the edge of the town with fantastic views across to the southern Lake District fells. It was much smaller and with no outside space, unless she counted the two-foot ledge surrounded by bowed, wrought-iron railings outside her bedroom window, but it was hers. She didn't have to accommodate somebody else's tastes, needs, or mess.

There was a pile of junk mail waiting in ambush on the hardwood floor which she quickly scooped up and threw onto the hall table where her answer phone was blinking a warning. She tapped "play."

'Hi, Kate, love…' Garry's voice sounded more whiney than usual, his nasal tones accentuated by the metallic digital reproduction. At least he'd followed her instruction to never call on her mobile, unless it was an emergency – the last thing she needed at work was a call from her ex. Kate hit "delete." She wasn't interested in anything he might have to say, especially if it was about his new baby daughter and his not-much-older girlfriend. She'd been stupid to offer to stay in touch with him. At the time, she had thought it was the mature thing to do. But it had just opened her up to more of his shortcomings. Now, a father again at nearly fifty and shacked up with a twenty-year-old hairdresser, he still found plenty to complain about; Kate really didn't want to hear it.

Slipping off her work shoes, she padded into the small kitchen in search of sustenance. She'd not managed to eat since grabbing a quick sandwich from a supermarket at lunchtime. Opening the fridge, she considered her options: two-day-old pizza, an out-of-date pasta meal, and a packet of ham. She grabbed a two-pint milk carton from the fridge door and rummaged in one of the cupboards for the box of cornflakes she remembered buying a few days ago. A quick sprinkle of demerara and she was heading to the sitting room like a teenager sneaking a midnight snack.

She'd angled the sofa to face the largest window in the whole flat, the one that looked out over the field towards the town centre. At this time of night, if she turned the dimmer switch to its lowest setting, she could see the lights of the town across the inky expanse of Town Field like a giant UFO perched on the edge of a Midwest cornfield. It wasn't a busy view; there were no roads, and the flight path from Robin Hood Airport passed to the back of the flat. It was almost like looking at a blurred photograph or an artist's impression of a night-time cityscape.

She'd just picked up the spoon when the first sob wracked her whole body. She'd known it was coming, and she'd been relieved she had managed to get all the way home without breaking down in tears. It had been a truly shitty day. Seeing Aleah's body had been the worst of it, then dealing with her parents, but another part was being back in Thorpe after so many years. Driving along familiar streets, noting the changes, but being shocked by familiarity at every turn, had been emotionally exhausting, and she'd known for the last few hours her feelings were waiting to ambush her. At least she'd held it together in front of Hollis. She'd rather he thought she was a hard-faced bitch than an emotional wreck.

She'd never expected to come back – even after the divorce. Twenty years on the Cumbria force had convinced her she would retire there, maybe buy a little house on the edge of the Lakes, and spend her retirement walking the fells that had been the backdrop to many of her most interesting and challenging cases. Bloody austerity! She held George Osborne personally responsible for her transfer. She still felt like screaming when she remembered Colin Bland telling her she was too young to retire, but there was no room for any more detective inspectors on his patch. Her transfer to South Yorkshire was meant to be a promotion, but earlier that day, standing a few yards from the house where she'd been born, it felt like a backward step, not a demotion exactly but somehow retrograde.

Wiping her eyes on her sleeve, Kate took a deep breath and dug into her "dinner." She was halfway through the bowl of cereal and thinking she ought to check her email when her phone pinged with a text. Hollis.

George Reese was in bookies when A went missing. With Craig!

'What the fuck?' she asked as soon as Hollis answered his mobile.

'He's just turned up at his house. PCSO took a quick statement. He's paralytic. Reese, that is, not the PCSO.'

'Don't tell me we can afford surveillance on subjects of minor interest these days? What was the PCSO doing outside Reese's house?'

'He wasn't,' Hollis said. 'A concerned neighbour rang the police when Reese started trying to kick her door down. Looks like Reese had lost his key and needed somewhere to spend the night.'

'Where is he now?'

'Local nick, sleeping it off.'

'Have you phoned it into Raymond?' she asked.

'Yep. He wants us to pick up Craig Reese first thing in the morning and find out why he's been telling us porkies.'

'Not tonight?'

'No point, we won't be allowed to question him overnight.'

'Right. I'll meet you back at base at seven. We'll go and get him.'

Hollis's instincts had been right, Kate thought, Craig Reese did have something to hide.

She stacked her bowl and spoon neatly in the dishwasher, had a quick shower, and went to bed, running through the questions she'd like to ask Reese in the morning.

Kate hated interview rooms in the summer. They were bad in the winter when they were invariably cold due to countless attempts at cost-cutting – including only heating the interview rooms when they were being used with heaters that took an age to cut through the icy air. But in the summer, they stank. It was mostly BO, but underlying that, was the smell of the rubber tiles on the floor as they heated and gave off a rancid, chemical smell. The air didn't move – even when somebody came in or left – and there was always a lingering odour of stale cigarette smoke, despite the ban that had been in force for years.

She took a deep breath as she pushed open the door to the room where Craig Reese had spent the best part of an hour waiting for her to start the interview; an hour in which she and Hollis had compared notes and devised a strategy. Nothing as simple as "good cop/bad cop," though – this needed a lot more finesse. They weren't sure whether Reese knew that they'd noticed Jackie's throwaway comment about him being out somewhere the night before they found Aleah's body. He'd not mentioned it so far, so it was going to be their trump card.

He looked up as she followed Hollis into the room. His eyes were resigned, defeated, and Kate could see giving him time to stew had made him submissive rather than inducing the aggression that some people needed to vent when they'd been left alone with no idea what the police were thinking. Reese wasn't going to attack.

'Do I need a solicitor?' he asked, looking from Kate to Hollis. 'Am I in trouble?'

Kate sighed theatrically. 'That depends. Are you ready to tell us the truth about what happened on Tuesday?'

Reese nodded eagerly. 'It's all my fault. I can't believe I didn't keep an eye on her. Fucking stupid. All for a quick bet.'

His eyes were tearing up, but all Kate felt was disgust. A girl was dead, probably murdered, and this piece of shit was sitting here feeling sorry for himself.

'Let's start at the beginning,' she said. 'You're not under arrest for anything, and we won't be recording this conversation. At the moment, you're helping us with our enquiries and not under caution, so you are free to leave at any time. Do you understand?'

Reese hung his head, greasy hair falling across his eyes as he nodded once.

'Good. Right, Craig, where were you at around 11am on Tuesday when Aleah went missing?'

'At the bookies,' Reese mumbled.

'That would be Allan's bookmakers on Main Street?'

Reese nodded.

'You previously stated,' Kate slid a piece of paper from the slim cardboard folder Hollis had brought with him, 'you'd sent Aleah out to play because, and I'm quoting, "I couldn't stand listening to any more of those bloody cartoons." Is this correct?'

'Yes.'

'But this statement wasn't accurate?'

Reese shook his head. 'No.'

'So why don't you tell us what really happened yesterday?'

Reese took a deep breath and fixed his eyes on a point on the wall behind Kate's head, unable to meet her eyes. 'I got a phone call from my dad at about half ten. He'd got a good tip from somebody who worked at Doncaster, at the race course. I'm a bit skint at the minute, and a good win would have helped Jackie with the bills and that. So, I took Aleah with me up to the bookies.'

'Which way did you go?' Hollis interjected. 'Did you go across the old quarry land?'

Reese shook his head. 'No,' he said. 'I walked down the hill to the main road and went up to the village that way.'

'And Aleah walked with you?'

'Yes.'

Kate pretended to consider this for a minute. She wanted Reese to think she didn't believe him, to get him to add more desperate detail to back up his story.

'She was with me, I swear,' he said. 'We passed an old school mate of mine, Darren Thomas, you can ask him.'

'We will,' Hollis said, his tone grim. 'So, you got to the bookies, what then?'

'I went inside to meet my dad.'

'With Aleah?'

Reese hesitated, and Kate could see him trying to work out which was the safest answer. Children weren't allowed in bookmakers, but she had a hunch the rules might have been waived for Reese.

'She came in with me. I know she's not supposed to, but Bob turns a blind eye. She just sits in a corner and reads or does a bit of drawing.'

'So, the betting slips in her room weren't given to you at the pub?'

Reese shook his head. 'Bob gave them to her the last time I went in to put a bet on. Said they'd keep her busy.'

'So, you lied to your wife?'

His expression became even more desolate. 'I suppose.'

'So, if Aleah was with you in the bookies, how did she disappear?'

'I sent her outside.' Reese said. 'I didn't have enough money for a decent bet and my dad couldn't lend me anything, so I wanted to ask Bob for credit. I didn't want Aleah to hear.'

'So, you told her to wait outside?'

'No, I gave her fifty pence and sent her off to the shop for some sweets.'

'And that's the last time you saw her?'

Reese nodded, his eyes suddenly brimming with tears.

'The last time you saw Aleah was when you sent her off to the shop?'

'Yes,' Reese said. 'Bob wouldn't take my bet, so I went back out to look for her and she'd gone.'

'You do realise,' Hollis said, his voice toneless, 'you've wasted a lot of time and resources. If you'd told the truth, we might have found Aleah on Tuesday.'

He didn't say "alive," but the implication was clear. Kate cleared her throat, hoping Hollis would take the hint and rein it in a bit; she could sense he was growing increasingly irritated with Craig Reese, and it wouldn't help any of them if he lost his temper. They didn't want Reese too defensive at this stage.

Reese stared at the table-top. 'Can I get a glass of water?' he asked. 'It's a bit hot in here.'

'Do you need a break?' Kate asked. 'Toilet, fag?'

Reese looked up at her gratefully. 'Please. I've been stuck in here for ages.'

'Okay,' she said, standing up and picking up the folder of notes. 'I'll send somebody in to show you where you can get a drink and have a cigarette.'

She left the room with Hollis in tow, trying to work out where to go next. Reese was being cooperative, but as soon as they shifted focus to his whereabouts on Tuesday night, she expected him to clam up, unless he had a damn good explanation.

'Let's grab a coffee,' she said to Hollis. 'Regroup.'

Doncaster Central was a fairly new building, and the designers had obviously decided police personnel would appreciate a good view when they found time for grabbing a quick coffee or a bite to eat. The canteen took up half of the top floor, three storeys up and flanked on three sides by floor-to-ceiling windows which afforded the diners views across the town. It was more like a viewing deck than a functional space.

Kate pushed open the swing doors, which always reminded her of a hospital with their port-hole windows, and pointed to a corner table. 'I'll get the drinks. White, two sugars?'

Hollis nodded and pulled out a chair.

The canteen was quiet; the breakfast rush a memory of bacon smells and empty cereal packets, and lunch was still an hour or so away, so Kate didn't have to queue. She took advantage of a minute of time to herself to consider their approach to Craig Reese. Hollis was getting a bit frustrated and wanted to push on with the interview, but they had agreed to take it slowly, earn his trust, and then, ask him about Tuesday night. She was worried Hollis was losing focus on that objective.

She grabbed the two mugs of coffee, took them over to the milk and sugar station, and studied the view out over the museum. The squat building was mostly hidden by trees in full foliage, but the breeze afforded her occasional glimpses of the swirl of block paving which flagged the approach to the main entrance. She remembered a visit there with school when she was eight or nine, a winter trip with a frigid picnic in the park before the coach took them home. The only exhibit that stuck in her mind was the beetles, massive examples of stag beetles, longer than her hand, which reminded her of something Doctor Who might have to tackle on a remote planet. She shuddered at the memory.

'Too much history,' she muttered to herself, tearing open sugar packets and pouring them into the two drinks.

'Right,' she said, plonking a mug in front of Hollis and causing a tiny tsunami of coffee to spill onto the table. 'Regroup time. How do you think Reese is feeling at the minute?'

Hollis shrugged. 'Hard to tell.'

'If he had nothing to do with her disappearance, then he's grieving. Don't forget Aleah was his stepdaughter. And he's frightened. We've caught him out in a lie, and that makes him vulnerable. And if he did harm her, then he's going to be panicking.'

Hollis wrapped both hands round his mug, as though he needed the warmth of the hot drink, and studied its depths. 'Have I done something wrong?' he asked.

'No, not at all. But I think you're getting a bit ahead of yourself. Accusing him of not cooperating and insinuating Aleah might have been alive if he'd told the truth could make him defensive. We don't want him defensive, we want him biddable, willing to tell us everything, so when we do ask him about Tuesday night, it'll be obvious if he's lying.'

'Do you think?' Hollis sounded sceptical.

Kate took a long drink of her coffee before she answered. Hollis still had a lot to learn, but he was quick and keen. 'You lead the next session,' she said. 'I think he's getting a bit wary of you. Be gentle, encouraging. Don't let him think you're disgusted with him for lying.'

'But I am. The girl's dead, and she might be alive if he'd told us the truth straight away.'

'I know, and he knows as well, believe me. But keep a lid on it. Show some sympathy, encourage him to open up. We'll show him his dad's statement, and then, you ask about Tuesday night.'

Hollis shook his head. 'Why don't you do it? I just want to punch him.'

Kate laughed, surprised at the younger man's sudden anger. 'We both want to punch him, Dan. We want to punch most of them most of the time. The real skill is reining in that energy and using it to your advantage. You up for it?'

The DC nodded. 'Is this a teaching moment?' Hollis asked, with a sudden grin. 'Are you mentoring me?'

'Now I want to punch *you*,' Kate said. 'Come on, drink up and let's get back to it.'

The stale cigarette smell was stronger when they returned to the interview room. Reese was standing opposite the door, leaning against the back wall. A PC was standing next to the table, and the two had obviously been chatting as Reese's facial expression was open and unguarded. The change when Kate beckoned him over to a chair was like a sudden cloud passing over the sun on a bright day. His eyes deadened, and his brows straightened into a faint frown. Kate crossed everything that she'd got this right and that Hollis was up to the job.

'Feeling a bit more comfortable, Craig?' Hollis opened.

Reese nodded.

'So, can we pick up where we left off? You went outside the bookies to look for Aleah. Tell us about that.'

'I went to the sweet shop,' he began, his voice low and uncertain. 'She wasn't there. I asked the girl behind the counter if she'd seen her, and she said she'd bought a couple of small packets of Haribo and left.'

'So, what did you do next?'

'I walked up and down the street a few times, thought she might have gone in a different shop, but there was no sign of her, so I went back to the bookies. My dad was still there, and I told him Aleah was missing. He said she'd probably gone home, and I should go back and see if she was there.'

'And that's what you did?' Kate wanted clarification. At some point, Reese had asked his father to corroborate a lie, and she wanted to be clear exactly when this had happened.

'Yes. I kept an eye out on the way, in case she was having a slow walk back, and then, I looked around at home.'

'You looked around, where?'

'Her bedroom, the garden, the shed. I was panicking a bit by then.'

'So, you phoned her friends and your wife?' Hollis prompted.

'I think so. I phoned Lucie's mam and then Evie's. Then, I rang Jackie and Jackie's mam and dad.'

Kate nodded as though she approved of what he'd done to find his stepdaughter. 'And you phoned your father,' she said.

Reese blushed. 'I phoned my dad and asked him not to tell Jackie I'd been to the bookies. I know I told you I'd phoned to ask if he'd seen Aleah, but that weren't true. I just didn't want Jackie finding out what I'd done.'

'And your dad said that he'd lie for you?' Hollis's tone was neutral.

'Yes.'

'So, you called Jackie, and then, you called the police? Is that right?'

'Yes.'

'Right. Two police officers came to the house, and you told them what you've told us, apart from the bit about being in the bookies?'

'Yes,' Reese admitted miserably.

Hollis slid a piece of paper out of his folder. 'This is a statement from your father that he signed this morning when he'd sobered up. Have a read and tell us if you agree with his account.' He placed the sheet in front of Reese who stared at it for a second before he dragged it closer and began to read. He nodded and slid it back.

'You accept what he's told us? It's accurate?'

'Yes.'

Hollis placed the paper carefully back in the folder, leaned forwards across the table and, using his arms to support his head, folded his hands beneath his chin. Kate could almost hear him thinking about how to approach the next part. He was half smiling, as though he was pleased with what Reese had said. Reese looked unhappy but not at all defensive.

'Where did you go on Tuesday night, Craig?' Hollis asked, his tone conversational.

'Wha– why…?' Reese stammered.

Got him, Kate thought. He hadn't been expecting that at all, and Hollis's calm manner had lured him in completely.

'Tuesday night,' Hollis repeated. 'You left your house. Where did you go?'

Reese looked at Kate, trying to understand what they wanted from him now, but Kate just raised her eyebrows and shrugged, letting him know she thought Hollis was asking a reasonable question.

'I went to look for Aleah,' he said.

'Where? Where did you look?'

'Just around the streets and that. Not far.'

'How long were you gone for?'

Reese's eyes flicked backward and forward from Kate to Hollis. 'I'm not sure. An hour?'

'And that was your sole purpose in leaving the house, to look for Aleah? And you stayed on the estate?'

Reese hung his head, defeated. Kate had sensed from the beginning he wasn't the type to stand up to hours of questioning – there was something a bit pathetic about him, like a puppy who just wanted to please its owner.

'I went to see if I could find my dad. I needed to make sure he'd back up my story to Jackie. I went up to his house,' Reese admitted.

'Why not just ring him?'

'I tried. He wasn't answering. He said yesterday he was going to the club, and I thought he might have had a few too many and fell asleep when he got home.'

'Which way did you go?' Hollis asked, and Kate wanted to give him a pat on the back. He knew exactly what to ask, and he was staying calm, reeling Reese in again.

'Over the quarry. It's quicker.'

'Did you go near the pond?'

Reese shook his head.

'You didn't go to the pond? You seem very certain about that. Were you not tempted to have a look around, just to see if you could find Aleah, be a big hero and bring her home?'

'She wasn't at the pond that night,' Reese said.

Kate sat up straighter. Was he about to confess? Had he kept her somewhere else and dumped her later in the night when his wife was asleep?

'How do you know if you didn't look,' Hollis pushed.

'There was a bloke there. Search and Rescue. I saw his Land Rover at the gates when I went through the fence. Wanted to know what I was doing, so I told him I was Aleah's stepdad, and I was having a look around. He said he was looking for her as well. He'd just checked up by the fence and at the pond, and there was no sign of her.'

Fowler, Kate thought. The man she'd seen earlier, the one who had told her he'd checked the pond last night. Could he have been dumping the body and wanted to keep Reese away? A bit unlikely, he had a good reason to be there, and he'd admitted it to her without being prompted. Worth checking him out, though.

Hollis was taking notes, writing down details of the conversation Reese claimed he'd had. 'And this would have been at what time?' he asked.

'Probably between half nine and ten. It was starting to get dark.'

'Can you describe the man you spoke to?'

Reese's description fitted Kate's memory of Ken Fowler exactly, down to the close-cropped hair and huge hands. Reese might be a bit of a numpty, but he was an observant one.

'And after you spoke with this man, where did you go?'

'My dad's. I knocked, but he wasn't in. So, I went home.'

Hollis nodded and finished scribbling. 'And that would have been what time?'

'Dunno. Half ten maybe? Jackie was in bed. The doctor gave her something to calm her down, and it knocked her out. I don't even know if she heard me come back.'

So, nobody to confirm when Reese had gotten home, Kate thought. And only Ken Fowler to confirm the story about being at the quarry. If Jackie Reese was doped up to the eyeballs, as Reese claimed, then he could have been out half the night, and she would have been clueless. She glanced at Hollis, hoping he was thinking roughly the same thing. It was time to wind this up, let Reese go, and perhaps find Ken Fowler for a quick chat. Hollis caught her eye and her intention.

'Right, Craig,' he said, closing his folder. 'We'll get your statement typed up and then send somebody along to get you out of here. We'll probably need another chat, so expect us to be in touch. And I'm sorry about Aleah. Go home and be with your wife.'

Reese's eyes filled with emotion as he looked gratefully at Hollis. He'd clearly been keeping a lid on his emotional state, but Hollis's kind tone had pierced the wall his feelings were hiding behind, and the whole thing was about to come tumbling down. Kate didn't want to be there to see it. She stood up and left the room, desperate for fresh air and another coffee.

It was going to be a long day.

CHAPTER 5

2015

Kate's phone beeped when she was halfway up the stairs to the canteen. She was tempted to ignore it until she was fully re-caffeinated, but there was a chance it might be news about Aleah Reese's post-mortem, and she didn't want to miss any details. It was from an anonymous number.

In Doncaster this afternoon. Can we meet? Drew Rigby. PCSO.

'Shit,' Kate sighed. She'd forgotten about her conversation with him the day before, and it looked like she was going to be too busy to see him. As she studied the screen, trying to decide how to respond, another text pinged in, this time from Raymond.

Team meeting, five mins.

Just enough time to grab a coffee and head back down to the incident room.

Raymond had already started his briefing when Kate pushed open the door to the small meeting room on the first floor. Hollis was there, leaning against the back wall, and the other two members of her small team, Cooper and Barratt, were sitting at the oval desk. A detective she didn't recognise was sitting opposite Barratt. The DCI looked up as she found a seat and balanced her mug on the table in front of her. He looked tidier and less flustered than when she'd met him at the scene the previous day, and he'd put on a clean suit and shirt – obviously, this was intended to be a formal occasion. She half expected him to make a sarcastic comment about her being the last to arrive, but she was well within the ten-minute deadline, and he clearly wasn't in a petty mood.

He'd started by putting information on the whiteboard which dominated the wall at one side of the room. Aleah's school photograph, the same one Jackie Reese had given to Rigby, was in the middle with lines radiating out to other pieces of information. One of these was another photograph. The girl's body beside the pond. Yet another photograph was a close-up of the hands, bound loosely with yellow cord.

Further lines led to the names of people who had been interviewed. A vertical line had been drawn down the board to separate the diagram from a handwritten timeline starting with Aleah being with her stepfather at 11am and ending with the discovery of the body. Reese's evidence needed to be amended to support his recent statement.

'Fletcher. What did you get from Craig Reese?' Raymond asked without preamble. He stood, poised next to the whiteboard, marker pen in hand.

Kate gave him a brief outline with times and potential witnesses, and Raymond used the side of his hand to scrub out the false information and replace it with the most recent.

'Right, good. We need to check up on this Darren Thomas, see if his story corresponds with Reese's. Got details?'

Hollis opened his folder and read out an address and phone number.

'Right, Fletcher. Send somebody in your team to find this Darren Thomas and check Reese's statement with him. We also need to find Ken Fowler, check he saw Reese last night and told him to stay away from the pond.'

One of Kate's DCs raised his hand.

'Yes, Barratt?'

'Might Fowler have wanted Reese to stay away so he didn't see the body? Is there anything to suggest Fowler had checked the pond, apart from what he told Fletcher this morning?'

Raymond glanced at Kate, eyebrows raised as if to ask, *Well?*

'Not yet,' Kate said. 'He told me he'd checked twice yesterday. Reese and Fowler seem to alibi each other at the moment. Somebody needs to talk to Fowler.'

'I think you just volunteered yourself.' Raymond grinned.

Kate suppressed a groan. She didn't want to be hunting down alibis; she wanted to do something more practical, useful. She didn't doubt what Fowler had told her; he had no reason to lie, unless he had killed the girl, and he would have had to be some special kind of psychopath to kill a kid just so he could watch people look for her. Still, anything was possible.

'What else?' Raymond was asking.

'CCTV?' Cooper suggested. 'We might pick up Aleah after she left the bookies, see if she spoke to anybody. We haven't checked yet because we had no idea she'd been on Main Street when she disappeared.'

'Get on it, Cooper,' Raymond said. 'Fletcher, work with Cooper on that. Get a phone number for this Ken Fowler and ask him to come in to give a statement. No point you chasing all over the county looking for him.'

Kate nodded, and Hollis grinned at her.

'Right,' Raymond said. 'Look at these pictures.' He stretched out one of his improbably long arms, the suit sleeve riding up his wrist, exposing a starched shirt cuff complete with silver cufflink. 'Aleah Reese. Seven years old. Bright, happy and dead. We need to find the bastard who turned this,' he tapped the school photograph, 'into this,' a tap on the scene image.

'At the moment, her stepfather is looking a bit dodgy, and as we all know, it's rarely a stranger in a case like this. We need to check the records of Reese and his dad, and anybody else who had contact with Aleah. We also need to contact her real father as well. It seems he's in Scotland, but we need to verify the details. Hollis, see if you can get some more information from Jackie Reese.'

Hollis nodded and jotted the instruction in his notebook.

Kate took out her own notebook and copied down Jackie and Dave Porter's names, CCTV, and Ken Fowler. She could make a couple of phone calls while Cooper and Hollis tracked down the footage, if there was any.

'Right. Let me introduce Detective Sergeant O'Connor.' He pointed to the man sitting opposite Barratt. 'He's been working in Thorpe, and in particular, on the Crosslands Estate, to break up a smuggling gang, cigarettes and booze, small-time stuff. I don't see any reason to assume a connection with Aleah Reese's murder, but he knows the area, and he knows the people. Use him, Fletcher.'

Kate nodded, avoiding eye contact with O'Connor. She was just getting to know the strengths and weaknesses of her team, and she didn't want the dynamic disturbed by a new member. She also suspected O'Connor was to be Raymond's eyes and ears as she and her team dealt with the Reese case, and she didn't appreciate the gesture.

'If anybody wants me,' Raymond continued. 'I'll be at Doncaster Infirmary watching the pathologist cut open the body of this little girl. I'm assuming nobody wants to come with me.'

A murmur of assent came from around the table.

'Good. Let's crack on, then. Anything comes up, let Fletcher know straight away.'

Ken Fowler proved easy to find – a quick call to Search and Rescue got Kate his home and mobile numbers. Fowler was able to confirm he saw somebody fitting Craig Reese's description on the old quarry site the previous night. He didn't want to come to Doncaster, though, so Barratt was dispatched with a photograph of Reese to confirm his identity.

O'Connor was sent to find Darren Thomas in order to verify Craig Reese's statement. It wasn't a job for a DS, but Kate wanted him out of the way until she'd had time to think about what it meant to have him on her team, and how she could use him. She didn't want him sniffing around while she was working out which lines of enquiry were worth pursuing.

Her priority was to track down Dave Porter, but this was proving to be harder than she'd imagined. She'd hoped to be able to find him without having to contact Jackie, but a quick trawl through 192.com told her there were thirty-seven Dave or David or D Porters in Scotland, and she didn't have the time to call each one to ask if he'd fathered a child with a woman called Jackie seven years ago. She'd have to call his ex-wife.

The phone was answered on the third ring, but it was Tatton who spoke. Kate explained what she needed, expecting Tatton to see if she could get any more information, but the call was interrupted.

'Who is this?' a voice at the other end demanded.

Kate recognised the slightly nasal tone of Jean Loach, Jackie's mother. 'Mrs Loach? It's DS Fletcher, we spoke yesterday?'

'Aye. I remember you.' The words could have been a simple acknowledgement of their conversation yesterday, but the tone implied history. Jean Roach knew who she was, or rather, who she'd been.

'I'm really sorry to bother your family at this difficult time…'

'Bother my family? That's just what I'd expect from you. Jackie can't talk now.'

'Please, Mrs Loach, I need some information about Dave Porter, Aleah's dad.'

A snort from the other end of the phone. 'I'll give you some information about him. He's a shit dad and a crap excuse for a human being.'

Kate sensed she was losing ground. Jean Loach clearly had a shed full of axes to grind despite her grief or, perhaps, because of it. 'I need to find him,' she pressed on. 'I need to find out if he's had anything to do with Aleah in the last few years.'

'He's in Scotland. Look up there for him.'

Grief or no grief, Kate had had enough. 'Mrs Loach,' she snapped. 'There is a possibility he might have had something to do with what happened to Aleah. I need to find out if that's the case. If he has any information, it is imperative I speak to him as soon as possible.'

Silence. Kate wondered if the other woman had hung up, but she was sure she could hear the faint rasping wheeze of a twenty-a-day smoker at the other end of the phone.

'He was living up near Dumfries,' Mrs Loach said. 'I don't know his address. You'll have to ask his mam.'

'And where can I find her?' Kate asked.

'She lived down Low Thorpe, near Craig's dad. Jubilee Terrace, I think. Probably still there.'

Kate made a note of the street name. 'Is she still called Porter?' Kate asked, pushing as far as she dared without risking further antagonism.

'How the bloody hell should I know? I've only said hello to her about four times since our Aleah was born. You're the copper, you find out,' and the line went dead.

'Helpful,' Kate muttered as she logged back on to 192.com. 'Right, let's see if there's a Porter on Jubilee Terrace.'

A few keystrokes later, she had discovered there was a Mrs A Porter at number seventeen, and not a great believer in coincidence, she switched browser windows and crossed everything the woman wasn't ex-directory. Bingo. The number was listed.

Kate jotted it down then kicked her feet against the newly laid carpet tiles and wheeled her chair over to a quiet corner of the incident room where Cooper and Hollis were pouring over a computer screen.

'Got anything?'

Hollis shook his head, keeping his eyes fixed on the screen. 'Bugger all. The council say there's no coverage in the village, apart from at the bus stop and that's pointed at the benches and the toilets. Sam rang the bookies and got lucky there. There's a security camera over the door and one inside. New ones, so they record digitally. The manager emailed me copies of the files from the day before yesterday. Funny format, though, so Sam's downloading a media player that might be able to play them.'

'Got it,' Cooper said. 'It's a media player I've used before. It will play pretty much anything. The problem is these files only use the proprietary player for the recording software, so we might be out of luck if it's something specific to the manufacturer.'

Kate just nodded, barely able to decode what she'd just been told. She knew Sam Cooper knew her stuff when it came to computers. She was also learning Cooper preferred her machines to people, most of the time.

Cooper tapped the enter key twice. 'Right, got it. Select and play.' She sat back slightly allowing Kate and Hollis a clearer view of the screen, and Kate leant forward to make sense of the images. The first few seconds were snowy, and then, the picture suddenly sprang into sharp focus, a view of a short section of pavement from above. She glanced at the clock in the top corner of the frame.

'Too early. Can you fast forward?'

A quick tap and there were people coming and going at breakneck speed. The clock was whizzing towards eleven.

'Right, slow it down again.'

Cooper followed her instructions, and at 11.24, a man and a girl approached and entered the bookies.

'That them?' Hollis asked.

Cooper tapped the keyboard, rewinding and then freezing the image. Even though it was in black-and-white, Reese's shaggy dark hair was unmistakable, and Aleah's pigtails were clearly visible.

'Looks like it,' Kate said. 'Let's have a look at the footage from inside.'

Cooper closed the file and loaded a different one, fast forwarding to 11.20. As she allowed the footage to play at normal speed, Kate watched Craig Reese and Aleah enter the bookmakers and cross to a waist-high counter littered with betting slips. A figure approached Reese from an area that was outside the camera's range. George Reese. The two men seemed to be talking, and neither noticed when Aleah wandered out of shot.

'Where's she gone?' Kate asked.

Hollis just shrugged and kept watching.

Aleah appeared again, ninety seconds later, and seemed to be asking her stepfather something. Reese grabbed a stack of betting slips and a pencil and thrust them towards her, but she shook her head and folded her arms.

'Stubborn,' Kate said.

Reese dug a hand in his jeans pocket and pulled out a handful of change. He poked through it, extracted a coin and passed it to Aleah who grinned and left the building.

'No, let it run,' Kate said, reaching out a hand to prevent Hollis from pressing stop. 'Let's see if there really was some sort of altercation between Reese and the manager.'

Reese watched Aleah leave and then had a quick conversation with his father. The older man shook his head emphatically and marched over to the counter. Reese followed and spoke to the person behind the glass. The view was obscured by a reflection, but it was clear whoever Reese was speaking to, he wasn't getting the answer he wanted. Eventually, he stalked over to the window and slumped in a chair.

'Fast forward a bit. What time does he leave?'

DC Cooper sped up the recording and stopped it just as Reese was heading for the door. The clock said 11.35. So far, everything he had told them was supported by the recording.

They switched back to the outside camera, watched Aleah leave and then, ten minutes later, her stepfather. No suggestion that there had been anybody hanging around, lurking by the door waiting to approach either of them. A quick check found Reese back again, fifteen minutes after he'd left gesturing frantically to his father.

'Well, that was a waste of time,' Hollis said, pushing his chair back.

'It corroborates Reese's story, though,' Kate said. 'It looks like he did finally decide to give us an honest account. Have you got the council footage yet, Cooper?'

'Some time this afternoon. For what good it'll do. I can't see whoever snatched her sitting around in full view at the bus stop,' Cooper said.

'Probably not,' Kate had to agree. 'But you never know. Fancy a trip back to Thorpe while we're waiting, Hollis? I've found Dave Porter's mother. I was going to ring, but it might be best face-to-face, especially if she's upset about Aleah. Who knows what she might let slip?'

CHAPTER 6

2015

Jubilee Terrace was a neat row of Victorian houses tucked away on the edge of Low Thorpe. They fronted directly onto the street, without the benefit of even a small garden to separate them from prying eyes, and each one seemed to have staked its place on the street with a small touch of individuality. One had hanging baskets on both sides of its main window; another had a boot scraper next to the door, and further down the street, the lintels above a door and downstairs window had been painted a bright blue, which seemed to give the house a slightly quizzical expression.

'It's different here, isn't it?' Hollis asked. 'On Jackie Reese's estate, I got the sense people are proud of their houses and take care of them. Old Mill near the main shops seemed like a bit of a dump, but I'm not sure what to make of this part of town.'

'Village,' Kate corrected him automatically.

'Village? Bit big for a village.'

'Thorpe's always been a village, even though it's probably technically a town,' she said. 'It was mostly council and pit housing when I was growing up. I was ten years old before I knew that ordinary people could own their own homes. I thought everybody rented from the council or the NCB. This part, Low Thorpe, was all pit houses. When I was at school, I thought the kids from Low Thorpe were a bit rough. Crosslands Estate, where I lived, and where the Reeses live, was a bit snobbier, even though it was all council housing. Looks like things have improved here, though.'

Aileen Porter's house had a red sandstone front step and an ornate door knocker shaped like a thistle. Kate wondered if the family had a Scottish connection, or if this was a present from her absent son. She rapped the knocker on the door smartly and stepped back, scanning the net curtains of the front room and the bedroom above. No sign of life, but if there was anybody home, they were probably in the kitchen at the back.

Just as she was about to knock again, the door opened to reveal a tiny woman wearing a thin coat and a headscarf. She looked like she'd either just come home or was just about to go out. Kate estimated her age at mid to late sixties. The headscarf stood proud on her head, indicating freshly styled hair underneath, and she was wearing a bold dash of lipstick on her thin lips, with a smear of rouge on each high cheekbone. Wrinkles carved deep slashes down each side of her mouth, and there was a furrow between her eyes, but she didn't have that dry chamois look Kate had seen in a lot of women her age. Obviously somebody who cared about her appearance.

'Yes?' the woman asked.

'Mrs Porter,' Kate flashed her ID. 'I'm Detective Inspector Kate Fletcher, and this is DC Dan Hollis, we're here about…'

'About our Aleah. I thought somebody might be in touch. I expect you want to know where our Dave is?'

'Er, I, er…' Kate stuttered, completely wrong-footed by the woman's directness.

'He's living near Aberdeen, and he's not been back here for over a year.' She glanced up and down the street, as though checking whether the conversation was likely to be overheard, then seemed to come to a decision.

'I suppose you'd better come in,' she said, opening the door further and stepping out onto the street to allow Hollis and Kate to pass into the narrow hallway. 'Go straight through to the kitchen in the back. I'll put the kettle on.'

The kitchen had been extended beyond the original footprint of the house, and the extended part had a window in the sloping roof that allowed the strong sunlight to illuminate the cream walls and light oak units. It was a functional space, with a small table to one side, a fridge, cooker and an assortment of cupboards and drawers, but one that had been thoughtfully decorated and recently cleaned. An air freshener, a bottle with sticks poking out, masked any stale cooking smells, and another plug-in one guarded the swing-top bin. Kate could see the woman was as proud of her house as she was of her own appearance.

'Sit,' Mrs Porter said, slipping off her coat and headscarf and pointing to the two pine chairs flanking the table. 'Can I get you a drink?'

Hollis asked for a glass of water, Kate for tea.

'I'm sorry to bother you,' Kate said. 'I can't imagine what you're going through. We're doing everything we can to find out what happened to Aleah. That's why we need to ask about Dave.'

'He'd have loved to have been a dad to her, you know,' Mrs Porter said, her voice raised slightly to compete with the sound of water as she filled the kettle. 'But that Jackie wouldn't let him. They'd already separated – I don't know why he married her in the first place, but I bet Aleah wasn't her first "pregnancy." Wouldn't put it past her to trick him into it. Wasn't much of a wedding, anyway – registry office and then a small do at The Lion. I think she just fancied having a husband, and when he didn't turn out to be what she wanted, she got rid of him. Said he was a waste of space and told him to sling his hook. Did you know she told him she'd gotten rid of the baby? Aleah was nearly a year old before Dave knew about her, and by that time, he'd gone up north.'

Hollis pulled out his notebook and started jotting.

'Put it about that he'd run off. As if. Our Dave might have his faults, but he's a good lad. He'd have done the right thing by her and the kiddie, even though the marriage was over. And now, she's… gone… before he could even get to know her.'

Her hand trembled as she filled a glass and placed it on the table. 'And I never got a chance, neither. I suppose you think I'm daft, being upset about a kiddie I didn't even know, but I'd always hoped when she was older, she'd want to know about her family.'

She turned back to the kettle and mugs on the worktop, keeping her back to the two police officers, but Kate could see her shoulders were shaking as she tried to control the range of emotions that she was battling with. Even though she'd had little or nothing to do with her granddaughter, the grief was obviously raw, and she was struggling.

'Here you go,' she said, passing a steaming mug of tea to Kate. 'Sugar's just there.' She pointed to a tin with the word *sugar* stencilled on the side. She placed her own mug on the table and drew up a chair.

'I've not told our Dave yet. To be honest, it hasn't sunk in with me. I was just at the hairdressers, and I heard off Winnie who lives up Crosslands, around the corner from Jackie. Terrible shock, it was.'

'I bet,' Kate said, blowing ripples across the surface of her tea in an attempt to cool it. 'I don't suppose anybody will tell your Dave before you can ring him?'

Mrs Porter shook her head. 'No chance. He can't take incoming calls. He works on the rigs, and he's at sea for the next week or so. He does a fortnight on and a fortnight off. Been there since last week. I rang him just before he went, and he rang me two days ago. I'll have to wait for him to ring again.'

It seemed typical to Kate that Aileen Porter would follow the rules to the letter. It reflected her tidy appearance and her sense of order and propriety.

'If you ring the company, they can probably get hold of him for you,' she suggested. 'Or we could do it for you?'

The older woman shrugged. 'I don't see what good that will do, really. They could helicopter him off, but then what? If he came down here, *she'd* probably not let him be involved. It might be best to wait.'

'I think he'd want to know,' Hollis said gently. 'She was his daughter, even if he didn't have anything to do with her. If we let him know, at least he'll have the option of coming home. Then, it's up to him what he does.'

'Aye, you're probably right,' the older woman conceded. 'I think it would be best if one of you did it, though, make it official. Then, he can ring me, if he wants.'

Hollis nodded. 'We can arrange that, if you can give us the details of his employer.'

'I'll just drink this tea. I've got contact details in my address book in the other room, I'll get them in a bit.'

She was stalling, Kate sensed, probably for a number of reasons; reluctance to hurt her son, fear of being left on her own with her grief and possibly the inertia bereavement brought. Kate sipped her own tea. No rush.

'How did Dave end up on the rigs?' Hollis asked.

Mrs Porter smiled at him, grateful for the distraction. 'He'd had a lot of dead-end jobs for years after he left school. Factory work and warehouseman – but he couldn't work out what he wanted to do. Then, he decided to go to night school, in Doncaster. Did engineering for two years. Paid his own way by working in The Lion and doing a milk round at the weekends. Never had any money, but he knew he could make something of himself. I was heartbroken when he got that Jackie Loach pregnant, but he told me he'd make it work. He could finish his studies, then they could move to somewhere where he could get an apprenticeship. Course, it didn't end up like that. I think it was just a bit of a fling for both of them, really, and when Jackie said she'd got rid of the kiddie, I think he was a bit relieved. Then, he got a job up in Dumfries, and when he got a chance, he applied for the rigs.'

'So, he never met his daughter?' Kate wanted to know.

'He saw her once when she was nearly a year old. Jackie'd taken up with that Craig Reese by then and didn't want to have anything to do with Dave. Told him that his name wasn't even on Aleah's birth certificate. To be honest, I think she thought he wasn't good enough for her. He didn't talk about his plans, his ambitions, much. Aleah would've been a lot better off with our Dave than with that Reese bloke.'

'You don't like Craig Reese?' Hollis prompted.

'I don't like his family. His dad's a troublemaker, and his sisters were a right pair. I was glad when they moved away.'

'Troublemaker?' Kate asked.

'Aye. Jud Reese worked at the pit with my Eddie. Caused a lot of bad feeling during the strike, stirring up men against the scabs. Not that they needed much stirring up. But he was the sort who would cause trouble then leave others to it and keep his own nose clean. Sneaky, like.'

Hollis was jotting again, and Kate knew exactly what he would have written. It might be well worth doing a background check on George Reese, just to see what sort of trouble he might have caused thirty years ago. There might be some old resentments there which could shed some light on Aleah's kidnapping and murder. It was a long shot and a long time ago, but worth a look.

Mrs Porter pushed her empty mug away and stood up. 'I'll get you the phone number for our Dave's company.'

As soon as she left the room, Hollis whispered, 'Jud is George Reese, right? Check his record?'

'And his son's. I'm not getting a good feeling about this family.'

'Here you go,' Mrs Porter announced, thrusting a piece of paper at Kate. 'Like I said, he's at sea, but they'll be able to get hold of him, won't they? And please, ask if he can ring me.'

Kate passed the paper to Hollis who slipped it into his notebook. 'We'll do just that,' she said, standing up to leave. 'Thanks for the tea, Mrs Porter, and we're so sorry about Aleah.'

Mrs Porter nodded her appreciation. 'Aye, well. Just catch whoever did it and string him up.'

I sometimes wish we could, Kate thought, as the front door closed behind them.

'What now?' Hollis asked, as they got back into the car. 'I don't think there's much else we can do here.'

Kate agreed. The best decision would be to head back to Doncaster and start to collate information from the rest of the team. She checked her email. One from O'Connor confirming Reese's meeting with Darren Thomas, and one from Raymond informing her about the next briefing, in just over an hour. She quickly emailed Cooper with a request for background checks on Craig and Jud Reese, and as an afterthought, she threw Carl Loach, Jackie's dad, into the mix as well.

CHAPTER 7

2015

Atext pinged in to Kate's phone just as they were pulling in to the car park at Doncaster Central. She checked the time. Much later than she'd anticipated. The traffic around Balby had been slowed down by a lorry crash, and she was surprised they had made it back in time. The text was from Raymond. Apparently, he wasn't impressed with her time-keeping. The preliminary PM results were in, and the team was assembled for their next briefing. Where was she? As Kate closed the text, she saw the next one down in the list of messages.

'Shit,' she said. 'Forgot all about him.'

'Who?' Hollis asked.

'Rigby. The PC who searched the Reeses' house yesterday. He missed the betting slips. I wanted to give him a bit of a pep talk.'

Hollis grinned. 'Is that code for an arse-kicking?'

'Something like that,' Kate said. 'And we'll be in for one ourselves, if we don't get upstairs to see what Raymond has to say.'

Her prediction proved correct. The team was already gathered around the conference table as Kate and Hollis entered the room, the sense of anticipation almost palpable. It was always the same with a serious case – any meeting needed to add information to the investigation, and the PM would certainly give them something else to look at.

'Good of you two to join us,' Raymond growled as they slipped into seats around the conference table. 'Had a lovely morning?'

'We–' Kate began, but Raymond held up a hand to cut her short.

'I don't need to know just yet. I'm just back from the PM on Aleah Reese. There's still a few test results to come back, but Doctor Kailisa gave me the basics.'

He picked up the remote control from the table in front of him and the interactive whiteboard sprang into life.

'First, no sign of sexual assault.'

There was a collective exhalation as the team recognised their worst fear hadn't been realised.

'She was wearing the clothes she'd been wearing when she went missing. There's no sign she was interfered with in any way. So, we're probably not looking for a paedophile.'

'Unless he didn't get to finish with her,' Barratt interrupted. Raymond scowled him into submission.

'Cause of death, manual strangulation. There's bruising on her throat consistent with adult thumbs, and her hyoid bone is fractured. No water or froth in her lungs. She was already dead when he put her in the pond.'

O'Connor was frantically scribbling notes.

'Now, the interesting bit. The yellow cord around her wrists was probably tied post-mortem. There's no bruising or abrasion consistent with that cord being used to tie her hands in front of her.'

'So why tie her up after she's dead?' Hollis mused. 'It makes no sense. It's not like she needed restraining. Why bother?'

'That's what we're going to find out,' Raymond said. 'The cord is unusual. It's quite thin but very strong, some sort of nylon blend. And the colour, bright yellow. The knot was a standard reef knot. Nothing special.'

'It could be tent guy line,' Barratt suggested. 'My tent's got high-vis ropes so that you don't trip over them. They're thin and strong. Just a thought.'

'And a good one,' Raymond said. 'We need to check whether the Reeses have a tent and whether any of the ropes are missing.'

'Do we have a time of death?' Kate asked. 'We've narrowed down the time she went missing to sometime after half past eleven on Tuesday. The CCTV footage shows her leaving the bookies around then. Do we know if she was strangled soon after that?'

Raymond shook his head. 'Hard to say. Stomach contents show the remains of some sort of breakfast cereal. Kailisa thinks either she was killed soon after she was snatched, so her stomach didn't have time to fully digest her breakfast, or the fear might have slowed down the digestive process. He thinks she'd not been in the water more than ten or twelve hours. He can't be more specific, at this point.'

'No sweets?' Kate asked.

'What?'

'Craig Reese sent her off to buy sweets. She bought some Haribo, but it doesn't look like she ate them, if there was only breakfast cereal in her stomach. What happened to the sweets?'

'I don't know,' Raymond sighed as though Kate was deliberately trying to throw his train of thought. 'All I know is what I've just told you. Breakfast in her stomach, so she was probably killed soon after she was taken.'

'So, Craig Reese could have kept her body hidden and then dumped her when he went out on Tuesday night?' Cooper suggested.

'Or Ken Fowler,' Barratt countered. 'He was at the pond that night.'

'Look,' Kate said. 'I don't think we have evidence to link Craig Reese or Ken Fowler to the murder. We need to keep our minds open. Reese and Fowler have no known connection, and they alibi each other. We should find out if they are linked in some way. Does one have something to gain by covering for the other? What about the background checks?'

She looked at Cooper whose normally pale, freckled face was pink. She'd obviously taken Kate's outburst as a telling-off, which wasn't Kate's intention. She'd seen too many cases get side-tracked and stalled due to people making assumptions and not looking at other possibilities. Her gut was telling her to look more closely at Craig Reese, but she knew it was only one possible line of enquiry.

'I checked Reese and his father first,' Cooper was saying, looking flustered by the sudden focus of attention on what she had to say. 'Craig Reese has three points on his licence for speeding, which is a bit moot as he doesn't have a car at the moment. George

Reese is clean. He's mentioned in a couple of cases of affray in 1984 and 1985, but he's never been charged with any offence.'

Exactly what Dave Porter's mother had suggested, Kate thought.

'Carl Loach's record tells a different story,' Cooper continued. 'Two cases of ABH in 1985. Nothing since.'

'More detail,' Raymond demanded.

Cooper consulted her notes, shuffling the print-outs like an expert card sharp. 'He was arrested outside the Miner's Welfare Club in Thorpe for an attack on a Paul Hirst in October 1984. Apparently, he attacked the man after calling him a scab. The two fought, cheered on by a crowd, according to statements given by two onlookers. Both men were arrested, but Loach was found to be the instigator and fined. The second one was in January of the following year. He attacked the same man.'

Raymond stared at Cooper, obviously thinking about the implications, while she sat like a rabbit in headlights, wondering what was coming next.

'We need to find this Paul Hirst. Maybe he's harbouring a grudge.'

'He's not,' Cooper said.

Raymond looked sceptical. 'How can you possibly know that, Cooper?'

'He killed himself in June 1985.'

Raymond snorted his disgust at the loss of a promising lead.

'How?' Kate asked. She'd seen a couple of cases where the initial assessment was suicide, but they later turned out to be murders.

'Hanged himself off Samson Bridge. That's…'

'The bridge to the pit. I know,' Kate said. 'Don't suppose it's there now, though?'

'The site was landscaped sometime in the early nineties,' Barratt said, eager to please. 'They built some sort of outdoor education place on it. You know, bush tucker and all that.'

Kate found that hard to imagine. When she'd been growing up in Thorpe, the whole area around the pit was grimy gravel tracks, black with coal dust, moonscape spoil heaps, and red-brick buildings that housed the pit head baths and the canteen. Not exactly the great outdoors. She'd walked the old railway track behind the pit once with her dad, and they'd had to cross Samson Bridge to access the start of the path. It had spanned a narrow-gauge railway line and a rough road, allowing miners safe access to the squat buildings that surrounded the winding gear. A bit public for a suicide.

'Fletcher?' Raymond was talking to her. 'Find out what you can about this Paul Hirst. Ask around. You know the area and the people – see what they'll tell you.'

Cooper and Barrett both looked at her, suddenly suspicious. It looked like Hollis wasn't the only one who hadn't been aware of her background.

'You're local?' Cooper asked.

'Thorpe born and bred.' Kate could hear the defensiveness and pride in her own tone as though Cooper had challenged her South Yorkshire credentials. It was instinctive, even though she'd have denied any loyalty to her hometown. She'd felt uprooted when her father had moved them south, but that had been wrong – the roots were still there, entwined in the streets and parks of her childhood, and she knew that, given the chance, they would spring to the surface and trip her up.

'Didn't see that coming,' Barratt said under his breath.

'Enough about DI Fletcher's family history,' Raymond said. 'Let's get back to the slightly less interesting matter of this girl's murder, shall we?'

Murmurs of "sorry" rose from Cooper and Barratt.

'So, where does this leave us? What are our next steps?'

'The rope,' Kate said. 'We need to find out what it is and where it came from. Craig Reese has been a bit cagey. I wonder if it's worth having a look around the house and garden – see if he likes camping.'

'Those Search and Rescue blokes are usually outdoorsy,' Barratt added. 'Ken Fowler might have a tent.'

Kate sighed. Barratt was obviously trying to make a name for himself on the small team, but his relentless pursuit of Fowler was getting boring. They were all taught to "think outside the box," to ask difficult questions and to challenge everything, but this was getting a bit tedious. If she'd been in Raymond's position, she'd have been tempted to let Barratt run with it and get it out of his system. Fowler had no motive and hadn't even been asked for an alibi for the time when Aleah went missing.

'Why don't you find out?' Raymond said, as Kate suppressed a grin. 'If you really think he's a viable suspect, then go and do some legwork.'

Barratt grinned broadly. 'Okay, I'll get on it.'

'Fletcher, Hollis. I want you to have a look around at the Reeses' house. Ask nicely. A warrant takes time, but we'll get one if we need to. If they've got nothing to hide, they won't have a problem with you poking around.'

'O'Connor, I'm interested in this spat between Loach and Paul Hirst. I want to know what Loach had against him, and I want to know why Hirst killed himself. It might be nothing, but then again, it might be somebody wanting revenge on Loach. You know people in Thorpe – ask around.'

'Cooper might be best digging around to see what she can find,' Kate suggested. 'She could try the *Free Press* and the *Times*. See if there's anything in there about the fights and the suicide. It might help to pick out the facts from any gossip and speculation O'Connor gets from anybody.'

Raymond nodded his approval. 'Come on, then,' he said, clapping his hands together. 'Let's do our jobs.'

O'Connor pulled Kate to one side as they left the briefing room. He waited until the others had passed before speaking.

'Are you really from Thorpe?' he asked, his mouth twisted into a half grin above his dark brown beard.

Kate nodded, waiting to see where this might be leading.

'Well, I've been doing a lot of work over there. Somebody's distributing smuggled cigarettes and booze. It's mainly small scale, but that's how these things often start. I've got contacts.'

'And?' Kate prompted.

'I just think I need to tread carefully. There are one or two who trust me, and if I start digging around in the past, they might clam up about everything. They don't talk about the strike.'

Kate sighed. 'O'Connor, I think a murdered girl is slightly more important than the sensibilities of your would-be informants, don't you?'

'I know that. I also know that Raymond assigned me to this team because of those contacts. I just want you to know I need to tread carefully. I can't go asking people what side they were on in 1985. It'll just put people's backs up.'

He stuck his hands in his pockets and leaned back against the wall as though he'd decided to stay where he was and he seemed to be expecting Kate to support him. She didn't know him very well; he'd been around for a few days when she'd first joined the team, but barely been in the office since then. She'd gathered that Raymond thought highly of him, and she couldn't help but wonder if he'd been expecting promotion to DI before she'd arrived. If that was the case, then going against Raymond's orders wasn't the best way to secure his advancement.

'Look,' she said. 'Find out what you can. Ask people who you think might trust you. If you need to, mention that it's to do with the murder: that might get people to cooperate.'

He nodded gratefully, but his expression was still cynical as he pushed himself off the wall and pulled the door open.

'And O'Connor?'

He stuck his head back around the door jamb. 'What?'

'Please don't ask whose side anybody was on during the strike. There was only one side, if you lived in Thorpe.'

CHAPTER 8

2015

The Reeses' house was unchanged since their previous visit, but Kate felt the weight of grief on the whole estate. The streets and shops would be buzzing like a hive with the news; gossip passing from one cell to the next and no doubt getting distorted with each re-telling. She wanted this to be a straightforward search, no resistance from the family and, hopefully, no evidence to link either of Aleah's parents to her murder. But the reality was rarely that simple.

Craig Reese scowled at them as he opened the door. 'What do *you* want? Can't you just leave us alone to get on with it now?' he grumbled. 'Our Jackie's asleep, and I don't want her bothered.'

'I'm sorry,' Kate said. 'And I'm so sorry about Aleah. The thing is, we have some new evidence, and we need to follow it up. Would you mind if we had a look around the house and garden? It'd be a big help.'

Behind her, she felt Hollis tense. This was the key moment. If Reese refused, then they would need a warrant, and any delay could be crucial. If he complied, did it mean he had nothing to hide or that he believed he'd covered his tracks? There was no way to be sure, other than searching.

Reese held on to the door handle and looked them both up and down. The apologetic, frightened man of this morning's interview had been replaced by a person who clearly had cast himself in the role of protector of his family. He shook his head. 'You've already had a look around. What's this new evidence, anyway?'

'I'm afraid we can't say at the moment. I think it would be in your interest to cooperate with us. If we have to get a warrant, it might look like you've got something to hide, Craig.' Kate stood her ground and met his stare.

'Look. I've told you everything. You kept me at that bloody police station for most of the morning, when I should have been here with my wife. The doctor's given her something to calm her down, and I don't want her disturbed.'

'How about we start outside?' Hollis offered. 'We can have a look in the garden and the shed, and if we're satisfied, we won't have to come in.'

'Fine,' Reese said, making a move to close the door. 'Knock yourself out, just leave us alone.' He slammed the door.

'Well, that went well,' Hollis said, with a grin.

'He's a mess. Probably doesn't know how he feels or what to do. Good thinking, though, offering him a compromise. Let's have a look in the shed first.'

Kate led the way into the back garden. A gravel path led across a newly mown lawn to the shed, and off to one side, a pair of raised beds had been constructed and both were overflowing with greenery. It wasn't quite the vegetable patch that had occupied the back half of Kate's dad's garden, but it looked like they'd have a good crop of carrots and beetroot late in the summer.

The shed was positioned on a slope, the front propped up on what looked like railway sleepers to provide a level floor inside. The door was fastened with a bolt and a hasp but no padlock. Instead, a six-inch nail had been bent at the top and threaded through the loop that was screwed to the shed door to provide a rudimentary fastening. Either the Reeses trusted their neighbours, or they didn't think there was anything worth stealing in the shed. Hollis drew back the bolt, removed the nail and pulled open the shed door, stepping back to allow Kate to enter. She took a pair of nitrile gloves from her jacket pocket, and Hollis followed her lead.

It was gloomy inside, the windows clouded with cobwebs and a layer of grime, so Kate stood on the threshold and allowed her eyes to adjust. There was nothing unexpected at first sight, the usual garden tools; hedge cutters, an electric mower and a pair of shears in one corner and a spade, fork and rake in another. The far end of the shed had obviously been used as a retreat or a hiding place. An ancient looking bedside cabinet and garden chair were huddled together as testament to somebody's need for privacy, or peace. Kate wiped a gloved finger across the top of the table. No dust. The ashtray was quite full but not overflowing, and the seat of the chair looked sunken and well used.

'Looks like Jackie doesn't like Craig smoking in the house,' Kate commented, remembering the woman sucking on an e-cigarette when they'd visited earlier.

Hollis just nodded, his attention distracted by the metal cabinet in the far corner. It looked like it had come from a 1950s office, solid and sturdy with a T-shaped handle on the door. He gave the handle a twist and pulled the door open.

'Bingo,' he whispered. 'Looks like somebody likes camping.'

On the top shelf of the cabinet was a tent, which had been roughly stuffed in its bag, some of the fabric and guy lines oozing out of the top like a slow-motion explosion.

Kate watched as Hollis lifted it down and pulled gently on one of the yellow cords. 'Could be a match,' she said. 'We need to bag it.'

A quick trip to the car and they approached the shed again, armed with an assortment of evidence bags. Kate took out her phone and snapped pictures of the cupboard and the tent *in situ* before labelling the largest of the bags and instructing Hollis to drop the tent into it. She sealed it and signed the seal with her initials and the date.

She scanned the shelves lining the wall opposite the window, but all she could see was an assortment of used paint tins and plant pots, no suggestion anything had been moved for months.

Hollis bent and pulled open the door on the bedside cabinet. There were two shelves inside. One held a couple of jars of screws and nails – nothing incriminating or even slightly suspicious. And nothing to suggest Aleah had been in the shed.

'If this matches, we'll need to get forensics around here,' Kate said. 'I suggest we leave it for now and see what they find out about the tent. We can't take Reese back in on this, but we need to let him know he's not off the hook yet.'

Craig Reese glanced at Hollis's gloved hands then back up at Kate. 'What have you been looking for?'

'As I said, we've been looking for evidence, and we need to send what we've found for analysis.'

Reese's face visibly paled. 'So, you've found something? In my shed?'

Kate noted the use of "my," but remained silent, hoping Hollis would have the common sense to follow her example.

'Is it something to do with Aleah?'

Silence. Kate wanted him to squirm; silence could be hard to take, and most people's instinct was to fill it. It was tougher than she'd expected, though. Reese stared stonily at her; no chance of a quick confession.

'We need to come inside and have another look at Aleah's bedroom.'

Reese shook his head violently. 'No! Jackie needs to be left alone.'

'I understand that,' Kate said. 'But this new evidence has raised some issues. We need to have a more thorough look around.'

Reese crossed his arms and raised his eyebrows in challenge. 'Or what?'

Kate sighed. She hadn't expected him to be this difficult. He'd been over-eager in their previous interview – apparently keen to tell the truth. 'Or I get a warrant – and I will be granted one – and we come in here and tear your house apart.'

'Wha... you can't,' he spluttered, all trace of his bluster evaporating. 'We're not hiding anything. We just want to be left alone.'

'That's what we need to establish,' Hollis said. 'If you refuse to cooperate with us, it'll go against you. We might think you've got something to hide.'

'Besides,' Kate added. 'What will folk think if we come back with a warrant and a forensics van? People in white overalls traipsing in and out. There's bound to be talk.

'But I…'

Kate sensed he'd taken her seriously, and he was genuinely conflicted about his duty to his wife and the opportunity to save himself humiliation. The houses might have been bought up and the occupants proudly sitting on their mortgages, rather than paying rent, but the community still felt the same – close-knit and closed minded. Nobody wanted to be the subject of gossip.

'Craig,' Hollis said, his tone measured. 'Let us come in and have another look at Aleah's bedroom. It won't take us long, and if we don't find anything, we'll be out of your hair.'

Reese sighed and frowned as though he was considering his options. Kate didn't want to go through the process of getting a warrant and making this difficult; she just wanted to check there was nothing she'd missed in Aleah's room, no lavish gifts or a stash of money that couldn't be explained. She hated the term "grooming," but it was a possibility she had to consider. Reese had lied before; why should they believe him now?

'Come on, then,' Reese said. 'Our Jackie's having a lie down upstairs, so be quiet. Just Aleah's room?'

Kate nodded, thinking, *For now*.

The girl's bedroom was exactly as she'd left it yesterday. The bed was neatly made, and the desk was still scattered with drawings on the backs of betting slips. Kate gathered them together and put them in an evidence bag. They'd get a psychologist to give them a look over and see if there was any indication in the drawings that something in Aleah's life wasn't right.

She pointed to the bed, and Hollis knelt down, running his hand along the frame to see if anything was taped underneath. He lifted the mattress to check for anything that had been concealed. Nothing. Kate pulled out each drawer from the chest of drawers, ran her hand through the contents and then lifted each one so she could check the bottom. Clean. She picked up the first paperback book from the pile on the bedside table and flicked through, looking for any papers that might have been hidden there. The first one was empty so she picked up the others, checking each one in turn. The only thing that fell out was a bookmark with a rainbow pattern.

'There's nothing here,' Hollis said, standing up and brushing carpet fibres from his trousers. 'If somebody was grooming her, he wasn't giving her anything she kept and hid.'

Kate sat on the bed, frustrated. The tent might be helpful, but the shed wasn't kept locked, so anybody could have got in. She'd been hoping a more thorough search of Aleah's room might yield more clues, but there was nothing to suggest she was anything other than a normal seven-year-old girl. She glanced at the bag of betting slips she'd left on the desk and suddenly remembered the text she'd received earlier. Rigby was the one who'd conducted the initial search. Had he noticed anything she hadn't? Unlikely. He hadn't been aware of the ropes binding Aleah's wrists, so he couldn't have been expected to understand the significance of the tent and the betting slips looked like a pile of kids' drawings.

She took out her phone and texted him, asking him to meet her at Doncaster Central when she got back.

The bedroom door opened as she slid the phone back into her pocket, and she glanced up to see a woman in her sixties bearing down on her, her face murderous. Startled, Kate stood up and took a step sideways, in case the older woman lunged at her.

'I know you,' the woman said. 'I remembered as soon as you'd come upstairs. You're that bitch who got our Rob excluded from school. The one that accused him of all sorts. It's Kathy, isn't it?'

She stood in the doorway, arms crossed as though she was trying to prevent herself from lashing out, daring Kate to disagree.

Kate smiled as she recognised the woman facing her. 'I've not been Kathy for a long time, Mrs Loach. But, yes, Rob did get himself excluded from school for writing me a threatening note.'

Mrs Loach snorted. '*Get himself excluded.* Everybody knows you went to your scab of a dad, telling tales, and that's what got him chucked out. We had to send him to Mexborough, and he never really settled. He failed his O-levels because of you.'

'He had nobody but himself to blame,' Kate said. 'Actions have consequences.'

'Ooh, Miss Lah-de-dah. You always were a stuck-up bunch, you lot. Thought you were better than everybody else because your dad was a deputy.'

Kate had had enough. She took a step towards Mrs Loach. 'With respect, Mrs Loach,' she said, her tone making her words a lie. 'Your Rob would have failed his O-levels if he'd gone to Eton. He never was the sharpest knife in the drawer. He was in the same classes as my sister, and she told me exactly what he was like. A bully and a coward. He never did own up to what he'd done. Tried to blame somebody else, as I recall.'

The other woman took half a step back, but the self-righteous expression on her mean face didn't flicker. 'That's because it wasn't him.'

Kate smiled. 'Much as I'd love to continue this conversation, Mrs Loach, my colleague and I need to get back to the police station and continue our investigation into Aleah's abduction and murder. I have no interest in raking up the past.'

Mrs Loach sneered. 'I bet you don't. Your family had a lot to hide, if I remember. Your dad worked all through the strike, while the likes of us were starving. Be careful, *Kathy Siddons*, people round here have long memories.'

She used Kate's name like a swear word, almost spitting it as she backed through the door and allowed Kate and Hollis to pass her.

CHAPTER 9

1984

Kathy wasn't used to wagging school. A lot of her friends had done it once or twice, but she'd always worried too much about getting caught and the effect it would have on her dad. He was always telling her and Karen they should get a good education. O-levels and A-levels were better than money because they'd always have them to fall back on. He'd been thrilled when Kathy had mentioned university a few months ago and had been helping her to find out about courses at the grammar school sixth form. If she could get in there, he'd said, she could do really well.

But none of that mattered today. Kathy had managed to ignore the stares and sniggers on the bus, but the note had tipped her over the edge, and she had to get away. She only had four more weeks anyway, and then, she'd leave for good. The only reason she had to come back was for her exams, and most of the whisperers wouldn't be there – they were doing CSE courses, the boys were destined for the pit and the girls would mostly end up in the clothing factories in Rotherham. Not that Kathy would ever give voice to her snobbery. She just knew she was different from most of the girls in her year – she had ambition. The careers teacher had said so.

The teachers probably wouldn't notice if she wagged it. She'd briefly considered showing the note to her form teacher, but he'd probably have said it was a joke and not to be so sensitive. So, she'd stuffed it into her jeans pocket and stormed out of the main school entrance, not caring who saw her or who they told.

She wasn't sure where to go. School gave structure and order to her day, and without it, she was at a loss, so she decided to wander down into the village and wait in the park near the bus stop until she was sure her dad would have gone to work. Then, she could go home to watch telly or read something for school. Hardly a serious effort at truancy, but anything was better than being *there*.

The village was starting to change in an indefinable way. It looked the same as it always did, but it felt quieter, as though the buildings and the concrete beneath her feet were brooding, waiting; something felt coiled and dark, like a sea serpent about to surge up from black water, smashing everything to kindling. The view from the higher part of the village, where most of the shops were located, was familiar in its topography of slag heaps and railway line, but something felt different. The winding gear at the pit head was still and silent – which wasn't unusual: it wasn't used between shifts, except in an emergency – but there was a finality in the stillness, as though, when all this was over, the mine and the village would never be quite the same.

The people she saw seemed exaggeratedly huddled down in their coats and jackets like spies, unwilling to be confronted, reluctant to exchange pleasantries. The strike was beginning to bite, and its steel jaws had the village firmly in their grip. In the flats and rows of terraced houses she passed on her way to the park, Kathy sensed the edge of a precipice – families would soon start to slide slowly over into poverty and hunger as the great beast padded slowly on through their lives.

Not her life, though. And that was the problem. So many of the kids in her year were the children of miners; so many were facing the stigma of "free dinners" and second-hand clothes. Kathy wasn't one of them. It had never mattered before that her dad worked at the pit, but he wasn't an ordinary miner. Nobody had ever singled her out before because he was a pit deputy – not management but not a hewer, either. Since the strike, that had changed. Other kids whose dads worked on the railway or the steelworks or in one of the various factories surrounding Rotherham and Doncaster were immune from the teasing. They had nothing to do with the pit or the strike, but they were happy to join in when others were being tormented.

Kathy pushed open the gate to the park, a metal one, she noted, so it hadn't been stolen for somebody's fire place, and sat on the roundabout, pushing slowly with one foot. She took the note from her pocket and flattened it against the faded, chipped paint of the wooden seat and read it again. There was no mistaking the malice. This wasn't a harmless bit of fun. This was a threat.

DIE SCAB BITCH!

She'd managed to get away with wagging school on the day she'd found the note, and it had become her routine for the week. She'd head out for the school bus in the morning, but she never made it to the bus stop. Instead, she'd turn in the opposite direction and walk up to the park by the shops at the top of the estate on Crosslands Road. She had a story rehearsed, in case any of their neighbours stopped her; she was going into school later because she had to get some cough medicine for her sister, but so far, she'd been lucky.

The park was a good place to wait for her dad to leave for work. Surrounded by high privet hedges on three sides, it faced a quiet street which wasn't a through-road to any other part of the estate. It had a slide, swings, a roundabout, and a monkey climb all huddled conspiratorially together in the middle of the grass, and it was the climbing frame where Kathy had started to spend the first hour of her morning; perched high above the ground reading a book for school or thinking about what she would do when she finally got away from home.

After the first day of her truancy, when Karen had been at home with her fake period pains, she'd had the house to herself until her sister came home from school at four o'clock. Plenty of time for watching telly, reading and doing some revision. At least if she was challenged, she'd be able to truthfully say she'd been at home studying for her exams.

Kathy hadn't meant for her dad to find the note. She didn't want anybody to see it, ever. Just looking at it made her burn with shame and a deeply smouldering anger towards whoever had left it in her locker. She had a few ideas, the usual suspects, people who had pretended to be her friend and then turned on her. Nothing definite, though; and she didn't want to get rid of the note until she'd confronted its author with the evidence.

Her dad had been going through her pockets, sorting clothes for the Saturday wash and barking instructions to Karen about what to put where, when he went suddenly quiet. Kathy looked up from the copy of *Twelfth Night* she'd been reading for the fourth time in the hope some of it might stick in her already full-to-capacity brain and saw her dad, ashen faced, gripping a piece of paper.

'Where did you get this?' he asked, his voice barely a whisper.

'What?'

'This note, Kathryn. Where did it come from?' He waved it at her as though she was the one writing threats; as though she was the one to blame.

'What is it?' she asked, trying to buy some time while she worked out what to say.

'It came out of your jeans pocket, so I'd expect you to know.'

'Oh, that.' She laughed, trying to counter his anger. 'It's nothing. Just a joke.'

'Do I look like I'm laughing?' her dad hissed.

She'd never seen him so angry. His cheekbones were highlighted by vivid red slashes, and his lips had contracted into a thin line even paler than the rest of his face. His normally slicked-back hair had fallen over one eye giving him a slightly unbalanced look, and his fist, still clutching the note, was trembling.

'Kathy, this is serious. This is a threat. Is it the first one that you've had?'

She considered lying; telling him it was nothing, that she wasn't sure it had been meant for her, but she could almost anticipate the relief the truth would bring.

'No. It's not the first. But it's the worst one. I didn't know what to do with it,' she confessed.

'Is it just the notes?' her dad asked.

Kathy shrugged.

'Kathy. I want the truth.'

The dam broke. All the weeks of pent-up anger and shame and fear came spilling through the cracks as Kathy told him everything. The other notes, the teasing on the bus, the whispering and pointing at school. Everything.

'Right,' her dad said. 'This is going to stop. Here and now. I'm going up to that school, and I'm going to make sure those people get what they deserve. Bullies and cowards, every one of them.'

'No, Dad, don't!' Kathy pleaded. Intervention from a parent was the worst thing that could happen to any teenager. The ridicule would get worse, the bullying more subtle but relentless, and even the teachers would despise her weakness. And there was another problem. If her dad went up to school, he'd find out she hadn't been there this week.

He was determined, though, marching down the hallway to phone up and make an appointment, even though it was Saturday.

'I'm not having it, Kathy,' he yelled. 'I'm not having any daughter of mine bullied by these ignorant, cowardly bastards.'

She heard a gasp behind her. Karen had just come in from the garden where she'd been pegging out the clean washing. Their father never swore. Ever.

'What's up?' Karen whispered.

Kathy picked up the note from the floor where her dad had thrown it in his rage.

Karen glanced at it, and her lower lip started to tremble. 'Shit, Kath. I think I know who wrote it.'

'What?'

'I know who wrote this note.' Her face reddened in embarrassment. 'I heard two lads talking about it at break. They thought it was a right laugh. I'm sorry. I didn't realise it was this bad, and I didn't realise they'd sent it to you. I thought they were having a bit of fun.'

'Who?' Kathy demanded.

Karen shook her head.

'Who left me this fucking note?' she screamed, grabbing her sister's long, red hair and curling it round her fist. 'You'd better tell me, or I'll bray you!' Kathy yelled, raising her other fist.

'It was some lads in fourth year and a couple of boys in my form. I think the one who wrote it is that lad who asked you out last year. You turned him down. He was calling you all sorts of names. He said you were a bitch, and that you deserved it. I didn't realise it was you he was talking about, though. It could have been anybody.'

'What lad?'

Karen shook her head as far as she could without increasing her sister's grip. 'Robert something. He lives up Old Mill near that lass you used to play with in juniors. I don't know his name, Kathy. Honest.'

'Loach,' she said, releasing her grip on her sister's hair. 'His name's Robert Loach.'

'And he's that one that wrote it, is he?' her dad asked from the kitchen doorway. Neither girl had realised he'd been listening, and Karen's blush deepened as her dad frowned at her possible complicity.

'Right. I'll have him. First thing on Monday, I'm going straight to your headmaster and telling him what our Karen just said. And you two are coming with me.'

Karen's mouth had formed an O of horror. 'He'll get expelled, Dad,' she whimpered.

'Good riddance,' her dad said, snatching the note from Kathy's hand, folding it and placing it carefully in the letter rack on the mantelpiece.

'And don't either of you dare pretend you're poorly on Monday. You're coming with me if I have to drag the pair of you there by your hair.'

CHAPTER 10

2015

Kate signed off the evidence bags in the property room at the station then headed upstairs to the incident room. She was already starting to feel the frustrations of the case and needed to hear what the other detectives had found out. The evidence she and Hollis had gathered at the Reeses' house was insufficient to warrant bringing in either Craig or any other member of Aleah's family, and there didn't seem much point in initiating a forensic search, with the added costs and extra staff, based on what they had seen this morning. Craig Reese had lied in his initial statement, but that didn't make him guilty of the kidnapping and murder of his stepdaughter. It was starting to look like this could be a stranger abduction which meant widening the search parameters and a lot of "what ifs" and "maybes."

She'd have to wait for the results on the tent, but when she'd glanced inside the canvas bag in the shed, she hadn't noticed anything unusual about the guy ropes. They didn't look like they'd been cut, but she couldn't tell if anything was missing.

As she reached the landing on the second floor, a figure barged through the double doors and nearly knocked her back downstairs.

'Watch it!' she snapped.

He stopped suddenly and backed up until she could see him properly. Drew Rigby.

'I was looking for you,' he said, frowning as though she'd stood him up on a date. 'I thought you wanted to meet me back here.'

There was no respect for her rank in his tone, and his deep blue eyes glowered belligerently from beneath dark eyebrows.

'And I said I'd be here in twenty minutes.'

'That was nearly an hour ago,' Rigby complained.

'Sorry. It's not like I have anything better to do,' Kate said, and Rigby's head pulled back, shocked by her sarcasm. 'I'm trying to find out who killed Aleah Reese, but I'm sorry if that got in the way of your tight schedule.'

At least he had the good grace to look embarrassed as he mumbled an apology. 'What did you want to see me about?' Rigby asked.

Kate sighed. This suddenly didn't feel like the time or the place to criticise a junior officer. 'Come back through,' she said, holding the door open and gesturing for Rigby to pass through. 'We can chat at my desk.'

The incident room was fairly quiet as Kate ushered the PCSO over to her desk. She told him to sit down while she wheeled another chair over from an empty desk. Barratt and O'Connor were chatting on their phones, mouthpieces half covered as though they were whispering, but Kate knew they were trying to mask the sounds of the office around them. Barratt glanced her way, pointed at his phone, and shrugged as if to express his own frustration with the case. She shook her head and sat down opposite Rigby.

'You searched the Reeses' house yesterday?' she asked, even though she'd already checked this with him earlier.

Rigby nodded warily.

'Did you check the shed?'

Another nod.

'Thoroughly?'

'I went inside, had a look behind some of the junk, opened the cupboard. There was no sign of the girl.' He recited his actions as though he was giving evidence in court.

'What about the house?' Kate prompted.

'I looked in Aleah's bedroom, in the parents' room and in the sitting room. There was nothing that struck me as unusual.'

Kate thought about the pile of drawings that she'd found. 'Did you see the pictures on Aleah's desk?'

Rigby nodded. 'Just a pile of kid's drawings.'

'They were drawn on the back of betting slips,' Kate said. 'Craig Reese had taken her to the bookies, despite his wife's wishes he stop gambling.'

'And? I'm sorry, but I don't see why this is relevant. They didn't tell me anything.'

'But did you turn them over and look on the other side?'

'No,' Rigby admitted, but Kate could see from his closed off expression he didn't see anything wrong with not checking.

'If you'd spotted the betting slips, we might have got an accurate statement from Craig Reese much earlier than we did. We could have at least added the bookmaker's shop to our list of enquiries.'

'Do you think it would have made a difference to the outcome? Am I in trouble in some way?' Rigby asked. He tilted his head up and fixed his eyes on a point on the wall next to the desk as if he was a child awaiting an undeserved telling-off from an angry parent.

Kate wanted to yell at him. He couldn't see this from her point of view at all. He was only concerned about the implications for himself. '"I honestly don't know" is the answer to your first question. And, no, you're not in trouble, I just wanted to urge you to be more thorough next time.'

He nodded. 'I will be. Is there anything else?'

Kate shook her head.

Rigby suddenly grinned at her, the chastised schoolboy look gone in an instant. 'I know you, you know.'

'What?'

'From when we were kids. I know you. Well, I knew your sister, Karen. You were a couple of years above me at school.'

Kate didn't know how to respond. First, Jean Loach, and now, this PCSO. It seemed there was no escape from the past today. 'I'm sorry,' she said. 'I don't remember you.'

Rigby shrugged. 'There's no reason you should. My family moved away when I was in third year. I only remember you because I used to fancy your Karen, but she never looked twice at me.'

Kate smiled, remembering her sister's view of boys when she was fourteen. As far as she was concerned, boys were smelly and "only after one thing." Her ideas had changed somewhat since then, and a string of "the ones" had left her disillusioned and in need of a new direction.

'She wouldn't have,' Kate said. 'She wasn't bothered about lads when she was that age.'

'What's she doing now?' Rigby asked, and Kate wondered if he had ideas about using her as a matchmaking service.

'She's trekking in India. She's away for six months trying to "find herself."'

Kate was about to tell him about Karen's failed attempts to find enlightenment through yoga and meditation, but something about his expression stopped her. She could tell he'd lost interest as soon as he'd discovered Karen was out of the country. And she was aware sharing personal information with a PCSO might be seen as inappropriate. She felt ambushed by the sudden familiarity and intimacy, as though she'd let her guard down for a few seconds and Rigby had slid under her defences.

Instead of saying anything else about her sister, she told him she had work to do, hoping he'd take the hint and leave.

'Have you found anything?' he asked. 'About Aleah? Had she drowned?'

Kate shrugged. 'Nothing conclusive as yet. I need to catch up with the team and find out what everybody knows.'

Rigby nodded but still made no move to leave. 'I fancy doing your job,' he said. 'CID. I was in the army for a bit and then did security for a cable works near Sheffield, but it didn't suit me. Do you think I'm too old to apply?'

Kate couldn't believe his audacity. She'd brought him here for a telling-off about his lack of diligence, and here he was, asking if she thought he'd make a detective. 'You could always try,' she said, spinning her chair around until she was facing away from him. This time, he took the hint.

She'd just logged onto her computer when her mobile rang. She glanced at the screen but didn't recognise the number. A quick flick of her thumb and a voice was asking for 'Detective Fletcher.'

'Speaking,' Kate said.

'Hi, you rang somebody at Ballater earlier today, asking about David Porter?'

Kate confirmed that she had.

'Oh, good,' the man said, his Scots accent extending the second word. 'I'm Steve McCready from human resources. I believe you'd been told he was working offshore by a family member? Well, he isn't on the rig this week. I don't know what you were told, but he's not at sea until next month now.'

Kate felt her pulse pounding in her forehead. Somebody had lied, but who? Had Dave's mother lied to her, or had Dave been lying to his mother? 'But he does work for your company?' she asked. 'And he works offshore for part of the time.'

'That's correct. He's on leave, at the moment.'

'Have you any idea how I might be able to contact him?'

A second of silence at the other end of the line.

'You might try his home number. Or his mobile. I'm assuming you have those?'

'I don't. I spoke to his mother, but she didn't give me any contact details as she seemed convinced he was on the platform this week.'

'As I said, that information is incorrect.'

'I don't suppose you have those numbers?'

A sigh and more silence.

'It is essential I contact him, Mr McCready. A family member has been involved in an incident, and we need to inform Mr Porter as soon as possible.'

'Okay, I've got his details on my screen. Have you got a pen?'

Kate grabbed a chewed biro and wrote down both numbers, checking each one with McCready before he hung up. 'Interesting,' she mumbled to herself.

'What is?' asked Hollis. He'd obviously crept up on her while she'd been on the phone.

'That was Ballater Engineering. Dave Porter isn't on the rig this week.'

'Where is he?'

Kate frowned and tapped the screen on her phone. 'That's exactly what I'd like to know.'

The phone rang at the other end of the line. Twice, three times. Kate tapped a finger on the desk impatiently. After the sixth ring, an answering machine kicked in with a generic message. Kate hung up, checked her note and tried the mobile number.

'Hello?' A woman's voice.

'Hello,' Kate said. 'Is this David Porter's phone?'

'Who wants to know?' Her tone turned instantly suspicious.

Kate introduced herself and explained she needed to speak to David Porter as a matter of urgency. The phone at the other end was dropped with a clunk, and Kate waited, twisting in her chair and raising her eyebrows quizzically at Hollis.

'Dave Porter speaking. What's this about?'

Kate turned back to her desk and repeated her name and rank, while she considered her options. She hadn't been confident she'd be able to speak to Porter, and now that she'd found him, there was no way she could avoid telling him about the death of his daughter. But she hated to do it over the phone.

'Mr Porter,' she began. 'I'm ringing with some bad news. Your daughter has been involved in an incident.'

'Incident?' he repeated.

'She was reported missing on Tuesday. Our initial search failed to turn up any evidence as to her whereabouts. Yesterday morning, she was found in a pond on an area of disused land. I'm sorry, Mr Porter, I'm afraid Aleah's dead.'

Silence.

Kate waited, allowing him time to process what she'd just said.

'Are you sure?' he asked eventually. 'Are you sure it's Aleah?'

'I'm afraid so. We've had a positive ID.'

'How…' He cleared his throat. 'How did it happen?'

'I can't say at the moment,' Kate said. 'We're still trying to track Aleah's last movements to try to find out what happened. I'd like to send a police officer to talk to you, if that's possible. Somebody local. Are you at home?'

'No. No, I'm… oh, shit. I can't get my head around this. I never had much to do with Aleah, but she was mine, you know, flesh and blood. I thought, maybe when she got older, that she might…' his voice tailed off.

'Mr Porter. Are you at home?' Kate prompted.

A sigh. 'Have you spoken to my mam? Does she know?'

'About Aleah? Yes. We spoke this morning. She thought you were offshore this week.'

'That's what I told her.' He sighed. 'I didn't want her to know where I am.'

'Which is where?'

'I'm in Sheffield. If I'd told her, she'd have wanted me to go home and visit. I lied. I've been seeing somebody, and I wanted to spend some time with her. She's got a house near Endcliffe Park.'

'I'll need an address,' Kate said. 'I'd like to come and talk to you myself.'

Kate noted down the address he gave and told him to expect her within the hour. 'Shit,' she breathed. 'This changes things.'

'What?' Hollis asked. 'Where is he?'

'He's been in Sheffield for the last few days. It's only half an hour from Thorpe. We need to get over there. Now.'

CHAPTER 11

2015

The sky over Endcliffe Park was bruised-looking with heavy thunderclouds as Hollis followed his satnav and turned onto the street that Dave Porter had named. It was lined with terraced houses, but these were very different from the ones where Porter's mother lived. Each was set back slightly from the street with low brick walls demarcating property boundaries. Some even sheltered patches of grass or clumps of shrubs – obvious attempts at a front garden – beneath generous bay windows. The houses themselves were bigger than the ones in Thorpe, and many had been extended further with the addition of Velux roof lights or dormer windows indicating the addition of attic rooms.

'Here,' Kate said, pointing to a gap in the parked cars which lined both sides of the street. 'We can walk from here. Looks like parking's a bugger.'

She reached for the door handle, but Hollis spoke before she could get out.

'Are you okay? You've hardly said two words since we got off the Parkway. You look like you are miles away.'

Kate shrugged. 'Just thinking about Aleah. It's a bit of a coincidence her dad happens to be having a secret liaison in Sheffield on the day she disappeared.'

Hollis nodded, accepting her response, and Kate tried hard to stifle a sigh of relief. How could she tell him she'd been dreading coming to Sheffield? Since they'd driven up through the city and she'd caught a glimpse of the university buildings, she'd been reliving her last conversation with Ben, the one where he'd told her he'd rather rely on his dad for support when he went to university. That had been nearly a year ago. She'd called to see whether he needed anything and to let him know she was living in Doncaster, and while he'd been polite, he'd made his lack of interest clear and had refused to accept her offer of financial assistance. They'd exchanged texts a few times since, but her son gave away very little about his new life as a student, and it was only through Garry that she knew he'd chosen to study environmental science.

They hadn't been close since her split with his father, and even though Kate knew it made sense for Ben to stay with Garry so he could finish his A-levels without moving schools, she hadn't expected to become so out of touch with her son's life so quickly.

'Come on. Let's see what Porter has to say,' she said, opening the car door and allowing a blast of heat to enter.

The address Porter had given was a few doors away from where they'd parked. As she approached the front door, Kate noticed a handwritten sign fixed to the glass on the inside.

PLEASE USE BACK DOOR.

She glanced down the alleyway which led between the house and its neighbour. Darkness.

'After you,' she said to Hollis, following as he led the way to a tall gate blocking the garden end of the passageway.

The back door opened before Hollis had even raised his fist to knock, and an attractive blonde woman smiled at them. She wore no make-up, and her shabby clothes looked like she'd been gardening in them, but her high cheek bones and confident gaze were a striking combination.

'Hi,' she said. 'Are you the police? Dave's in the front room.'

She opened the door further and ushered Kate and Hollis inside. The back room was a kitchen, modern and bright with a series of black-and-white photographs dotting the walls which weren't occupied by cupboards. The woman saw Kate looking at the images and said, 'I'm a photographer. I do seascapes mostly. That's how I met Dave. I… er. I'm sorry. I'm Sara Evans. I should have introduced myself.'

She led them through to the living room and then quietly backed away and closed the door, allowing them some privacy while they talked to Dave Porter. The room was calming; pale walls, ornate fire surround and discreet electrical equipment. One alcove next to the chimney breast was shelved from top to bottom and completely lined with books, the other housed a flat-screen television. Like the kitchen, the walls in here were adorned with examples of Sara's work, including a huge print of Whitby Abbey Kate coveted immediately.

Dave Porter was sitting in an armchair facing the front window and didn't acknowledge them until he heard the door close behind his girlfriend.

'Mr Porter?' Kate said quietly. The man seemed to be in some sort of trance, just staring into space. Then, he blinked and shook his head as if to shake himself awake. He stood up and extended a hand.

'Yes, sorry. I've been feeling a bit out of it since you rang.'

He shook hands with Hollis and Kate and gestured to the leather sofa which ran along one wall of the room. They sat, and Kate leaned forward, elbows on knees, as she studied the man opposite. He was well built, muscular rather than fat, and even slumped in the chair, he seemed to dominate the room. His blond hair stood up in spikes and tufts as though he'd been running his hands through it, and the skin around his eyes was red and puffy. He was perceptibly upset about the death of his daughter.

'The thing is,' he continued. 'I don't really know how to feel. It's not as if I had much to do with Aleah. Well, nothing, really. But she was my flesh and blood, and that means something, doesn't it?'

He glanced up at Kate as though he expected her to understand.

'Mr Porter. I'm so sorry for your loss, but I need to establish your whereabouts for the past forty-eight hours. We believed you were working offshore, but that's obviously not the case.'

Porter's eyes narrowed. 'You think I had something to do with this? You think I killed my own daughter?'

'That's not what DI Fletcher is saying,' Hollis stepped in. 'It's routine, sir. You must understand that. We have to ask certain questions.'

A nod from Porter. He seemed to be responding well to Hollis, so Kate sat back and allowed him to take the lead.

'Your mother told us you were at sea this week,' he repeated. 'Clearly, we don't know why you told her that, but I'm sure you had your reasons. We just need to establish where you've been for the last couple of days.'

'Here,' Porter said, sitting back in his chair. 'I've been here with Sara. I didn't tell my mam because she would have expected a visit, and I promised I'd spend this week with Sara.'

'And Sara is…?'

'My girlfriend.' He smiled as though the word still felt unfamiliar but pleasant. 'We've been seeing each for about six months. We met on the coast outside Aberdeen. I was out for a walk, and she was photographing the sea. I fell for her, literally. Her legs were across the path, and I tripped over her.'

Hollis made a note. 'And when did you arrange this visit?'

'A few weeks ago. She's stayed with me a few times, and so, we decided it was my turn to visit her.'

'Does she know about your connections with the area?'

'Hard to hide them with this accent,' Porter said. 'She picked up the South Yorkshire twang as soon as we met. She's an Essex girl, but she stayed here after uni. I thought it was a strange place to live if you like the sea, but Sara says she can get to pretty much any part of the coast in less than a day from here. It's very central.'

Kate could see he was lost in memories of his girlfriend, and the interview was losing focus. 'Tell us about this trip.' she prompted.

Porter looked at her as though he'd just remembered he had company. 'Sara wanted to show me her home. It's years since I spent any time in Sheffield, so I wanted to have a look around, to see what's changed. I couldn't tell my mam, though. She'd have wanted to see me, and this trip wasn't about family. It was about me and Sara.'

'What did you do on Tuesday?' Hollis asked.

'Not much. Got up late. Went to the café in the park for breakfast. Walked up to Forge Dam and had a coffee. Walked back. Then, that night, we went out for dinner to an Indian restaurant just up the road.'

'Can anybody vouch for this, other than Sara?'

'I dunno.' Porter shrugged. 'The woman who served us breakfast knows Sara. She'd probably remember. And Sara took some pictures of me eating on her phone. You can probably tell where I am.'

'You didn't take Sara to Thorpe?'

Porter shook his head. 'I've not been back in months. I went for my mam's birthday in February but not since then.'

'Does Sara know about Aleah? Have you told her that you have a daughter?'

'I told her a few weeks ago. It felt funny, saying it out loud. I always knew she was mine, but I never really felt a connection with her. Now she's gone, though… I just always wondered if she might want to get to know me, when she was older.' He rubbed his face with his hands, trying to control his emotions.

Kate could see he was struggling. 'I think we'll need to see those photographs,' she said. 'The ones on Sara's phone.'

Porter nodded and called for his girlfriend. She pushed open the door a minute later, and Kate imagined her listening at the other side and then counting off the seconds before she made an appearance. Was her evidence going to be worth anything? It was obvious from the way she looked at Dave Porter that she had fallen for him.

'Hi, Sara,' Kate said, trying for her most reassuring smile. 'We just need to ask you a couple of questions about Tuesday. Can you run through your day for us?'

Sara glanced at her boyfriend and then back at Kate. 'What do you mean?'

'Just tell us what you did. What time you got up, that sort of thing.'

She nodded uncertainly. 'Well, we got up late.' Another glance at Porter confirmed in Kate's mind the reason why they had difficulty getting out of bed. New love. She couldn't help but feel a bit envious, and a bit sorry for them. It didn't last, that feeling.

'Then, we went across to the park for breakfast. The café there does a really good full English.'

'What time would this have been?' Hollis wanted to know, pen poised above his notebook.

Sara shrugged. 'Eleven? Half past?'

'And did you see anybody that you knew? Somebody who could confirm where you were?'

She nodded. 'The woman who served us, Sally, owns the café. She knows me. I'm not sure she'll remember what time it was, though.'

'You took some photographs of Mr Porter eating breakfast?'

'Yes! They'll have the time on.' She dug in the front pocket of her tight-fitting jeans and pulled out her mobile phone. A few flicks and she turned the screen around so Kate could see it. 'Flick forward from there. If you tap the screen, the date and time come up.'

Kate thumbed through the pictures. The first showed Porter sitting at an outside table with a huge breakfast in front of him. He was pretending to frown in concentration as he held his knife and fork, ready to tuck in. A quick tap revealed the photograph was taken at 11.24 am. The others formed a short photo journal of the meal. Some were close-ups of Dave Porter's face, others showed the plate with the contents slowly disappearing. Even though they were quick snaps, they demonstrated a keen eye for composition and framing and a clear sense of humour. Kate found herself warming to Sara through her work.

The last image was of Dave holding an empty plate in one hand, the other raised in a victorious fist. The time stamp was 11.37am. They'd need to check with the café owner, but it looked like Dave Porter had nothing to do with the abduction and murder of his daughter.

Kate couldn't decide whether she was pleased or disappointed.

'Well, that didn't get us any further,' Hollis said, as Kate slammed the car door, and he turned on the engine. 'I hoped, in a way, he'd be a lot shiftier, but he seemed like a genuine bloke. Another dead end.'

'We still need to check at the café. Fancy an ice cream? I'm buying.'

Ten minutes later, they were perched at a plastic table outside the park café, Hollis with double chocolate ice cream and Kate with salted caramel. The proprietor, Sally, had told them to wait outside while she served a big family group, and Kate had been happy to follow her instruction. The café overlooked a huge grassy area which had been taken over by groups of people of all ages. There was what looked to be a football team for five-year-olds at the far side, a group of young men playing Frisbee, and a number of families either picnicking or throwing something around. The mood was relaxed, despite the threat of rain from the darkening clouds.

'I used to come here as a kid,' Hollis said. 'My dad would drive us up from Chesterfield, and we'd walk through the parks, feed the ducks, have a sandwich, and go home. I loved it.'

Kate smiled and snapped part of her ice cream cone off so she could use it as a scoop. It was the most personal thing Hollis had revealed, and she liked the idea of him running around on the grass: the innocence was appealing.

'How about you? Have you been here before?'

She shook her head. 'Sheffield was the great unknown when I was growing up in Thorpe. Doncaster was our sun. Sometimes, people went to the market in Rotherham but never Sheffield.'

'And then, you moved away?'

'We went to live near Nottingham. A newish town. It was good, better than where we'd come from at least.'

'So why move to Cumbria?'

Kate took her time finishing her cornet, and then, she wiped her mouth with the inadequate square of tissue that had come wrapped around the base. She considered telling Hollis to mind his own business, but she knew he wasn't prying; he was just making conversation and to rebuke him would be unnecessarily churlish.

'Love,' she said. 'Isn't that why anybody moves to anywhere?'

'Love of the hills, or love of a man?'

She laughed. 'Love of a man who loved the hills.'

Hollis frowned at her, surprised at her answer. Or perhaps surprised she'd given an answer. 'So, where is he now?'

'Still in Cumbria. Still loving the hills and still loving a woman half my age.'

'Ah.'

They both glanced across the field, watching the kids playing football, and Kate hoped she'd put an end to the conversation, but Hollis wasn't easily daunted.

'Did you have kids with the mountain man?'

Kate nodded. 'A son, Ben. He's just turned nineteen. He's in his first year at university. He got my husband and the house in the divorce.'

'And what did you get?' Hollis asked.

Kate thought for a few seconds. 'Peace of mind.'

'Where's he studying, your Ben?'

Kate pointed in the direction of the university. Hollis looked baffled until realisation dawned, and his eyebrows met his hairline in disbelief.

'He's here? In Sheffield?'

'Environmental science at the uni.'

'Don't you want to see him, while you're here?'

Kate shrugged. 'I doubt he'd appreciate it. We don't talk much, at the moment. Hopefully, when he's a bit older, we'll get on better again.'

'Oh. It just seems–'

Hollis was interrupted by the appearance of the café owner. She smiled at them both and pulled out a chair opposite Kate.

'Bloody hot in there,' she said, untying the red bandana she was wearing to keep her unruly dark curls in check and wiping her face with it. 'School holidays are great for my bank balance but not so good for anything else.'

Kate felt immediately drawn to her open manner. She was probably about the same age as Hollis and very pretty. Her dark hair and deep brown eyes suggested Mediterranean heritage, and she had the poise and measured movements of a dancer.

'You wanted to ask me something about yesterday?'

Hollis took out his notebook and flipped back a few pages. 'We just need to confirm the details of a statement we were given earlier.'

'Okay.'

'You know Sara Evans? She's a friend of yours?'

The woman nodded. 'She comes in a lot. Has done for a couple of years.'

'So, you know her as a customer?' Kate asked.

'At first. She's a photographer. Outdoorsy stuff mostly, but she did some shots of my nephew's picnic, here in the park.'

'So, she did some work for your family?'

The woman nodded. 'My brother wanted some proper photos of Lewis, his son. He… er… he has leukaemia. We wanted some memories of him while he was healthy. Sara did a brilliant job.'

Hollis nodded and seemed reluctant to continue so Kate stepped in.

'And you're friends now?'

Sally nodded, the action sending tsunami-like waves through her hair.

'Did you see her on Tuesday morning?'

'She came in for breakfast, a couple of days ago. Late breakfast.' Her serious expression turned suddenly lewd, and Kate half expected her to add *nudge, nudge, wink, wink*. 'She's got a new boyfriend. Dave something. I think she wanted to show him off. Seemed like a nice man.'

'And they were both in here on Tuesday?'

'Yep. Came in around eleven. I was teasing Sara about the time, and how she needed a full breakfast to keep her energy levels up.'

'What time did they leave?'

She shrugged. 'Maybe half an hour or forty-five minutes later. He came inside to pay, and I told him to say goodbye to her from me.'

Hollis closed his notebook with a snap.

Nothing more to add.

CHAPTER 12

2015

Kate's phone rang as they were pulling into the car park at Doncaster Central.

'Where are you two?' Raymond barked as soon as she tapped the screen.

'Car park. On the way up now.'

'Well, get a bloody move on. We've got another one.'

'Another one?'

'Missing kiddie. From Thorpe.'

She gave Hollis an account of the phone call as they jogged upstairs to the incident room. Stunned faces turned to the door as they entered, like sunflowers following the light. Kate felt like she was back at school again, and she'd walked in late to an exam. On the whiteboard was an image of a boy who looked to be about four or five years old. It was a school photograph – pale yellow polo shirt with a logo, neatly parted hair and a grin that revealed a gap in his front teeth.

Raymond had obviously been in the middle of his narrative. He pointed to two empty seats, and Kate and Hollis obediently slipped into them.

'Okay. For our new arrivals,' his voice dripped sarcasm. 'This is four-year-old Callum Goodwin. Last seen playing on his scooter on the street in front of his parents' house on Aspen Grove this afternoon. Mum was in the garden – went inside to get a drink – came out, and little Callum was gone.'

'Where was his scooter?' Hollis asked.

'Also gone. What we know so far is bugger all. Uniforms have been canvassing the area, but nobody saw anything.' Raymond's tone suggested he thought the uniformed officers were incompetent.

'Is there a link with Aleah Reese?' Kate wanted to know.

'That,' Raymond's voice boomed, 'is the sixty-four-thousand-pound question. The family live two streets away from the Reeses, in a square.'

Kate started making notes as she envisaged the area. The "square" was a cul-de-sac – a short road surrounded by eight or ten semis.

'How come nobody saw anything? It's like a goldfish bowl down there.'

Raymond glanced down, consulting his notes. 'Most of the neighbours were at work. A couple were out shopping.'

'But the place must be crawling with marked cars. What sort of person snatches a kid from under our noses?' Kate couldn't make sense of the arrogance it would take to do something like that.

'A bloody clever one,' Raymond snapped. 'Or just lucky.'

'Do the family know the Reeses?'

'Everybody knows everybody on that estate.'

'But there's no connection? No family link? Work? Nothing?'

'Not so far. It looks like this and the taking of the Reese girl might be random. Opportunistic. We need to get digging. If there is a connection between these two, then we need to find it. Fast. If there isn't a link, then we need to be extra thorough. If this is a nutter with a thing for kids, we might have another body on our hands.' Raymond paused, surveying the grim faces in the room before focussing on Kate. 'Fletcher – in my office!'

The DCI stormed out. Kate followed him into his office and closed the door behind her as he marched to the seat behind his desk and flopped down as though he was exhausted. A vague wave in the direction of the other vacant seat invited Kate to sit opposite him.

'I don't like this,' he said. 'Two kids from the same estate.'

Kate nodded. 'Too much of a coincidence.'

He pulled a file out of a drawer in the desk and pushed it over to her. 'We've got more details from Aleah Reese's PM. Nothing to contradict what we were first told. Manual strangulation. No prints, no useful trace evidence, no sign of sexual assault. But she'd been held somewhere after she died. There are some marks which suggest perhaps the floor of a van. Livor shows some odd lines as though she was left on a ridged surface like the metal floor in a delivery vehicle. She'd eaten some type of breakfast cereal with nuts, and as I said before, it hadn't had time to digest, suggesting she was killed soon after she was snatched. Kailisa puts it at somewhere between midday and four that afternoon. He doesn't think she was held anywhere for any length of time – even if she was terrified, the stomach contents would have been more degraded.'

He pulled the file back towards him as though he'd changed his mind about sharing the information with Kate. 'And there's this.'

He pulled out a photograph and slid it across the desk towards her. It showed an image of Aleah's head and neck. Nestled in the hollow between her clavicles was a gold pendant, the chain snaked back around her neck and looked like it was stuck to her damp flesh.

Kate bit down hard on the sorrow that threatened to engulf her. 'Have you got a close-up?' she managed to ask.

Raymond slid her another photograph.

'It looks like a letter T.'

Raymond grunted his agreement. 'I had Cooper Google it. It could be a letter T or it could be a Tau cross, a particular type of Christian cross without the top bit.'

Kate considered his statement. 'The cross makes more sense. Why would a kid wear a pendant with a letter that isn't part of her own name? Is the family religious?'

Raymond shook his head. 'That's the thing, Fletcher. It isn't her necklace. Barratt rang to check. They had no idea what he was talking about.'

'Shit,' Kate said. 'This isn't random, is it? Somebody targeted Aleah Reese for a specific reason? Maybe some religious nutter who wanted to use this to brand his kill?'

'That's what I'm thinking,' Raymond said. 'Nutter of one flavour or another. Which makes it all the more important we find out what's happened to Callum Goodwin. I'm not ruling out Craig Reese. Aleah might just have been him getting started, and now, he's moving on. I need you to share this with your team.'

He slid the folder across the desk, and Kate understood what he was saying. This was her case now. Raymond had seen enough of her work to allow her to run her own investigation. As senior investigating officer, he'd still have an overview, but the hour-to-hour decisions and actions of her team were down to her. This was what she'd moved for; this was what her promotion had been about.

She stood up, clutching the folder to her chest and turned to leave.

'And Fletcher?'

She turned to see Raymond scowling up at her.

'I'll be watching. Don't fuck this up.'

Hollis grinned at her as she threw the folder down onto her desk. 'Bollocking?'

Kate shook her head. 'Just the opposite. I need to get the others up to speed. A hand?'

She sent Hollis to the scanner with the photographs and quickly read through the autopsy notes. She'd seen much worse, but the description of such a young life so brutally snuffed out made grim reading. And there was nothing much to move them forward. Time for a brainstorming session.

The other detectives looked apprehensive as she turned to address them in the meeting room, and she was sure Barratt glanced over her shoulder to see if Raymond was following her through the door. They were all there, *her* team, all three of them – and O'Connor. Hollis smiled encouragingly, but she sensed he was anxious for her, and not for the first time, she was glad that he had her back.

She picked up the remote for the projector, and it came on with a beep. A quick swipe of her finger across the trackpad of the laptop and the first of the new PM photos was displayed on the whiteboard. Kate turned to check it was clear and then back to the four expectant faces.

'Right. Raymond has handed the day-to-day of this investigation over to me. He'll still have oversight, but this is now my case, which means it's *our* case.'

A surprised exhalation from O'Connor.

'I know I've not been here for very long, but I'm not an outsider. I was born in Thorpe, two streets away from where the Reeses live. I grew up there. I knew the village, and I still know some of the people there. But *you* know the area *now*, not in the past.'

Nods of approval from O'Connor, Cooper and Hollis.

'We've got the full PM report on Aleah Reese.' She pointed to the image behind her, a close-up of the dead girl's face, slack and inanimate as though she was in a deep sleep.

'Something's come up we need to think about. I don't know what it means and nor does Raymond, but one of you might have some ideas.'

She flicked forward to the photograph showing Aleah's neck.

'This necklace was found on Aleah's body. The family say it's not hers. Cooper thought it could be something called a Tau cross.'

Cooper flushed at the mention of her name.

'So, if we get a suspect called Tony or Ted, we're sorted,' Barratt said, with a soft chuckle.

'I doubt it's that simple,' Kate said. 'But we can live in hope.'

'Does Raymond think the Goodwin boy is connected?' O'Connor asked.

Kate ignored the implied slight and shrugged. 'We can't rule it out. It's a hell of a coincidence, and his disappearance is similar. Kid on his own, nobody saw anything.'

'Despite an obvious police presence on the estate,' Cooper said. 'Might suggest it's somebody local. Somebody everybody was used to seeing so they wouldn't think his, or her, presence in the area was unusual. Somebody who wouldn't be noticed?'

'Craig Reese lives just around the corner,' Barratt said. 'I still like him for Aleah. He might have taken another one to throw us off. I bet he's got a decent alibi.'

'His story about Aleah stacks up, though,' Cooper said. 'It's obvious from the CCTV he's upset when he can't find her.'

'Or it's obvious he knew he was on CCTV. He could have followed her to the shop, grabbed her and tied her up, and then gone back to the bookies.'

Hollis shook his head.

'So, where did he put her when he went back? He couldn't just leave her in the street.'

Kate flicked forward on the laptop to another photograph. This one showed the lividity marks on Aleah's back. Clear vertical stripes, as though she had been laid on a ridged surface.

'She was kept somewhere after she died,' she said. 'Raymond thought maybe the back of a van with a metal floor. Reese doesn't have a van. Any other thoughts?'

Three heads tilted from one side to the other and back again as her team studied the photographs.

'I'd be inclined to agree with the DCI,' Barratt said, and Hollis nodded. 'But it doesn't rule out Reese. He may have transport we know nothing about. He could have borrowed a van.'

'But the time frame doesn't add up,' Kate said. 'He'd have had twenty minutes to grab her, strangle her, and dump her in a van. We know he walked up to the village with Aleah. Where did he kill her? He could hardly do it on Main Street.'

'He could have taken her to the van and killed her there. She'd have gone with him. All he has to do then is rush back to the bookies and look frantic with worry,' Hollis suggested.

Kate thought for a minute. It was possible, just. But was it plausible? Did Craig Reese fit the profile of a child killer? And what was his motive?

'Okay,' she conceded. 'We should have another look at Reese. He might have borrowed a van from a friend, or have one that's not registered.'

'Or he might have nicked it,' Barratt said.

'Okay. So, we'll have Reese back in and see if he can add anything to his previous statement. What else?'

'I still think Ken Fowler is either as dodgy as hell or Mister Right-Place-Right-Time,' Barratt said. 'And he drives an old Landy. Might be worth a look in the back. If he and Reese alibi each other for Tuesday night, then either one of them could be lying. There's the tent ropes thing as well. I bet our Ken's a keen camper.'

'Where are we at with Reese's tent?' Hollis asked. 'Have you heard anything?'

Kate shook her head. It could take a couple of days for forensics to check the tent to see if the guy ropes had been cut or were missing. And then, they would have to try to match the ropes found on Aleah's body to the ones from the tent found in Reese's shed.

'Cooper, what did you dig up about Paul Hirst's suicide? Anything useful?'

Cooper shook her head. 'Not yet.'

O'Connor said, 'I asked around this afternoon. Couldn't get anybody to talk about him or Jud Reese.' Kate wasn't surprised. Getting anybody to talk about events during the strike was next to impossible without a great deal of alcohol.

'Look,' she said. 'We need a list of actions, and we need to factor Callum Godwin into the investigation. At the moment, he's a missing child – and let's hope he turns up – but if he doesn't, we might be looking at two dead children.'

She studied the faces that were hanging on her every word. Eager, intelligent, and keen for direction.

'So, actions for tomorrow. Barratt – follow up on Fowler. Talk to him, check his alibi, and try to get a look in his Land Rover. Cooper – you did excellent work digging into the background of the Reeses, so keep digging. And add Callum Goodwin's parents to your search. There might be a link. And check phone records – find out if Reese contacted anybody who might have a van. And if he had contact with the Goodwins. Hollis, with me. We'll have a chat with the Goodwins, and I want to go back to the first scene.'

'What for?' Barratt asked. 'Forensics will have gone over it already.'

'We're missing something,' Kate said. 'Why dump the body there? Aleah wasn't drowned. She could have been left anywhere. This place might mean something to the killer.'

As she said it, Kate felt that she was right. The choice of site for the body wasn't random or opportunistic. The whole thing had the feeling of being staged, and the necklace tied in perfectly. There was a message there, if only they knew how to read it. Whoever had killed Aleah Reese felt he had some sort of justification. He had a reason. Kate just prayed he wasn't on some sort of mission and just getting started.

'Cooper? Who owns that site? Did you find out?'

Cooper shook her head. 'I was working on the CCTV and the background checks. I'll have a look. It should be fairly easy to find.'

Kate nodded, satisfied. At least they had a plan.

CHAPTER 13

2015

Barratt knocked on the door and then took a step back to assess the house Ken Fowler had given as his address. A new build at the end of a cul-de-sac, it sat in a slightly elevated position and commanded a view of the entrance to the road and most of the other houses. A strip of drying grass ran along one side, flanked by a wooden fence. The attached garage was locked with padlocks and hasps, and above the door, a burglar alarm box indicated the occupants of the house took their security seriously. Or they had something worth stealing.

The latter seemed unlikely. The area was popular with retirees looking to downsize and first-time buyers trying to get a foot on the property ladder. The main entrance road to the estate ran off a dual carriageway which took a back route into Rotherham. On the other side of the main road, connected by a footbridge, was a large Tesco supermarket and a chain pub which advertised pensioners' specials and two-for-one meal deals. Obviously targeting their local market.

Barratt knocked again. He hadn't warned Fowler he was coming. He believed the element of surprise was always useful when dealing with a suspect, but he was beginning to wonder if he'd had a wasted trip. Just as he was about to leave, the door was suddenly snatched open.

'Christ, what's your problem? I was in the shower.' Ken Fowler was dressed in tracksuit bottoms and a T-shirt which revealed bulging biceps as he towelled his head and neck, making a point about being interrupted.

'Sorry to bother you so early,' Barratt lied. He held out his warrant card and introduced himself. 'I'm here about Aleah Reese.'

Fowler just stared at him.

'The little girl whose body was found on the old quarry site?' Barratt prompted.

'I know who she is. I just don't know why you want to talk to me. I've given a statement.'

'Yes,' Barratt agreed. 'And that's why I'm here. I just want to clarify some details, if that's okay with you.'

Another long, assessing stare, then Fowler stepped back and gestured for Barratt to step into the hallway. He led the way into an immaculate sitting room and pointed at a large leather sofa.

'Sit,' he said. 'I'm going out in about fifteen minutes. I trust this won't take long?'

'Anywhere nice?'

Fowler didn't answer, and Barratt suspected his reticence was his default setting rather than a response to being interviewed.

'Right. Well, I just need to ask about your encounter with Craig Reese. It seems that you're his alibi for the night Aleah went missing.'

'And he's mine,' Fowler said. 'I've thought about that. If you suspect one of us, then it's my word against his regarding what happened that night.' He sat in a chair opposite Barratt and waited. Barratt flicked back through his notes, trying not to let Fowler's manner bother him.

'You said you saw Craig Reese at "sometime between half past nine and ten o'clock" near the pond where the girl's body was found.'

Fowler nodded.

'And you'd already been to the pond?'

Another nod.

'Why did you go back so late?'

Fowler sighed. 'It seemed an obvious place to look. Kids play over there all the time. If she'd run away or been hiding from her parents, I just thought she might have gravitated to the pond at some point.'

Barratt made a note of "gravitated;" Fowler was obviously educated and eloquent, despite his reticence.

'But you'd checked there earlier?'

'No. Somebody in my team checked there.'

'So, why the need to see for yourself? Don't you trust your team?'

Fowler grinned disconcertingly as though he was unused to smiling. 'Of course I trust my team. But what would you do in the circumstances? A little girl was missing. I couldn't just clock off at five and go home. Is that what you do at the end of a shift? Whatever's going on, you just leave it until tomorrow? I doubt it. I couldn't come back here and just sit, so I kept busy.'

'Do you work?'

Fowler scowled at him and seemed reluctant to answer. 'Retired,' he finally said. 'Royal Logistics Corp.'

'And you live alone?' Barratt asked, glancing round the room that seemed to have been lifted wholesale out of an interior design magazine. There wasn't a chair or a cushion out of place. The curtains were held back with tasteful tiebacks, and the distressed hardwood floor looked expensive. He found himself wondering if Fowler were gay and then gave himself a mental slap for lazy stereotyping.

'I do,' Fowler confirmed. 'I bought this place before it was even built. I like the area, and I liked the plans. My sister's an interior designer, and she took charge of the decorating. I have a regular cleaner who does a much better job than I ever could of keeping the place tidy. I'm not very domesticated.'

'So, there's no Mrs Fowler?'

The stare again.

'Okay. Back to Tuesday night. How did Craig Reese seem to you?'

'Seem?'

'Was he agitated? Distracted? Upset?'

'Distracted.'

The answer was so definite Barratt immediately regretted even suggesting it. Was he leading Fowler? 'Distracted how?' he asked.

Fowler thought for a minute. 'He didn't see me at first, even though it wasn't dark. He was wandering along with his hands in his pockets and his head down.'

'Was he walking towards the pond or away?'

'Towards. He said he couldn't settle so he'd decided to carry on looking for Aleah. I told him I'd just checked the pond.'

'And then where did he go?'

Fowler shrugged. 'He just turned away and kept on along the path.'

'Towards the village?'

Another shrug.

Barratt snapped his notebook closed and slipped it into the breast pocket of his suit jacket. 'I do have another reason for being here,' he said, with what he hoped was a convincing smile. 'My boss told me you were driving an old Land Rover, and I hoped to get a look at it. It sounded like a classic, but I couldn't be sure from her description. I didn't see it on the drive, though.'

Fowler gave him an appraising glance, and Barratt wondered if his fifteen minutes of internet research would be enough to convince Fowler he was an enthusiast.

'You know Land Rovers?' Fowler asked, his head tilted sceptically to one side.

'Not really,' Barratt hedged. 'I'm just a beginner. My grandad had one when I was a kid and I loved it, so I started to find out a bit about them.'

'And what have you found out?'

'All sorts. I quite fancy finding a 1970s Series 3 and doing it up. I've heard that the parts aren't too hard to find.'

Fowler nodded, satisfied. 'Come on then.'

He led the way through the kitchen, which was as impressively clean and tasteful as the living room, to a door which appeared to lead into the garage. It was bolted top and bottom and deadlocked. Whatever Fowler had in the garage was obviously valuable to warrant so much security. Fowler caught Barratt looking at the lock as he turned the key.

'Can't be too sure,' he said, with a half-smile. 'Right then, here you go.'

He reached around Barratt and flicked a switch which lit a row of strip lights that ran the length of the garage ceiling. Like the rest of the house, the place was orderly and, for a garage, very clean. Garden tools were bracketed to the end wall, and the side walls were lined with steel cupboards and cabinets which, Barratt assumed, contained tools. In the middle of it all was the Land Rover. Barratt was impressed, despite himself. He'd done a bit of research about classic Land Rovers, just to see what they were worth, and he knew this one was something special. Or it could be. It was obviously used, and used often. The tyres were worn, and the wheel hubs dusty. The windscreen needed a wipe, and the olive-green paintwork was splashed with dirty water marks, probably from one of the recent showers.

'Wow,' he said appreciatively. 'She's quite something. I'm surprised you drive her.'

Fowler turned and frowned at him. 'What else would I do with it? It's a functional vehicle.'

'But she must be worth a fortune. What model is she?' Barratt couldn't help but stick with the female pronoun, despite Fowler's use of "it."

'A 1959 series II. If I gave it a good clean and replaced the brake pads and the back canvas, it'd probably sell for about fifty grand,' Fowler said. 'In this condition, somewhere between thirty-five and forty.'

Barratt whistled. He'd seen models on some of the websites he'd browsed that were worth a similar amount, but he hadn't expected Fowler to have something so valuable. He seemed to be doing well for somebody who was retired. Barratt considered asking Fowler about his financial situation, but it was more curiosity than anything relevant to the enquiry.

'Did you do the restoration?' he asked instead, trying to draw the man out with conversation about his hobbies.

Fowler shook his head. 'It was about half done when I got it. I've done a lot of bits and pieces, but there are still a few bits I could do, like the canvas, and the seat covering's been replaced with cheap vinyl at some point.'

'Do you mind if I…' Barratt stepped closer to the vehicle, bending to peer through the passenger side window. The seat was strewn with maps and papers, obviously left over from Tuesday's search. 'I used to sit in the back of my grandad's,' he lied. 'Can I have a look?'

Fowler stepped past him, rolled up the canvas and unlocked the rear door, swinging it open for Barratt to inspect the back. He glanced at the floor. Rubber matting with the Land Rover logo covered the space between the small bench seats. It was ridged, but the grooves seemed narrower than the ones on the autopsy photograph.

'Does it have a sick hole?' he asked with a grin. 'My granddad's had a hole in the metal between the seats. I was never sure if he'd put it there or if it came as standard. He called it a sick hole so that the vomit would drain away, if anybody got travel sick.'

The story sounded convincing to his own ears, but Fowler's eyes narrowed, and Barratt sensed he might be getting suspicious.

'Never heard of that,' he said, pulling back the rubber matting to reveal a plywood base. 'Must've been a later model. I'm not sure what's under the plywood, but from underneath, it looks like a solid sheet of metal. Haven't bothered to take the wood off yet, though. No point.'

Barratt nodded as though everything Fowler was saying made perfect sense, but he found it hard to mask his disappointment. He'd had visions of arresting Fowler for Aleah's murder and phoning it in triumphantly to Fletcher. There was still the mat, though. He could be mistaken about the pattern. Something beeped in the kitchen, and Fowler glanced over his shoulder then back at Barratt.

'I need to see to that,' he said, urging Barratt to follow him back in to the house.

'Okay,' Barratt said. 'Could I just have a look in the front?'

The older man sighed and went back through the door to the kitchen. Barratt dug in his pocket for his phone and managed to get images of the mat and the cab of the vehicle before Fowler returned.

'Summons from the boss,' Barratt said, waving his phone in Fowler's direction to disguise the real reason for it being in his hand.

'Was there anything else?' Fowler asked.

'I think that's all for now,' Barratt said, trying to place just the right amount of emphasis on the final part of the sentence. He didn't want Fowler to think he was above suspicion just yet.

Fowler led the way back through the house, and they parted at the front door. As he was heading down the drive, Barratt turned as though the thought had just struck him.

'You can't drive that Landy all the time. Have you got another vehicle?'

Fowler shook his head, his expression neutral. 'Nope. Just the Land Rover.'

Unless he was lying, this was another dead end. Fletcher wouldn't be impressed.

CHAPTER 14

2015

It was mid-afternoon when Kate and Hollis finally managed to get back to Thorpe. Raymond had had them both busy with paperwork, and Kate suspected he was trying to get her to back away from the face-to-face investigation and trust her team. Barratt had been gone all morning chasing Ken Fowler, and O'Connor was meeting yet another contact about the smuggling problem in the area. As she read through statements and signed overtime request sheets, she wondered if this promotion was going to be what she actually wanted, if it took her away from the front-line investigating she loved. Hollis had been getting irritated as well, she could hear it in his heavy sighs and the over-loud tapping on his keyboard. Only Cooper had seemed happy, headphones on, tapping away as she mined for information.

Now, back on the estate, Kate was starting to feel like she'd never been away; that the past thirty-odd years of her life had been just a spectacularly detailed dream. Here she was again, a few streets away from the house she'd grown up in, desperately noting the small changes in the houses and the roads which would signify that time had actually passed.

The Goodwins lived in one of the two "squares" on the estate, a quirk of the council planners that had never made much sense to Kate. Perhaps they had felt an obligation to break the monotony of ordinary, linear streets, or perhaps they saw it as making the best use of all the available land. On an estate where space didn't seem to be too much of a concern – green triangles had been laid at the end of each street like grassy parentheses, and the gardens were much bigger than on modern housing estates – Kate was inclined to opt for the former.

She'd been right when she'd described the cul-de-sac as a goldfish bowl. The street seemed narrower, and the houses huddled just a little bit closer together than on the "ordinary" streets, as though they sensed their difference and needed the protection of their peers. There was very little room for parking, and Hollis swore as he tried to manoeuvre the car into a space between a marked police car and a delivery van.

'Just park out on the street,' Kate said. 'It's not worth the stress.'

Hollis reversed out and did as he was instructed, leaving them a short walk to the Goodwins' house.

Kate had expected it to be at the end of the "square" facing the entrance, but it was one of the semis that flanked either side. It had a large front garden which was a swathe of grass divided almost perfectly in half by a strip of concrete leading up to a prefabricated garage – a rarity on the Crosslands Estate, Kate noted. A smaller strip of concrete ran from an inconspicuous gate in the hedge up the side of the lawn to the front door. The living room window overlooked the path, and Kate had a distinct feeling their approach was being watched.

She was dreading this interview. The family would have heard about Aleah and must be fearing the worst after a night of uncertainty and dread. She had no words of comfort to offer. The circumstances were too similar, the likelihood of the same person being behind the taking of both children was extremely high. But she knew they'd still be hoping for Callum's safe return, and she didn't want to kill that by saying the wrong thing.

Hollis knocked on the door, and it was opened almost instantly. The woman standing in the hallway was vaguely familiar to Kate, and she wondered if they'd been at school at the same time. She looked about the right age, although she'd dyed her hair a deep brown in an attempt to look younger.

'Liz McKintyre,' she said, offering her hand and ignoring Hollis's outstretched warrant card. The name didn't ring any bells. 'You must be DI Fletcher and DC Hollis. I was told to expect you.

I'm the FLO.' Kate nodded her understanding. People higher up the chain of command had obviously made the connection to the Reese case and had sent in somebody to be with the family.

McKintyre smiled at Hollis as she ushered him inside, but her expression changed when she got a clear look at Kate. Puzzlement, quickly replaced with recognition.

'Kathy Siddons?' she asked, her voice betraying her slight disbelief.

Kate just smiled.

'It is. I'd recognise you anywhere. You sat opposite me in English for two years. You've hardly changed at all.'

Kate stared at the woman, trying to imagine her as she might have looked thirty years ago. The grin was familiar, but the hair colour was wrong. The girl she was vaguely remembering had been fair-haired with a long fringe. The brunette spikes were confusing her.

'Libby Walker?'

The other woman's smile widened.

'Fancy meeting you here,' she said to Kate. 'It's been a long time. Would've thought you'd have moved away for good. Can't see why anybody would come back once they'd managed to escape.'

'Things change,' Kate said, hoping to curtail the conversation. 'I wanted a promotion, and this is where I ended up.'

The FLO shook her head again and looked Kate up and down. 'Detective Inspector, eh? You always were one of the clever ones at school. I'm not surprised you've made something of your life.'

'You're obviously not doing so bad yourself,' Kate responded, returning the scrutiny. 'No uniform? You've obviously done okay.'

Liz grinned. 'Trained as an FLO as soon as I joined CID. It suits me better than day-to-day investigation. I'm better with people than paperwork.'

Kate nodded appreciatively. She'd worked with some excellent FLOs in Cumbria, and they'd always been prepared to go above and beyond for whichever family they'd been assigned to. It wasn't a soft option for a police officer – the balancing act of having an active role in the investigation and providing support to the family was never an easy one to maintain.

'How are they?' she asked, nodding in the direction of the kitchen, assuming that was where the family would have gathered.

'Holding up. They'll not be best pleased to see you two, though.'

That was what Kate had been dreading. She and Hollis had no good news, no hope, just more questions, and she knew as soon as she mentioned Aleah Reese, these parents would start making assumptions they shouldn't have to make. But Cooper hadn't been able to find anything, and Kate had to know if there was any connection.

'Come through,' Liz said, leading the way.

Kate gestured for Hollis to go first, hoping his bulky presence might offer some reassurance before she started asking the questions the parents wouldn't want to answer.

The kitchen was almost a mirror image of Jackie Reese's. The units were a similar light wood and the counter tops almost the same shade of dark grey marble. Obviously the two women shopped at the same place. It wasn't much of a connection, though, the same taste in kitchens. Two people were sitting at the table, opposite each other. The woman was staring into a mug, but the man looked up when they entered, and Kate saw the unmistakable light of hope flicker in his eyes.

'Trevor? Anna? Two detectives are here to ask you some questions.'

The light in Trevor Goodwin's eyes died, to be replaced with a slowly smouldering rage. He resented their presence before they could even open their mouths.

'I'm Detective Inspector Kate Fletcher,' Kate introduced herself. The man scowled, his face reddening. He looked like a boxer who'd gone to seed. His slightly off-centre nose gave him a faintly boss-eyed look, and his large lips and ears looked like he might have been on the receiving end of a few well-aimed punches. He thrust his double chin out in a pugnacious challenge.

'I think we should be the ones asking questions.'

His wife continued to study the contents of her mug, refusing to acknowledge their presence.

'I can understand your frustration,' Kate said. 'But if–'

'Can you? Can you really understand what we're going through? Because unless you've had a child kidnapped by god knows who, I somehow doubt you have the first fucking idea!' Suddenly, he was on his feet and in her face.

Hollis took a step towards the two of them, but before he could intervene, rescue came from an unexpected source.

'Trev, sit down. They're only doing their job.' Anna Goodwin had put down the mug and was watching the confrontation unfold with an expression of boredom as though she'd been expecting this and just had to wait for it to be over before the real conversation could start.

Kate got her first real look at the woman and was surprised to see her smile apologetically.

'Trevor's always been a bit highly strung,' she said as though talking about a wayward pet. 'But he means well. Sit down, Trev.'

'Liz, will you get the detectives some tea or a glass of water?' She spoke to the FLO as though she was a treasured housekeeper or ancient retainer who had been on the staff for decades.

'I'm fine, thanks,' Kate and Hollis said in unison, and Anna nodded, satisfied that social niceties had been upheld. She was very different from her husband. Where he was round, she was angular. Where he was slightly asymmetrical, she was perfectly balanced and delicate. Her dark blue eyes studied Kate with shrewd intelligence from beneath her copper fringe.

'Please sit,' she said. 'And ask your questions.'

Kate pulled out a chair and sat next to Trevor Goodwin, while Hollis sat slightly away from the table on a stool against the wall. He took his notebook out of his inside breast pocket and waited.

They'd agreed they would try to stick to finding a connection between the Goodwins and the Reeses. The facts of the child's disappearance had been established earlier, and both she and

Hollis had read the parents' statements. There was little to be gained from going over too much old ground. But Anna Goodwin had other ideas.

'I feel so responsible,' she said, looking from Kate to Hollis. 'I only popped back in to get a drink. He was on his scooter, just going up and down the driveway and turning around on the street. I'd been in the garden, watching him. It was hot, so I went to get us both some juice, and when I came back, he was gone.'

She was struggling to retain control. Her husband reached across the table and covered one of his wife's tiny hands with a huge paw. She might be blaming herself, but he visibly didn't share her feelings.

'I just don't understand,' she continued. 'There have been police cars patrolling the estate ever since Aleah Reese went missing. I saw two that morning, and one even stopped at the entrance to the square. How could somebody just grab him like that without anybody seeing? It doesn't make sense.'

She wiped her eyes with a screwed-up tissue that had been sitting on the table in front of her.

'I'm sorry, Mrs Goodwin. We don't have any answers just yet, but we need to get some more information. You just mentioned Aleah Reese. Do you know the family?'

Anna shrugged. 'Everybody knows everybody around here. I've spoken to Jackie a few times. I don't really know Craig, though. I know who he is, but I've not had much to do with him.'

Hollis made a note.

'How well do you know Jackie Reese?'

'In passing, really. I'm not from around here. I moved here after I married Trevor. He's Thorpe born and bred.'

Mr Goodwin grunted as though reluctantly accepting a compliment.

'Do *you* know the Reeses?' Hollis asked.

'I've seen Jackie around,' Trevor said. 'I've had a pint or two with Craig in The Lion. It's not like we're friends or anything.'

'So, you've never worked at the same place? Been to the same school? Had the same friends?'

Goodwin shrugged. 'I probably went to the same school as Jackie. Don't remember her, though. Most folk around here went to Thorpe Comp. I'm not sure about Craig. I thought he was from over Rotherham way somewhere. I think he had an older sister who went to our school, but I'm not sure.'

It wasn't enough. There was no specific link. A few pints and a few years apart at school didn't make much of a connection.

'Do you know Jud Reese, Craig's dad?' Kate tried.

'Same, really. Might have said hello in passing. I know who he is because he used to work with my dad at the pit. I think he was something big in the union during the strike.'

Kate saw Hollis out of the corner of her eye. He was writing frantically. Apparently, this was something he thought they should pursue.

'Your dad was a miner?'

Goodwin just shrugged as if to say, "wasn't everybody's?"

'Did they work the same shift?' Hollis asked. 'Would they have known each other quite well?'

'I think so. I remember him coming around to my dad's during the strike. My dad was responsible for the money the union got – donations and that, I think – he decided who got what.'

'What about Jackie Reese's dad – Carl Loach. Do you know him?'

'I know *of* him,' Goodwin said. 'Can't say I know him. He's got a bit of a reputation for having a temper – or he did have, when I was a kid. I always steered clear.'

'Did he work with your dad?'

'Probably. Can't say I remember though.'

It wasn't much, but there was something there, Kate thought. Three men linked by the pit and the strike. Was somebody harbouring a grudge that had been festering for thirty years? Somebody who was punishing families for something that had happened a long time ago?

'We need to talk to your father,' she said.

Goodwin smiled sadly. 'Wish you could, love, but he's been dead for three years. Lung cancer.'

Kate nearly swore aloud. The threads of these two cases seemed to be knitting together, there was the faint outline of a connection, a link between Aleah Reese and Callum Goodwin, but if Trevor's dad was dead, the idea of Callum's kidnap being some sort of punishment for something he'd done in the past didn't quite work. She was missing something.

'I'm sorry,' she said to Goodwin, who nodded his acceptance of her condolences.

Then, another thought struck her, another possible link based on some of the information Cooper had dug up from Loach's record.

'Does the name Paul Hirst mean anything to you?'

Goodwin thought for a minute and then shook his head. 'Never heard of him. Should I have?'

'It was just a thought,' Kate said. 'You've been really helpful, Mr Goodwin. If there's anything that you or your wife think of that you haven't already mentioned, please let us know. And if there's anything you need…'

'We just need our Callum back safe,' Anna murmured. 'Nothing else matters.'

Kate nodded and stood up to leave.

'What was that about Paul Hirst?' Hollis asked.

'Cooper dug the name up earlier, remember? He was roughed up by Jackie Reese's dad during the strike. Some sort of fight.'

Hollis nodded. 'That's right. Something about him being a scab. Two assaults. Poor bloke killed himself in the end. I don't see what that's got to do with Callum Goodwin, though.'

'Nor do I,' Kate said. 'But there's a link between Callum's grandad and Aleah's. They both worked at the pit; they were both on strike. Goodwin said that his dad was involved with the union. He'd have known Hirst.'

'And so would half the men in Thorpe. Including your own father, I suppose. Everybody worked down the pit. But that was years ago.'

It was, but Kate could clearly hear Jean Loach telling her people around here had long memories. She was about to tell Hollis the same thing when her phone pinged – an email had just landed in her inbox.

She unlocked the screen and tapped the app. Cooper. The subject line simply said "Interesting?" and the email contained an attachment. Kate tapped again, and a newspaper article appeared on her screen, obviously a photograph Cooper had taken with her phone, judging by the quality. Kate drew her finger and thumb outwards and expanded the image until the headline jumped out at her.

GIRL DROWNS ON QUARRY SITE.

'Bastards!' she spat. The press had put their spin on the story before cause of death had been officially released. Hollis gave her a quizzical glance while trying to keep his attention on the road in front of them.

'Cooper's sent a newspaper article about Aleah. Raymond's still preparing his next press briefing about Aleah's death. He was due to give it today, but he's holding off because of this new case.'

'They were bound to come up with something,' Hollis said. 'People talk. The local news covered her disappearance on Tuesday evening, and there was all sorts of speculation on there. She's been on the evening bulletins ever since – it was only a matter of time.'

Kate nodded, trying to focus on the words. What she was reading didn't make sense. The names, the circumstances were completely different. The article wasn't about their case.

'It's not Aleah,' she said. 'It's another girl.'

She scrolled back to the top of the image. The dateline was just visible in the top right-hand corner of the image. June 10th, 1975.

'What the fuck?'

She scrolled down again trying to make sense of what he was reading, but the motion of the car was making it difficult to focus.

'Pull over,' she told Hollis.

'But we–'

'Now. Hollis. Just pull over.'

He flicked on the indicator and pulled into a bus stop.

Kate continued to read.

GIRL DROWNS ON QUARRY SITE

The body of seven-year-old Tracy Moore was recovered from the former Jepson's Quarry in Thorpe on Thursday. Her parents had reported her missing on Sunday, but it wasn't until an anonymous tip was received that the police started to scour the site. The girl's body was discovered in one of the ventilation shafts which had provided air to the brickworks flue which had occupied the north side of the site until its demolition in 1970. Cause of death was declared as drowning due to the violent storms and accompanying heavy rains last week.

Although the death is not being treated as suspicious, it remains unclear how the girl came to be in the ventilation shaft. The area is well known among local children, many of whom play there, despite the dangers. It seems likely she was exploring and got stuck. If anybody has any further information, please contact South Yorkshire Constabulary.

Below the headline was a grainy image of a school photograph, presumably of Tracy Moore. Kate switched from the article to her contacts list and tapped. 'Cooper, where did you find this?'

'Online. It was in the *South Yorkshire Times* archives. I printed it out and sent you a photo of the print-out. Sorry it's poor quality, but the image of the original article was pretty awful. I tried to sharpen it up a bit, but–'

'Cooper. Not the time.' Kate snapped, unwilling to get bogged down in one of Cooper's lengthy explanations of the limitations of the technology available to her. 'What else did you find out about the site? Was it filled in because of this girl's death?'

'No. It was already being filled in by then. It was finished in 1989.'

'And then, it was landscaped?'

Cooper laughed. 'And then, it was abandoned. The owners had the gates locked and left it to grass over. Nothing's been done to it since. I've checked company and land registries. It's still owned by the Jepson Company, but it's never been on the market. Useless, I suppose, because of the industrial contamination.'

Kate was suddenly lost in the memory of walking home from school accompanied by the constant rumble as lorry after lorry wound its way up the quarry track, with new loads of soot and rubble and other debris to fill in the massive hole in the village. It was still being filled in when they'd left.

'So, who's this kid?' Kate asked.

'Local, I think. Just playing. Wrong place, wrong time.'

'Poor bugger,' she murmured. 'Keep digging, Cooper. See what else you can find.'

She hung up and filled Hollis in.

'So, this was forty years ago?' he said.

Kate nodded. 'I remember my dad warning us about playing in the quarry. He said that there was all sorts of stuff from the factories in Sheffield being dumped there.'

'Did you know about the ventilation shafts?'

Kate thought. She had known. As soon as she'd read the article, something had stirred in her memory. She was quite young, still in the infants' school probably. Her mum was alive, because she could remember both her parents had been present when her father had given her his sternest warning to date. He'd reminded her about the piles of soot from the factory, but he'd seemed more concerned about the other part of the quarry, where the brickworks had been. Had he said something about tunnels? Or shafts? She wasn't sure, but she remembered his face had been deadly serious, and her mother had held her hand while she listened. The timing could easily have coincided with the discovery of Tracy Moore's body.

'I'm not sure. There were all kinds of stories about the quarry from piles of acidic soot that would melt your skin off to strange men who would take you off to live in their caves with them. It was just somewhere we weren't allowed to go and I never challenged that – just took it all at face value.'

'Do you think there's a link, though? This kid drowned forty years ago.'

Kate shrugged. 'I don't know, but I want to go back out there and have a look around. And I want a map of the site before it was filled in,' she said, calling Cooper back.

CHAPTER 15

2015

The PDF map Cooper had emailed wasn't brilliant on a five-inch phone screen, but it gave Kate some idea of the layout of the former quarry and brickworks. She could zoom in on some of the details, but for others, she had to rely on memory. Standing at the rusted gates, she checked her position against the map and set off across the waste ground with Hollis in tow.

'What are we looking for?' he asked, slightly breathless from the heat and the pace.

'I want to work out the position of the pond in relation to the ventilation shaft where the girl's body was found in 1975.'

'You think there's a connection?'

Kate stopped suddenly, turning her head left and right to try to get her bearings, and Hollis ran into her back.

'Shit,' he said. 'Sorry.'

Kate took a few steps away, eyes fixed on the screen as she pinched in and out of the map Cooper had sent. She knew where the brickworks had been. The buildings had still been standing when she'd been in junior school, and she could place them in relation to the road that ran up one side of the site. The rest of the area had been a quarry, varying in depth from about fifty feet to a shallow depression of no more than twelve feet on the side furthest from the road. Or at least that's what she remembered. But the memories of a teenager weren't the most reliable guide, and Cooper's map had her doubting her own recollection of the layout.

'The buildings were here,' she said, gesturing to an area to their right. 'Some of them had been knocked down, but there was a long, low row of offices still standing. The chimney had been over there near the top, which means the flues ran roughly east-west from over there.'

She set off again, following a faint dusty path through the sun-dried grass. As she trudged across vague depressions and gentle rises, she looked again at the map, trying to work out how long the flues would have been. The chimney had been quite tall; she remembered it from pictures she'd seen of old Thorpe when she'd been at school, so it would have needed huge ventilation shafts.

'Here.' Hollis managed to sidestep her this time. He looked around, baffled.

'The chimney would have been about here, and the ventilation shafts would have gone out in a rough fan shape in that direction.' She pointed to the far end of the site marked by a tall fence. 'Come on.'

She worked out if they headed west, following the rough line of the main shaft, they could then cut left and right to get an idea of where the other ones had been as they'd fanned out from the chimney. She continued towards the fence trying to imagine where they were in relation to the pond. Too far south. Another glance at the map showed her another flue would have run about ten yards to her right and a third about the same distance away to the left. If she turned left and walked about twenty yards, she would be almost at the pond. And almost directly on the line of another ventilation shaft. It wasn't very precise, but she knew she could get Cooper to overlay the original map onto an aerial photograph when they got back to Doncaster. It was close enough. There could be a connection.

'What do you think?' she asked Hollis, who was looking perplexed.

He shrugged. 'You'd know better than me. Can you actually remember these tunnel things?'

'I remember being warned about the whole area. The air shafts don't specifically ring a bell, though. There were lots of kids who used to play over here but none of my friends.'

Hollis chuckled. 'I thought you'd be a goody-goody.'

'Maybe,' Kate said. 'Or maybe it was easier to get into different kinds of trouble.'

Hollis raised his eyebrows in a question. 'Don't tell me you used to bunk off school and go shoplifting. Or you used to post dog crap through your neighbours' letter boxes? No, wait… you used to mug little old ladies for their pension.'

'Yes, yes, no, and no… in that order,' Kate said with a grin. 'Never got caught either.'

'That's what gives you such great insight into the criminal mind. I thought it was training and experience; didn't expect it to be empathy.'

Kate turned and started walking back to the gate. The banter was harmless, but it was a distraction she couldn't really afford. She needed to start making the pieces fit together, and her gut was telling her there was a solution to the puzzle, if she could only find the right pattern. The necklace the killer had left was bugging her. It had to be a message or a statement. Why go to all that trouble and then try to hide it? If it was a message, why not leave it somewhere more prominent? Unless it wasn't a message for the police. It might be something the killer felt compelled to do, like ticking off items in a list. And then, a thought struck her.

'Oh!'

'What's up?' Hollis said, nearly running into her again as she stopped suddenly.

'The necklace Aleah was wearing. It wasn't a cross. It was a letter T.'

'And?'

'How did I miss that? The girl who drowned was called Tracy. He left Aleah there to link her with Tracy Moore.'

'I'm going to need a bit more convincing,' Hollis said, looking sceptical.

'It's a message. In the killer's mind, Aleah represents Tracy in some way. He's recreating her death and labelling the body. This isn't a coincidence. We need to find out more about Tracy Moore and the circumstances surrounding her death.'

'Okay,' Hollis said, drawing the word out to demonstrate his scepticism. 'But if Aleah represents Tracy, who the hell does Callum Godwin represent?'

'I don't know. I just think it's part of a plan, a pattern, and I've got a feeling we might be too late. I need to get back to base and talk to Cooper.' She was already dialling Cooper's number to get her to find what she needed.

There was a buzz around their small team when Kate and Hollis got back to Doncaster HQ. Barratt was standing behind Cooper, looking over her shoulder at her computer screen, his expression intent.

'Did you find it?' Kate asked, striding across the office space.

Cooper nodded. 'Just doing the final overlay. I've scaled up the map to match the aerial photograph so they're a pretty good fit.' She tapped a key. 'There. I've fixed the two together so you can scroll around, if you need to.'

She stood up and stepped back so Kate could sit down, but Kate shook her head.

'This is your thing, Sam. Talk me through it.'

The DC sat back down and grabbed the mouse. 'Okay. This is the map I sent you.' She clicked twice. 'And this is an aerial photo of the same area. You can see the road in the map so I used that to scale it up to match the photo. I put the two together by making the map file semi-transparent, so you can see the photograph through it. The X on the photograph marks the pond where Aleah's body was found.'

Kate stared at the image. Dotted lines marked the ventilation shafts, and she could see where she'd guessed their locations to be was slightly inaccurate. The pond lay about twenty feet away from the most northerly shaft. Close enough, though.

'Do we know where the body of Tracy Moore was found?' Kate asked.

Cooper shook her head. 'None of the newspaper reports mention it. They just say she was found in a shaft.'

'Family?' Hollis wanted to know.

It was a good question, Kate thought. Was their mystery abductor a family member who was out for revenge?

'Parents and a brother. No names so far, but I've only checked the local papers. I was going to start digging after I'd done the map.'

Kate glanced at her watch and shook her head. It was past half past six, and they were all exhausted. Sam looked especially tired, and there was no point burning her out on a hunch. Better to start fresh in the morning.

'Let's hear what Barratt has to say about Ken Fowler, then call it a day. I'm expecting more from forensics about the tent ropes tomorrow, and that might give us a new direction.'

Barratt dug out his notebook and flipped through the pages. 'Fowler confirms Reese's alibi. He didn't see anybody else in the area. I managed to get a look at his Land Rover, but the floor in the back isn't metal. The mat has some ridge patterning on it, but I don't think it matches the marks on Aleah's back. I've PNC'd him, and the Landy is the only vehicle he owns. I also had a chat with a couple of his neighbours. They think he's a "good bloke," but he keeps himself to himself.'

He tapped his phone a couple of times and passed it around to show the images he'd taken of the inside of the vehicle. Sighs of frustration and a general shaking of heads.

'Send them to me, and I'll get a comparison done, but it's not looking likely,' Kate said. 'Right. Tomorrow, we come in refreshed and start early. We need to get more family information on Tracy Moore. I want to try to establish a link between the Reeses and the Goodwins, and I want that little boy found. If we need to, we go right back to basics and knock on all the neighbours' doors ourselves.'

Barratt grinned.

'Oh, I mean it, Barratt. Get some sleep. Tomorrow's going to be a busy one.'

Kate scanned her desk to make sure she hadn't left anything behind, trying not to look at the door to Raymond's office. She knew she should let him know about her theory, but she also knew he'd laugh her out of the building. He wasn't a big fan of hunches; he had a Gradgrind-like appreciation for facts and hard evidence.

Sighing heavily, she stuffed her hands into her trouser pockets, strode over to the door, and knocked gently as though she hoped that he wouldn't hear her.

'Come in!'

Kate opened the door and plastered her most winning smile across her face.

Raymond's expression told her he wasn't fooled for a minute. 'Well?'

'I have some new information pertaining to the Aleah Reese case.'

'Go on.'

Kate stood in front of his desk and outlined her idea about the link between Aleah's death and the forty-year-old accident. She also pushed the possible link to Callum Goodwin as though this might be the thread that held her entire theory together.

Raymond wasn't convinced. 'Fletcher,' he said, gesturing to the chair next to his desk. 'Sit down. Look, I like your tenacity, and you're obviously used to "thinking outside the box," as they say. But this sounds like nothing more than a coincidence.'

Kate nodded. She'd expected this. 'The necklace Aleah was wearing. It's not a cross, it's a letter T. That's why it looks a bit strange. We've been looking at it wrong.'

'I thought you'd decided it was an unusual type of Christian cross. That was one of the avenues of investigation, wasn't it? Some sort of religious link?'

Kate nodded, already regretting the time wasted on a dead end. 'But I just can't see the relevance. A letter makes more sense. We need to find out more about this girl's death in 1975. I'm certain there's a connection between Tracy Moore and Aleah Reese, and probably Callum Goodwin. If we're going to find that boy, we need to start digging into his family. I think this is rooted in the past.'

'And *I* think,' Raymond said, raising his voice slightly, 'you're getting bogged down because of your own past and your own links to this town. You need to get back out there and have a look at the people closest to these two children. You know random child snatches are a lot less common than the public believe. You need to look closer to home. Check Craig Reese's alibi for the time of the Goodwin boy's abduction. And look at Trevor Goodwin. You know how these things usually work.'

Kate nodded. There was no point in arguing. She knew how her theory sounded. The problem was, she was convinced she was right.

'Go home, Fletcher. It's been a long few days. You might think differently in the morning.'

Kate knew he was trying to give her the benefit of his wisdom, but his advice was just a bit too patronising to be convincing. She shook her head in frustration and left.

Her mood didn't improve when there was another message from Garry waiting on her answerphone. Why couldn't he just text like other people? Then, she remembered how many times she'd snapped at him for calling when she was at work. He probably thought a text would get him a good telling-off as well. *Poor bugger couldn't win*, she thought with a smile, as she tapped play.

'Kate? I just thought I'd ring to tell you Ben's been asking about you. He knows you're in Doncaster, and I think he'd like to get in touch.'

Her heart rate picked up. Was her son finally wanting her back in his life? Garry's next words were like being doused in icy water.

'He's struggling a bit, financially, and he thought you might be able to help out. He's burned through one of his loans, and he can't seem to find a part-time job. I've sent him a few quid, but I'm not sure how long that'll last. He'll get another loan next term, so he'll be all right in September for a bit. I thought you might want to help out.' He finished by reciting Ben's mobile number.

It wasn't the one Kate had stored in her phone, and she wondered why he'd changed it. Hopefully not an expensive upgrade.

She dug her own phone out of her pocket, navigated to the message app, and typed in the number Garry had given her. What to say? She hadn't heard from him in nearly a year, but she couldn't refuse to help him. He was her son, and she could never imagine any circumstances where she wouldn't do her best for him. It was just bloody irritating the only reason he wanted to get in touch was that he was skint.

She typed quickly, not allowing herself any more time to think about it. *Dad says you need some money. Get in touch and I'll see what I can sort out.*

A message came back almost immediately. *Great. Thx. I'll give you a buzz in the morning.*

Kate considered texting back, then hit the icon to call instead. She wasn't going to take his call at work, and she knew he'd just get huffy if she didn't have time to talk to him. It was one of the things they'd argued about the most. He hated her job and the amount of time it took her away from her family, and he resented her dedication to every case she'd been involved with. He wouldn't be inclined to mend fences if she had to brush him off yet again.

'Mum?'

She could hear voices and music in the background, then a door slamming as her son found some quiet and privacy.

'Mum. I said I'd call you tomorrow. I'm with some friends at a party.' He sounded a bit drunk.

'Sorry to interrupt,' Kate said. 'But I've got an early start tomorrow, and I didn't want to miss your call. I thought I'd try to catch you tonight.'

He didn't respond, so she continued.

'Dad says you've spent your loan money.'

'I have.' Ben sighed. 'And I know you'll just think I'm irresponsible, but I had a job lined up for the summer, so I thought I'd be okay.'

'What happened?'

'It fell through. It was in a restaurant. Waiting on, clearing up, that sort of thing. Minimum wage, but it would have kept me going. The restaurant closed down.'

'In Sheffield?'

'Yep. I don't want to go back to Dad's for the summer. I'd feel like such a loser.'

'Any chance of another job?'

'I'm looking, but there's not much about.'

'How much do you think you'll need to get you through?'

'Dunno. I've got rent to pay. I'm sharing a house with some mates next year, and we've already moved in.'

Kate wondered whether these were the same mates she could still hear faintly in the background. 'How much is rent?'

'Two-fifty a month.'

Kate calculated. Three months' rent plus expenses would be well over a thousand pounds. 'Has your dad given you anything?'

'A bit,' Ben admitted.

'How big a bit?'

'Five hundred quid.'

She was impressed. It wasn't like Garry to be so generous now he had a baby to feed and clothe. 'Okay. So, how about I pay your rent for the next academic year? Your dad's money should get you through the next couple of months, if you're careful, and at least your loan will go further, if you've not got rent to think about.'

Silence.

'Ben?'

'You'd do that? For a whole year?'

'Of course. But I'll pay it directly to your landlord. You'll have to send me the details. I don't want you tempted to spend it every month.'

He laughed. 'As if.'

'As if nothing. I know you. At least I'll know you've got a roof over your head.'

'Mum. I'm sorry I've been such a shit these last couple of years. I wanted to get in touch when I got to Sheffield, but I didn't really know what to say.'

Kate smiled at his drunken sentimentality, knowing he'd probably regret it in the morning. 'I'll always be here for you, Ben. You might think you're an adult, but I never will. It's my prerogative as your mum. Now, get back to your friends. I'll text you my new email address, and you can send me the details of your landlord.'

And that was that. No "I love yous." No promises to meet. They both just hung up.

But it was progress.

CHAPTER 16

2015

An email pinged in to Kate's inbox as she was gulping coffee and scanning the BBC News website. Her preparations for the day always involved coffee, news, and some sort of food, even if it was just a slice of bread or a bowl of leftovers from the night before. What she read in the email caused her to spray toast crumbs all over the table and her phone.

'Shit!' She scrolled to Hollis's number and dialled. 'Where are you?' she asked.

'Home. About to head out. Why?'

'Forensics just sent their report. The rope used to tie up Aleah matches the guy ropes from the tent we found in Craig Reese's shed. There were two guy ropes missing when they unpacked the tent, and the remaining ones are the same type. We need to pick him up.'

'Hang on.' She heard Hollis put the phone down and then muffled voices in the background. 'I can be there in about half an hour.'

She shook her head, even though he couldn't see the gesture. 'Barratt and Cooper should be at their desks by now. I'll send them. It'll probably be quicker. You can have first crack at him, though.'

She hung up and dialled Barratt's desk number. 'Barratt? It's me. Get yourself and Sam 'round to Craig Reese's house and bring him in. If he refuses to come, arrest him on suspicion of murder.'

'What? It was him all along?' Barratt sounded almost disappointed. Kate knew he'd been pushing for Fowler to be their main suspect, but the case against him just wasn't stacking up. She'd compared the photographs Barratt had taken of Fowler's Land Rover and the mat in the back didn't match up with the marks on

Aleah's body. It was a dead end. Hopefully, this would re-energise him. She briefly considered giving him the interview, but she knew Hollis was much more skilled in that department. She'd turn Reese over to Hollis and Cooper while she watched on video link.

As she showered and threw on a pair of tailored trousers and a light blouse, she considered what to tell Raymond. He'd instantly go into gloating mode, and she didn't really want to have to deal with his "I told you so" face this early. But if she didn't notify him, he'd be pissed off when he did find out. She opted for a quick text informing him Reese was once more "of interest" and was being brought in for questioning. She also mentioned they might be needing a warrant to search the Reeses' house. Raymond had plenty of other cases on his plate so that might hold him for a few hours until Reese's guilt could be established… or not.

Kate's gut was telling her this was wrong. Reese just didn't strike her as being organised enough to abduct his own stepdaughter and make it look like a kidnapping. She also didn't feel convinced he had it in him to kill a child. He'd struck her as too lethargic and set in his routines to go to any trouble. And what did he gain? He seemed to be in a stable relationship with a woman who was supporting him, however begrudgingly. If he'd not wanted to be saddled with a kid, why marry Jackie? There was only the evidence of the tent that seemed to point to him, and that just wasn't compelling enough.

'We'll just have to see what he says,' she said to herself as she pulled the door to the flat closed behind herself.

She grabbed her second coffee of the day on the way up to the observation room. Hollis had texted to say Reese was in Interview Three, and he'd been left to cool his heels for a few minutes. He hadn't come willingly, though, so Barratt had read him his rights, and he was currently under arrest for murder which meant they initially had twenty-four hours, minus rest breaks, before they had to charge him or let him walk.

She glanced at the monitor on the desk in front of her, trying to establish Craig Reese's demeanour. He was leaning with both elbows on the table in front of him, chewing on his fingernails. He looked dishevelled, as though he'd not had time to straighten his hair or choose any suitable clothes before he'd been bundled into the back of the police car. His grey tracksuit bottoms and navy hoodie looked almost like an afterthought.

Kate continued to watch on the monitor as Hollis and Cooper entered the room. Hollis was holding two cardboard cups from the canteen, and he passed one to Reese. Cooper had her own. They were settling in for a long session. Hollis explained the tape and the camera and reminded Reese why he was there. Reese looked up at the camera for a second, and Kate almost had to look away as his haunted eyes made contact with her own. Even though he had no idea she was there, it was uncomfortable to read his expression; she could see the despair and hopelessness even through the camera and monitor.

'Right, Craig,' Hollis began. 'I've explained to you why you're here, you've been read your rights, you've waived the right to have a lawyer present, but I need to remind you that you *are* under arrest.'

Reese winced as though he'd just been slapped with the final word.

'We're trying to establish the facts around Aleah's disappearance, and you've already lied to us once. Is that correct?'

Kate held her breath. This was the key moment. If he said, "No comment," then their day would be wasted. He'd just string them along until he was allowed a break, and eventually, they'd have to apply for more time. Raymond would go ballistic at the cost and effort, and they'd be no further forward.

Reese nodded.

'Please answer yes or no,' Hollis reminded him gently.

'Yes.'

From the angle of the camera, Kate could see his right leg crossed over his left under the table. His right foot was jiggling uncontrollably. He was nervous. Good.

'Okay, Craig,' Hollis leaned forward slightly. 'We need to ask you a few questions about the day Aleah went missing. We know

now she was at the bookies with you and not on the street as you first claimed.'

Reese nodded then whispered, 'Yes.'

'We've established a timeline using the CCTV from the shop, and this supports your statement.'

Hollis was being gentle, reeling the other man in, gaining his confidence. It was why she'd put Hollis on the interview, even though Barratt had been champing at the bit. Hollis was sensitive and had good instincts around suspects. She knew if anybody could get the truth out of Craig Reese, then Hollis was the man.

'You also told us you were on the old quarry site around 9.30pm the same day looking for Aleah, but you also went to your father's house?'

Another nod. This time, Hollis didn't ask him to confirm. Instead, he stated Reese had nodded.

'So, where were you after that? Where did you go between looking for your father and going home?'

Reese looked confused. 'Nowhere. I went up to my dad's and then went home.'

'What time did you get back?'

Reese thought for a minute. 'Must've been about half ten or eleven.'

'And can anybody confirm this. Your wife, perhaps?'

Reese shook his head. 'Jackie was out for the count. The doctor gave her something to help her sleep. I didn't want to bother her, so I slept on the sofa in the living room.'

Considerate, Kate thought, *and very convenient.*

'And you didn't go out after that?' Hollis checked.

'No. I went out the next morning, but just to the shed for a quick fag before Jackie woke up.'

He'd given Hollis an excellent opening to steer the interview, and Hollis pounced on it immediately. Kate felt like clapping as he deftly manoeuvred Reese into talking about the real area of interest.

'Do you spend a lot of time in your shed, Craig?' he asked.

Reese shrugged.

'In an average week, say. How often do you go into the shed?'

'Every time I want a cigarette. If it's cold or wet. Not so much in the summer. I just stand outside.'

'But you didn't stand outside yesterday, or the day before. You went into the shed to smoke?'

'Suppose so.'

'Had it been raining? Is that why you didn't stand outside?'

'On and off. I probably didn't want to get caught in a shower. I don't know why. I just went to the shed. Force of habit, maybe.'

'Is it *your* shed, Craig? Your man-cave?' Hollis leaned in further. 'A place where you can get away from Jackie and have a smoke and a think? I know I like to have a potter in mine. Gives me time to think away from distractions.'

Kate smiled. As far as she knew, Hollis lived in a second-floor flat.

Reese leaned back as though sensing Hollis's lie. 'It's just a shed. I smoke out there and keep all the garden stuff in it. I don't need to get away from Jackie and Aleah. Don't want to either.'

'Is all the "stuff" in there yours, Craig? None of it was there when you moved in?'

Reese frowned. 'I don't know. It's ours. We don't keep track of who bought the bloody lawn mower and who paid for the garden chairs.'

He was getting annoyed. Hollis needed to change tack.

'Ask him about the tent,' Kate said out loud.

As though he could hear her, Hollis glanced down at the small pile of papers in front of him, as though checking some piece of information, then looked up at Reese with no sign of his former friendly smile. 'What about the tent? Is that yours?'

Reese looked baffled. '*We* bought it last summer. It belongs to the family; it's not *mine*.'

Hollis nodded and looked back down at his papers. 'When did you last use it?'

'Easter. We went to Flamborough for a few days. It pissed down.'

'Did you put the tent away when you got back?'

'I did. What's this got to do with Aleah?'

'All in good time,' Kate murmured, watching as Hollis sifted through the papers, ignoring Reese's question.

'So, you put the tent away after your Easter holiday, and it hasn't been used since?' Hollis produced a photograph from his pile of papers, and Kate could see it was the one he'd taken of the tent, still in the cupboard, bursting out of its bag.

'For the tape, I'm now showing Craig Reese image 03/08/15AZ. A bit sloppy, weren't you, Craig?'

Reese took the picture and studied it. 'I didn't leave it like that. I hung it on the line to dry properly and then rolled it up. It'll perish, if it's left in a lump like that.'

Reese nodded. 'Who else has access to the shed?'

'Nobody. Me and Jackie and Aleah, I suppose.'

'But nobody else would go in your shed on a regular basis?'

'No.'

'Craig. When Aleah was found, her hands were tied. The ropes used match the guy lines of your tent.'

Reese's mouth dropped open. 'How… when… hang on, it's not an uncommon brand of tent. That rope wasn't forced to be from the one in my shed. I bought it online from GO Outdoors. They must sell hundreds.'

Hollis nodded as though he could see exactly where Craig was coming from. 'But when we took your tent away, the guy ropes were missing. Are you sure you put them away with the tent?'

Reese looked panic-stricken as he tried to work out what the best answer might be, and Kate was almost convinced he had nothing to do with Aleah's murder. His shock was too convincing. He looked like he'd been slapped by somebody he couldn't see or hear. If he was guilty, Kate thought, he'd try to stall. She held her breath as he opened his mouth to speak.

'I put everything back in the bag. Tent, pegs, ropes, awning. It was all there.'

'You're sure?'

'Aleah helped me. I gave her a list, so she could tick everything off.'

'Where's this list?'

Reese's eyes searched the room wildly as he tried to either remember or come up with a convincing answer. 'Threw it away when we'd finished.'

He was either telling the truth or a bloody good actor, Kate thought. He couldn't have just made up that fact about Aleah on the spot; he wasn't clever enough. Raymond was wrong. She knew in her gut Craig Reese didn't kill his stepdaughter. He hadn't mentioned the shed wasn't kept locked, which would have shifted suspicion to anybody who lived nearby, or who had access to the Reeses' garden. Which, literally, could be anybody. It would have been the perfect fact to draw attention away from himself, but he hadn't even thought about it.

A tap at the door drew her attention from the monitor.

'Kate?' It was Barratt, holding a piece of A4 paper.

'We've got a sighting of Aleah on the day she was snatched. Some old bloke saw her picture on the evening news last night – they're giving the murder top billing. He recognised her.'

Kate sighed. Too little too late. 'Shame he didn't remember earlier. She might have been found sooner.' She didn't say "alive," didn't need to; she could see Barratt shared her frustration.

'He's a bit confused. I think he might, you know,' Barratt made a "drinking" gesture with his thumb and little finger extended next to his mouth.

'Oh, great. Another bloody drunk witness. Just what we need. Give it here.'

He passed the sheet of paper over and fixed his eyes on the monitor. 'How's he doing?'

Kate glanced at the image of the interview room. 'Reese or Hollis?'

'Both. Either. I just wondered if Hollis had cracked him yet.'

Kate shook her head. 'I'm not sure there's anything to crack. He hasn't denied the tent was his and that he was the last one to put it away. It's not enough to charge him.'

Barratt nodded soberly.

'I'm not sure this statement'll help. But it does put Aleah somewhere other than on Main Street on the day she was taken.'

Kate scanned the statement looking for key pieces of information. It was a straightforward sighting of a child fitting Aleah's description and wearing similar clothes to those Aleah had been wearing on the day she disappeared. The person making the statement couldn't be sure of the exact time, but he knew it had been before midday as he'd been heading to one of the pubs in the village, and it didn't open until twelve.

And then, she saw why Barratt was so interested.

I saw the girl walking down the hill towards the main road. Instead of staying with the road, she descended the steps to follow the shortcut route of the old road.

Aleah hadn't been snatched from Main Street. She'd been on a little-used track which was only overlooked by the backs of a few terraced houses. Once there, nobody would have noticed her until she emerged at the main road. Kate tried to picture the lane. It crossed a brook at the bottom of the hill and then opened out into a parking area just before the main road. If the abductor had snatched her from there, it would have been a matter of seconds to bundle her into a waiting car or van.

But why had she left the shops? Where was she going?

The obvious answer was home, but she'd just been sent out to the shops by Craig Reese. Why not go back to the bookies and wait for him to take her home?

Kate glanced at the monitor again. Hollis was just winding up the interview. She could tell from his posture he hadn't got what he wanted. Reese hadn't admitted to anything, and there seemed little point in continuing – for now. But what might this new information do to him?

'Barratt. Get Hollis out of there. I want him to show Craig Reese this. See what he has to say.'

The DC left while Kate scanned the statement again.

'Why were you going home, Aleah?' she whispered. 'What happened to you to stop you going back for your stepdad?'

CHAPTER 17

2015

Hollis burst into the room with Barratt close on his heels. 'You wanted to see me? Is there a problem?'

'Not a problem. You handled him really well. What's your gut telling you?'

Hollis took a deep breath as he considered his reaction to the interview. 'I'm getting nothing from him. There's nothing calculated about his answers. I don't think it's him.'

Kate smiled. 'Fancy telling Raymond that?'

'Not a chance. You get paid more than me – you tell him.'

She passed Hollis the new witness statement and watched his face as he read it slowly.

'Shit!' he exclaimed. 'What does this mean?'

'Aleah wasn't taken from Main Street, which is why nobody remembers seeing anything unusual. This back lane is isolated but easily accessible. I think this is the snatch site.'

'Hang on. We know that Reese was in the bookies, and that he left to look for Aleah. Does the timeline fit? Could he have walked her home the back way and strangled her?'

Kate shook her head. 'I don't think so. Not according to the time stamp on the bookies CCTV. And even if he did, where did he put her? He didn't just dump her straight in the pond.' She glanced at the screen which showed Craig Reese sitting alone at the table with his head in his hands. A uniformed officer observed impassively.

'Ask him, will you?'

She grabbed her phone and dialled Raymond's number. He answered on the first ring, obviously irritated he'd been interrupted.

Kate gave him a quick outline of the new statement and then asked the question she knew Raymond would be dreading.

'Can we send a forensics team? We need to examine that lane and the car park at the bottom.'

Raymond huffed and puffed, but Kate could tell it was all for show. There was no denying the need to have the area closely examined. Raymond promised to make the call as soon as Kate hung up – a full forensics team plus uniform back-up to help with a fingertip search.

Kate grinned to herself, feeling like she'd won a minor victory, and turned back to the monitor watching as Barratt and Hollis entered the room. Reese looked around as if expecting somebody else. Perhaps he was hoping Cooper, as a woman, was a calming influence. Without her there, he had to face two aggressive-looking men who obviously wanted a confession.

Hollis resumed the interview, adding Barratt's name to the tape, and then practically threw the statement onto the table.

'More lies, Craig,' Hollis snapped.

Reese glanced at the paper on the table then back at Hollis, the fear in his face looked genuine to Kate. 'I haven't–' he began.

'Haven't what? Haven't been straight with us?'

Reese shook his head vehemently. 'I've told you everything. I don't know what happened to Aleah.'

'Ok.' Hollis took a deep breath. 'Let's start again. You sent her out of the bookies to get some sweets. When she didn't come back, you went to look for her. But it was all an act, wasn't it, Craig? You told her to go home, and then, you met her on the way. She trusted you – it's not like you had to kidnap her. And then, what? Where did you put her?'

Reese just stared at him, mouth open.

'We've got a witness who says he saw her heading down the back lane next to the road up to the village. She was going home. Why would she do that, Craig, unless you'd told her to?'

Reese sat back in his seat and looked from Hollis to Barratt and back again, his face completely disbelieving.

'Where did you go after you left the bookies, Craig?'

'I went to look for Aleah. I already told you.' He was tensing up, and Kate could sense he was getting ready to withdraw his co-operation. Whether out of guilt or self-preservation, she couldn't be one hundred percent certain, but her gut was telling her Craig Reese wasn't capable of this.

'Which way did you go home?'

'The main road.'

'You didn't use the shortcut?'

'Why would I? I was looking for Aleah. I didn't expect her to have gone down there.'

Hollis pretended to read the statement again, obviously buying himself some thinking time. Reese glanced from Hollis to Barratt, back again, and then towards the door, as though he was expecting somebody to come in and rescue him. Kate could see he still didn't fully grasp how much trouble he was in.

'Where were you the day before yesterday? In the afternoon?' Hollis asked, suddenly changing the focus of the interview. Kate knew, he'd done it to wrong-foot Reese, but it was a gamble. If Reese made the connection between the question and Callum Goodwin, he might clam up, but if he had a decent alibi, he might see it as a chance to get on Hollis's good side.

Reese's eyes narrowed. He'd seen straight through the question. 'I was at home. I needed to be with my wife. We just lost our daughter. Where would you expect me to be?' His tone was increasingly belligerent.

'Can anybody confirm that?'

Reese nodded. 'I was at home from the time I woke up until the time I went to bed. There were people coming and going all day. Jackie's mam and dad were there, the doctor called in, and one of your lot was around for most of the day.'

Kate knew he meant Tatton, the FLO, who'd been asked to stay with the family for another twenty-four hours, ostensibly to help with any legal issues, but in fact, to keep an eye out for any unusual comings and goings.

'What about popping out for a quick smoke?' Hollis asked. 'Did you go out to your shed?'

Reese shook his head. 'Jackie didn't care where I smoked. She said she'd only made me go out for Aleah's sake, and that it didn't matter anymore. Apart from when I went to the toilet, I didn't get much more than a few minutes to myself all day. There's at least four people who can back me up. I know why you're asking.' His face was grim. 'I didn't go anywhere near that little lad's house. I didn't take Callum Goodwin, and I never hurt our Aleah. I just wish you'd get your arses back out there and find whoever did.'

With that, he sat back, crossed his arms and fixed his mouth in a rigid line.

Interview over, as far as Craig Reese was concerned.

Kate watched carefully to see what Hollis would do next. If it had been her, she'd have left immediately. Leave the suspect to stew. Leave him wondering if he'd said enough to get himself off the hook. Hollis smiled, slid the statement back towards himself and picked it up. He stood up, thanked Reese for his co-operation, and told him they'd be back later. Before Reese could say anything, Hollis practically shoved Barratt out of the door, and Reese was left on his own. He sighed heavily and put his head on his arms as though he was going to try to get some sleep. He wasn't their killer. Kate knew it in her bones.

Kate met the two detectives in the corridor as they were heading back to the observation room for a debrief. 'No time for a break,' she teased. 'Hollis, chase up Reese's alibi for yesterday – check every minute, if you can. And then, check out this statement – see if this old man can add anything. Barratt, with me. There's a forensics team on their way to Thorpe, and I want to see if they find anything down that back lane. Although given last night's rain and the amount of foot traffic there might have been in the past few days, we'll be bloody lucky to find anything even remotely admissible.'

Little had changed since Kate had used the back lane as a shortcut to school more than thirty years ago. In a bigger town, it would have been littered with broken spirit bottles, used needles and condoms, but the teenagers of Thorpe obviously had better places to get high or laid. It had been the original route from the main Doncaster to Rotherham road up to the village, but had fallen out of use when a newer road was built with a huge sweeping bend which took some of the steepness out of the hill.

Kate stood at the top of a short flight of steps which led down on to the lane. A later addition, they would have presented too much of an obstacle to horse-drawn carts and early motor cars. The top part of the lane ran in front of three terraced houses which seemed to guard the entrance. The other side was bounded by a stone wall, too high to peer over from the new route. It would be a perfect place for an ambush. Looking further down, Kate could see that dense undergrowth and brambles encroached on the gravel, forcing the lane to downsize to a narrow track. She couldn't see very far – a bend and a group of white-suited crime scene techs blocked her view – but she knew it eventually crossed a railed bridge before ending in a parking area known locally as the old square.

A PCSO blocked her route down the steps, grinning as she approached. 'We meet again!'

Rigby. The bloody man was everywhere.

'PCSO Rigby,' Kate said, acknowledging their earlier meetings. 'Any news?'

Rigby shook his head. 'Just getting started. I can let you down there, but you'll have to get booted and suited. God knows what they expect to find by now. Kids'll have been up and down here every day on their way to school.'

'It's the holidays,' Kate said.

Rigby tilted his head. 'Is it? Oh, aye. Forgot.'

Even though she knew the man was only the same age as her sister, there was something of the elderly about him as though he'd been raised by grandparents who were set in their language as well as their ways. He spoke like her dad.

'Where can I get kitted out?' she asked.

Rigby pointed in the direction of a side street. 'There's a van down there.'

'Who's that?' Barratt asked, as they turned into the street that Rigby had indicated.

'The PCSO who took the Reese's initial statement. He was at the quarry the other day as well.'

'He's either dead keen, or he's pissed off somebody higher up. Crappy duty, guarding crime scenes.'

Kate nodded, remembering her early days as a "W"PC, when she was assigned jobs suited to her gender such as standing around and making tea when required. She knew there were still a few dinosaurs on every force who would be more than happy to see her doing the same sort of duties even now.

She struggled into a paper suit, shoe covers and gloves, cursing the heat as she zipped herself in and headed back to the steps. She could hear Barratt rustling and swearing behind her as she approached Rigby again.

'Right. Let them know I'm coming.'

Rigby tilted his head to speak into his radio. 'I've got a Detective Inspector Si… Fletcher here and a DC…'

He glanced at Barratt who snapped his name. The radio crackled, and then, they were cleared to head down the lane.

'What did he think you were called?' Barratt asked as they descended that steps.

'He remembers my family. Fletcher's my married name. It's not important.'

She could see from Barratt's face he was storing these small nuggets of personal information, reassessing what he thought he knew about her. *Well, let him*, she thought. It wasn't a secret she was divorced, or that she was from Thorpe.

It was cooler between the houses and the wall, and the greenery added to the sense of serenity, despite the hundreds of discarded crisp wrappers and crumpled soft drinks cans.

Kate led the way to the group of figures who were gathered about halfway down. 'What have we got?' she asked.

A woman squinted up at her from beneath an elasticated hood. 'Not much so far. We've just–'

She was interrupted by a shout from further down the lane. Kate nodded to Barratt, and they jogged towards the sound.

It wasn't much. Easily missed among the other litter. A small, sealed packet of Haribo Tangfastics. Kate took out her phone and texted Cooper. *Shopkeeper's statement. What did Aleah buy?*

Ten seconds later, a beep. *A couple of packets of Haribo. Tangfastics?*

Another agonising ten seconds. *Yep. She remembers teasing her about them making her eyes water, like the advert.*

'They could be Aleah's,' Kate said to the technician, who was photographing the packet from every possible angle. 'She bought some at the shop.'

Another shout took her further down the lane to an area of trampled grass and weeds. It could have been done by anyone at any time, but amongst the burdock and brambles was a child's hair clip with a ladybird design. Another suited figure picked it up carefully and eased it into an evidence bag as she watched.

'Hang on,' she told him. Kate got him to hold the item out on his palm while she took a picture with her phone. Much easier than waiting for images to come back from the labs. She could show it to Craig or Jackie Reese to see if they recognised it.

The afternoon dragged into evening, as she and Barratt alternated between observing the search and sitting in the van cooling off. Nothing else of significance had turned up, but the plastic boxes in the van were bulging with evidence bags that would need examining, analysing, and categorising. Kate knew from experience on similar scenes it would be mostly crap, but they might have already found a couple of needles in this particular haystack.

Her phone rang just as she'd bundled Barratt back into the car and told him he needed to go home for a long shower. It was Hollis. 'What have you got?'

'We got a warrant to search Reese's house because of the tent guy line. Raymond pushed for it – just to be sure. Guess what turned up under the floor of his shed?'

Kate felt her heart rate pick up. Had they been wrong after all? Was this where he'd kept Aleah's body? And Callum Goodwin's?

'What?' she asked, crossing her fingers it wasn't another corpse.

'About a grand's worth of duty-free cigarettes and a half-dozen bottles of single malt.'

'What? Where did that come from?'

'Looks like Craig Reese is involved with the smuggling that's been going on in Thorpe. O'Connor thinks he's small-time, and that he's working for somebody else. He's taken over the interview. Reese is alibied up to his neck for yesterday. There's no way he could have had anything to do with Callum Goodwin's disappearance, unless his in-laws, our FLO, and a GP are all lying, but at least we've got a reason to keep him. O'Connor's looking forward to getting stuck in.'

Kate sighed. She hadn't expected this, but she didn't think Reese was a murderer. If anything, he'd probably got himself in too deep with whoever was running the smuggling operation and was terrified of the police sniffing around his shed. No wonder he'd been so nervous every time they'd spoken to him. He wasn't even bright enough to fit a proper lock on the shed. He was either over-confident or really quite dim.

'What about the statement from the man who saw Aleah? Does that get us anywhere?'

'That's where it gets interesting. I talked him back through his walk to the pub, and he did remember one unusual detail.'

Kate waited, tapping her fingers on the steering wheel as Hollis built up the suspense like a reality show host announcing the winner.

'He remembers seeing a van in the square. He only noticed it because he thought it was an AA van, and he wondered who'd broken down. It wasn't the AA, though. It was a campervan. He said that it looked like somebody had bought an AA reject and was doing it up. It had a side window and a roof light.'

'Please tell me that he looked inside, and it had a bare metal floor.'

Hollis laughed. 'He didn't bother giving it a closer look because it was nearly opening time. But he did notice part of the registration, because it spelled his niece's name, Ness, short for Vanessa. It must've been NE55.'

It wasn't much, but it was more than they'd had that morning. Tomorrow, she'd send as many bodies as she could find over to the estate to see if anybody had seen a yellow camper. And she'd get Sam checking CCTV in the area to see if they could get a more complete index number for the van.

CHAPTER 18

2015

A heavy thunderstorm had kept Kate awake for much of the night, the loud crashes and blinding lights preventing her from falling asleep for more than a few minutes at a time until the early hours. At one point, she'd got up to make a mug of herbal tea and stood at the living room window watching as the weather changed her view from darkness to monochrome and back again. Her thoughts had drifted to Callum Goodwin. Was he out somewhere in this weather, wondering where his parents were, and why they weren't coming to get him? Or was he tied up in the back of a van, listening to the rain drumming on the roof? Or worse. There was no wonder she couldn't sleep, she'd thought, sipping her tea and brooding.

Her midnight questions were answered by a text just as she was slipping on her shoes, about to leave the house.

Callum Goodwin found.

It was from Raymond, and she knew he was being deliberately vague in case her phone records were ever to be used in a court case. The fewer communications written down, the better – there was much less room for ambiguity and misinterpretation.

She rang him to get the details.

'He's dead, Fletcher,' Raymond announced without preamble. 'Not much else I can tell you. Similar circumstances. The body's been abandoned on waste ground. You'll love who was there when the body was found, though.'

She waited for him to tell her, knowing that to ask a question would probably waste more time.'

'Our friend, Ken Fowler. He's not been far from this investigation this week, has he?'

Barratt would be happy – this would add more credence to his theory about Fowler being involved. Kate made a mental note to get Sam to double check Fowler's registered vehicles using a combination of his first and middle names and initials. Just because the Land Rover wasn't viable didn't mean he didn't have a bright yellow camper stashed away somewhere, and Barratt's PNC search might have been a bit cursory. It didn't hurt to have another look. He was a bit obvious, though, insinuating himself into the investigation. He'd struck Kate as much smarter than that.

'Where was the body found?'

'On a patch of land that belongs to that outdoor centre. Kids off on an early morning nature walk with Fowler made the discovery, and he called it in. Probably be in therapy well into their twenties, poor sods.'

'Shall I meet you there?'

'No. I'm in bloody budget meetings all morning. You be my eyes and ears, Fletcher. Take Hollis to interview the kids who found the body. And get Cooper checking for any CCTV on site or nearby.'

A quick text to Hollis and she was on her way, negotiating roads she used to know so well but which now seemed unfamiliar and alien. She was reminded of a French term she'd learned while studying for her A-levels – *jamais vu* – the opposite of *déjà vu*. This was what she'd been experiencing off and on since she'd returned to South Yorkshire and especially since she'd been back in Thorpe. A feeling of unfamiliarity in familiar surroundings. Everything looked the same but different, and she wasn't sure how she felt about her return. She was glad of the promotion, the extra responsibility, and the extra money she could use to help her son, but she couldn't help but resent the town that kept dragging her back and was threatening to drag her under.

She pulled into the carpark for the outdoor centre, squeezing her Mini between a liveried police car and a forensics van. There were three other police cars and a minibus as well as various unmarked cars and a Land Rover she recognised as Ken Fowler's. The main buildings of the centre were across a concrete bridge Kate remembered used to lead to the main road into the pit. It was called Samson Bridge and had been the main access point for anybody approaching on foot – as most of the miners had done when she'd lived in Thorpe.

They were all local men, and most would have lived within easy walking distance of their work. The road had turned right just after the bridge and went past the baths and the canteen up to the winding gear. Now, the road ended in tufty grass, and a cinder path led up to a reception building. She nodded to the PCSO who was standing next to the white and blue tape stretched across the track and showed him her identification. He lifted the tape, allowing her just enough height to duck under.

As she crossed the bridge, Kate glanced over the side where the railway used to run. There was a lot of activity beneath her. Uncomfortable-looking, overall-clad police officers observed as the forensics team started their work. The sides of the bridge had also been taped off, preventing anybody from actually looking directly over, so it was impossible to see where the body had been found.

Kate ducked into the reception building to see what she could find out. Inside, knots of people were clustered around low tables, each occupied by a uniformed officer furiously taking notes. She spotted Barratt huddled at a table on the corner talking to Ken Fowler. From Barratt's body language, she could tell he was questioning the older man aggressively, but Fowler looked unruffled as he sat back from the table with his arms folded across his chest. He seemed to be answering thoughtfully and carefully.

'What do we have?' she demanded, marching up to Barratt who gave her an irritated frown before realising who had just spoken to him. Slightly flustered, he stood up and walked over to an empty table, indicating Kate should follow him. She looked back at Fowler who gave her a grin of recognition. Much too cool for her liking.

'Right,' Barratt began. 'Fowler rang 999 at about half seven this morning. He was out with a small group of boys on an early morning nature walk. One of them had lost his mobile the night before and ducked down under the bridge to have a look for it. Apparently, they had a bonfire down there somewhere last night and told a few ghost stories.'

Kate glanced around. Most of the people in the room were teenaged boys, probably around thirteen or fourteen. They nearly all looked pale and frightened. No doubt this would eventually morph into an urban legend in their re-telling when they got back to school; a horror story that ended with a real body. One boy in particular looked really out of it, and Kate guessed he'd had the dubious honour of being first on the scene. He was shivering despite the mild morning, and his dark eyes looked deep set and smudged in his pale face. She held up a hand to stop Barratt's account and strode over to the boy.

'Hi.' She gave him the best smile she could muster under the circumstances. I'm Detective Inspector Fletcher. Did you find Callum?' She deliberately used the boy's name instead of 'the body' unwilling to highlight again the awfulness of the situation.

The boy nodded. His eyes flicked from her face to the police officer opposite him, to the window and back again.

'What's your name?'

'A…Aaron,' he stammered.

'Okay, Aaron. I'm going to want to talk to you but not right now. Right now, I want you to sit on the sofa over there. This police officer will go back to your room and get you a sweatshirt – tell him what you need and where it is – and then, he'll get you a hot chocolate. Does that sound okay to you?'

Aaron nodded, eyes wide at this sudden demonstration of compassion. He slid off the seat, followed by the police officer, and headed to the sofa Kate had indicated. She watched as the two of them had a hushed conversation, Aaron finally smiling as the policeman went to fetch him warmer clothes and a drink.

She clapped her hands together to get the attention of the people in the room. 'Right. Who's in charge here?'

A hand was raised by one of the few civilian adults in the room. The man was unshaven and dressed in a baggy grey tracksuit which might have passed for pyjamas, and she suspected he hadn't had time to get properly dressed this morning. He looked to be in his mid-twenties and was obviously dazed by the events of the morning. He stood up and approached her looking like a scolded puppy, obviously expecting to be berated.

'I'm the overnight supervisor,' he said, extending a shaking hand. 'Mark Thompson. I've rung the centre director, and he's on his way.'

Kate nodded her approval, hoping to put him at ease.

'Good. Look, I know you're probably out of your depth here, but you've got a group of traumatised young boys who need a bit of TLC. Can you take an officer to their rooms and get some warm clothing? We can't let them get their own. And, please, organise some hot drinks. Get a kettle from the kitchens, some tea bags, hot chocolate, coffee, and plenty of sugar. That young man's in shock.' She pointed at Aaron. 'And he's probably not the only one.'

Satisfied her instructions were being carried out, she returned to Barratt. 'Start again,' she said.

'Okay. Fowler rang in the discovery of the body this morning. A young lad went looking for his mobile phone, thought he'd left it down there last night when they had a bonfire and ghost story session. They were up 'til after eleven apparently – it's one of the highlights of a visit here. Anyway, he'd just left the path, eyes at his feet, and he found the body. It hadn't been hidden. It was lying next to the ashes of last night's fire.'

Kate noted Barratt's impersonal use of "it" for the body of Callum Goodwin and considered taking him to task about it, reminding him this was a four-year-old boy they were talking about, but she could see the DC was struggling with his emotions. Depersonalising the body was probably a coping mechanism, and she didn't want to snatch it away unnecessarily. Instead, she nodded for him to continue.

'I got here about twenty minutes ago. Some of the boys were already being interviewed, so I had a chat with Fowler. He does a bit of work here, outdoor skills, that sort of thing.' He lowered his voice. 'Bit of a coincidence, him being on both scenes.'

Kate nodded. It was a *huge* coincidence. But he had a legitimate reason for being on the site. 'What time did he get here?'

'Just before seven, according to Mark Thompson.'

'And he wasn't here last night?'

Barratt shook his head.

'So, where was he?'

'He played in a pool tournament at his local, then home alone until he left at six-thirty to come here.'

'Okay. Well, there's a start. I'll get Cooper to check his alibi. What's the pub called?'

Barratt told her, and she sent a quick text. No rush, though. She doubted there would be anybody at the pub much before ten o'clock.

'Have statements been taken from all the boys?'

Barratt shook his head. 'They've been kept separate, but I don't think anything official has been put in place. We've got enough bodies now, though. I think Thompson wants us to allow them to ring their parents.'

Kate shook her head. 'Not yet. If Thompson wants their parents here, that's fine, but we can't have a bunch of traumatised teenagers blabbing all sorts to their mums and dads. We need to keep this quiet until we've established the facts. Thompson will have contact details, and there's only…what?' She looked around. 'Ten or twelve kids? Hollis is on his way. I want him to talk to that boy, Aaron. The uniforms can chat to the others. It doesn't sound like they saw much anyway. You stick with Fowler for the minute. Okay?'

Barratt nodded and went to speak to Mark Thomas, who'd just appeared with a couple of sweatshirts under one arm and a tray containing a kettle, mugs, and various jars and boxes of drinks. He'd obviously followed her instructions to the letter.

A quick scan of the room satisfied Kate that all was in order so she could leave and face the scene under the bridge.

Just as she was struggling into her overalls and bootees, Hollis appeared striding across the bridge.

'Morning. Where do you want me?'

Kate quickly filled him in and gave him a description of the boy she wanted him to talk to.

'You off down there?' he asked, gesturing to the bridge.

'Yep. Just what I need after breakfast.'

Hollis sighed. 'I really hoped we'd find this one alive.'

'I know,' Kate said. 'We all did. All we can do now is try to work out what happened and try to stop this bastard from doing it again.' She stalked off towards another barrier of police tape, struggling to wriggle her hands into nitrile gloves.

It wasn't hard to pinpoint the location of the body. Clear plastic stepping plates led from the first area of slightly flat ground to a dark expanse of shadow beneath the bridge. Kate could make out several ghostly white figures hunched over something on the ground, which she assumed to be the body of Callum Goodwin. Around the bridge and into the woods, plastic containers of various sizes lay upended protecting possible evidence from the increasing threat of showers.

It was dry here, Kate noticed; no sign of the thunderstorms which had kept her awake for half the night. She moved closer to the body, treading carefully and breathing in shallow rapid breaths. She didn't know what to expect. Aleah had been her first child murder victim in nearly twenty-five years of policing, but she had felt removed from the girl – perhaps it was the distortion of the water in her hair and clothes or possibly the shock – but she felt a shiver of apprehension when she caught her first glimpse of Callum's sneakered foot.

'What do we know?' she asked, and even to herself, it sounded like bluster. Her voice wasn't quite steady as she tried hard to both look at and avoid looking at the tiny, broken body.

Kailisa glanced up, irritated at the interruption. He would only have been called because the body was in some way "problematic" and couldn't be signed off by the area surgeon – just like Aleah Reese. Kate was already making connections, and Kailisa's presence was another tick on her imaginary checklist.

'We have the body of a child. Approximately four or five years old. White. Cause of death unclear, as yet.'

Kate looked away from the body, examining the scene. The bridge was angular, shaped like a goal post – the road above forming the cross bar and thick concrete buttresses forming the posts. There was no sign of the railway line that used to run beneath; in fact, it was difficult to see why the bridge was there – it just spanned an expanse of elder and bramble which must have grown out of control after the closure of the pit.

'How did he get there?' Kate asked. The undergrowth around the body looked barely disturbed, and it would have been difficult to force a path through, especially in the dark.

Kailisa sighed. 'Judging by the positioning of the body and the post-mortem injuries, at the moment, we're working on the premise he was dropped from up there.' Kailisa pointed to the concrete above with a wooden spatula.

'Dropped?'

'There is very little disturbance to the area around the body, it was pure chance that unfortunate young man spied the feet through the bushes.'

'Shouldn't you be looking on the bridge, then?'

'All in good time. We have only been on site for an hour, Detective Inspector. You will no doubt have noticed the bridge is part of crime scene, but we also needed to provide access to the reception building for the children. It's unlikely to yield anything important as it is a busy thoroughfare when the centre is in use. Ditto the car park.'

Kate looked up again. The road was probably less than ten feet above her head, and the sides of the bridge added another three feet to that. A thirteen-foot drop – not enough to kill somebody, even a small boy. Unless he'd landed on something hard. Kate opened her mouth to ask another question, but Kailisa held up a gloved hand.

'All in good time,' he repeated. 'Please let my team do their jobs, and then, you can do yours. Observe, by all means, but please keep interruptions to a minimum.'

Kate stepped back, interpreting Kailisa's comments as "back off and shut up." There was nothing to be gained by pushing him, but she couldn't just walk away; she'd met the boy's parents. They would have their own questions, and she owed them the best and most honest answers she could give.

CHAPTER 19

2015

Kate watched Kailisa examine the body for well over an hour, biting her tongue when he shared findings with his team. He seemed fairly convinced the little boy had been dead when he was dropped over the bridge, but as usual, he couldn't tell her much about time of death or cause, although he was tentatively suggesting strangulation. The small body was scratched from the fall, but none of the injuries had any vital response. There were no other marks on his body. His clothing was intact and didn't look to have been removed at any point, but, again, Kailisa told her to wait until they'd examined him more closely at the mortuary.

She was vaguely aware of movement on the bridge above her as members of the team examined the area where the body might have been dropped from, but she knew Kailisa's assessment was probably right – there wouldn't be much to be found in the dust and debris that had piled up along the edges of the bridge. As Kailisa's team got ready to remove the body, Kate headed back up to the reception centre. Barratt and Hollis would have finished taking statements, and she knew she ought to send them back to base to collate all the information – and possibly get a bite to eat.

She examined the bridge, trying to imagine how somebody could possibly have hanged themselves from them. There was nothing to fix a rope to on the bridge or next to either side. She stepped closer to get a better look at the tops of the walls and saw the solution to her puzzle. Studded along the concrete surface of the wall were the rusting stumps of iron railings, barely half an inch high. Their regularity made them look like the holes left by the removal of stitches from a deep cut. They would have been taller at some point, tall enough to knot a length or rope around. Kate wondered if they'd been removed as a result of Paul Hirst's death, or if they'd been stolen and sold for scrap. Not that it made any difference now. Next to one of the low bridge walls, a crime scene case was standing open – a pile of evidence bags stacked on top. Each holding something that may or may not have some relevance to the case.

'Mind if I have a look?' Kate asked the nearest scene of crime officer.

He shrugged in a "help yourself gesture," so she bent down to get a closer look, picking her way through the layer of transparent bags. The contents were not very inspiring. A few sweet wrappers and cigarette butts, a nail, a stiff sports sock that had once been white but had transformed to the same shade of grey as the gravel track over a period of months or even years. One item was even more incongruous than the sock. She held it up to the light, hardly able to believe what she was seeing. It was a square of leather attached to a keyring and the side she was looking at still had a faint but unmistakable letter P carved into the surface.

'Where did you find this?' Kate yelled at the group of people who were still trawling through the gravel.

One of them looked at it and then pointed to the wall. 'It was in the gravel next to that bit of wall.'

Kate ducked under the tape and peered over. Kailisa was giving a few final comments to his team directly below her. 'How long do you think it's been here?'

The technician shrugged. 'Hard to say. It's not especially scuffed or worn. Could have been left any time in the last few months, I suppose. There's no way to know.'

'Well, get fingerprints and DNA from it, if you can. Prioritise it. It might be linked with another case.'

A T on Aleah Reese and a P near Callum Goodwin. Tracy Moore and Paul Hirst. Two tragic deaths, ten years apart. She needed to find the link.

Cooper answered on the first ring. 'Kate?'

'Sam, listen. Have you found anything else about Tracy Moore?'

'Not really,' Cooper said. 'I've got a DOB and a birth certificate which has her parents' names on it. I've not managed to find out anything about them yet, though.'

'What was her father's name?' Kate held her breath as she heard Sam tapping on her keyboard.

'Donald. Donald Moore.'

'Damn! Listen, Sam. I need you to find a link between Tracy Moore and Paul Hirst. There is one, I'm certain. They both meant something to somebody, and I think that somebody is our killer. I'm not sure why he's doing this, but it's linked to those two deaths. Text me the minute you find anything.'

She hung up and clenched her fists in frustration. The answer was tantalisingly close, she could almost smell it. Her thoughts swung back to Ken Fowler. He'd been on both scenes – legitimately – and he knew the area well. Could she have been wrong about him? Barratt didn't trust him, and Barratt's instincts weren't bad. It was worth another look. She rang Cooper again.

'Sam. While you're at it, see if there's any link between Ken Fowler and either of the other two names.'

Cooper sighed at the other end of the phone, but Kate knew it was mostly for effect. There was nothing Sam Cooper liked more than digging around on the internet and mining databases for information.

'And don't pretend you don't love it.' Kate laughed as she hung up.

As she'd expected, Barratt and Hollis were questioning the last of the boys. She raised her eyebrows in a question at Hollis as he snapped his notebook closed and thanked a tired-looking teenager. Hollis shook his head slightly. Nothing useful, then.

'What have you got?' she asked as Hollis approached, stretching his shoulders and neck.

'It doesn't look like any of the boys saw anything. I had a long chat with Aaron, and he's a bit less shell-shocked now. He was just looking for his phone and saw the shoes through the bushes. He didn't get near the body, but he feels responsible.'

Kate nodded. 'Only natural.'

'He ran to Fowler, who rang it in. Fowler didn't approach either.'

'Not even to check whether Callum was still alive?'

'He says he called the police and an ambulance just in case, but he didn't want to get too close. He had a look from the bridge, and he was fairly sure that the kid was dead.'

'But still?'

Hollis smiled. 'Don't know what's better. People who think they can help or people who think it's best to keep away. At least he didn't contaminate the scene.'

Which might have been his intention, Kate thought. If he was responsible, then surely, he'd have wanted to get close to the body in order to explain the presence of his DNA. If he wasn't involved, why not try to help? It didn't make sense.

'I need to talk to him,' Kate said. 'Where is he?'

Hollis looked around. 'Thought he was over there. Nobody's been given permission to leave.'

Kate quickly scanned the room. If Fowler had fled the scene, there could only be one interpretation of his actions. Guilt. 'Barratt!' Kate called. 'Here a minute.'

The DC approached looking worried.

'Where's Ken Fowler? Have you seen him?'

Barratt nodded. 'He's in the back, I think. Tea and coffee duty. Volunteered when nobody else wanted to do it.'

'What a saint.'

Hollis smiled at Kate's sarcastic tone.

'Can you see if he's still there?'

Thirty seconds later, Barratt was back with Fowler in tow. The older man looked slightly amused as though his disappearance had been a deliberate attempt to cause a commotion.

'Can I help you, Detective Inspector?'

Kate led him to a vacant table and gestured for him to sit down. 'Just a couple more questions,' she said.

Fowler nodded. 'Anything to help.'

'When you saw the body under the bridge, why didn't you get closer to see if he was still alive?'

Fowler gave her a condescending smile. 'Come on, Inspector. Everybody watches crime dramas these days. I could see from the angle of the body the chances of him being still alive were very slim. I've found dead bodies before. There was no point me charging in and messing up anything that might be of use to yourselves.'

Arrogant, Kate thought. 'Even if it might have saved a life?'

'As I said, I checked from the bridge, where I had a clearer view. In my opinion, the boy was dead, and there wasn't much to be gained by me trampling a potential crime scene.'

'What made you think it was a crime scene? The boy could have fallen by accident.'

That supercilious smile again which made Kate want to slap him 'DI Fletcher, I was helping to search for Aleah Reese, and I was aware of the search for Callum Goodwin. The Reese girl didn't die by accident, and I assume this little boy is probably the victim of the same disturbed individual. There was no doubt in my mind I was looking at the body of Callum Goodwin.'

'Where were you last night?' Kate asked abruptly, hoping to wrong-foot him.

'I took part in a pool competition, and then, I was at home, by myself. As I've already explained to one of your detective constables.'

'And you arrived on site here at what time?'

'Just before 7am.'

Kate nodded.

'I'm not the person you're looking for, DI Fletcher. I can see you don't like me very much, and, I admit, my proximity to both crime scenes may seem suspicious, but neither fact makes me a murderer. I'm willing to cooperate in any way I can. Take my DNA and fingerprints, if you wish – neither is on any database – and use them to eliminate me.'

Kate wondered if she had been mistaken about his attitude. Was his apparent arrogance just confidence? He seemed very sure of himself, which meant he was either very clever or completely innocent. Part of Kate hoped it was the former – at least that would give them a viable suspect after the case against Craig Reese had collapsed.

'Does the name Tracy Moore mean anything to you?'

Fowler's eyes flicked left and right as he thought. 'Nope,' he said, pursing his lips to add an air of finality to his answer.

'How about Paul Hirst?'

Fowler shook his head. 'Never heard of him either.'

Kate pushed her chair back, satisfied there was nothing else to be gained from the interview. 'We'll be in touch if there's anything else, Mr Fowler.'

He gave her a broad grin. 'I'll look forward to it.'

Kate knew Raymond would be keen to see her when she got back to Doncaster. It wasn't a meeting she was looking forward to as she knew he wanted progress, and he'd be pissed off with her for letting Craig Reese go yesterday. He was a good boss, fair, but he could be like a terrier with a bone when he got an idea fixed in his head. At least he'd spared her the trauma of having to inform the Goodwins about the body – he'd sent a couple of uniforms to talk to the FLO who'd have the dubious honour of that task. As she climbed the stairs to the incident room, Kate ran all the developments through her head. There was quite a lot to report, but in terms of progress towards finding a viable suspect, there was nothing. She only hoped Cooper had made some progress with the van index number or the family histories of Tracy Moore and Paul Hirst.

She could see through the glass top of his office door that Raymond was on the phone, so she quickly ducked off to the side of the room where she wouldn't be in his immediate field of vision. Sliding into the seat next to Sam Cooper, she made a finger-on-lips hushing gesture to the DC. Cooper smiled and passed Kate a pile of papers.

'What's all this?' she asked.

'Some of the research I've been doing. I think I've found your link between Hirst and Tracy Moore.'

Kate scanned through the thin pile of printouts – birth and marriage certificates and Paul Hirst's death certificate. 'Who's Barbara Wilkinson?'

'Barbara Wilkinson is Tracy Moore's mother. She divorced Tracy's father not long after their daughter was born and changed her name back to her maiden name. Tracy kept her dad's name, though – maybe he insisted. It wasn't as easy for divorced women back then.'

Kate glanced at the date of the marriage certificate – July 1967. Tracy had been born in February 1968. She didn't need a degree in further maths to work out the reason for the marriage. The divorce papers had been finalised in June 1969. At least one party had discovered marriage wasn't all it had been cracked up to be.

'So where does Paul Hirst come in?'

Cooper took the pile of papers and shuffled them until a different marriage certificate was on top. Barbara Wilkinson and Paul Hirst had married at the end of 1969.

'Christ, she didn't waste much time. Any kids with Hirst?'

Cooper did another quick shuffle. 'A son. Ian Andrew. Born August 1970.'

'So, she was still living in Thorpe. Two kids by two different husbands. Tracy dies in 1975, then what?'

Cooper shrugged. 'I can't find her after that. Not yet, anyway.'

Ian Hirst. He was the link. Half-brother to Tracy and son of Paul. Could he be the person they were looking for? Two deaths, ten years apart, his half-sister and his father. Had he come back for some sort of twisted revenge? And why now?

'What about this son? Ian. Where's he?'

Cooper shook her head. 'I'm not sure yet. I've got twenty-one Ian-Hirsts on the electoral register. I'm going to ring 'round and see if any of them is our man. Starting with the local area and working out.'

'Get some help. Barratt should be on his way back, and Hollis won't be long. You should be able to break the back of it in an hour or so with their help.'

Kate glanced at Ian Hirst's birth certificate again and was struck by the date. He was only a few months younger than her sister. An August birthday would have placed him in the same year at school. Karen might have the answer. Kate checked her watch. It was about half past six in India – not an awful time to try to get hold of her – but she might still be away on a trek. She decided she'd email later when she'd had time to think about how to approach her sister. Karen might give them the break they'd been hoping for. At least she had something positive to tell Raymond when he opened the office door and summoned her in like an executioner beckoning her towards the scaffold.

CHAPTER 20

2015

The rest of Kate's day hadn't gone well. Raymond wasn't impressed with her theory about Ian Hirst, and he dismissed the keyring as coincidence. He suggested the next actions should be involving the mysterious yellow van and running more background on Craig Reese and his known associates. He was starting to look at the smuggling ring as a possible reason for the abduction and murder of Aleah. Perhaps Reese had cheated somebody, and they wanted to teach him a lesson?

Kate knew her suggestions were a little outlandish and unsubstantiated, but she was convinced she was looking in the right place. She just couldn't convince her boss.

When she got back to her desk, Cooper had printed out a list of NE55 index numbers – over four thousand of them. She and Barratt were combing through the list; Barratt working down a sheet with a ruler, trying to find the ones that had been allocated to commercial vehicles. Neither looked happy when she approached.

'Needle in a haystack?'

Cooper nodded. 'We've got forty-four NE55 numbers registered to vans.'

'Okay. How about a different approach? The man who gave the statement thought it was an AA van. If he's right, then the fleet operator will have a record of it. They can't have registered many vans on that plate. It might narrow down the field quite a bit.'

'But it's already been sold on.' Barratt protested. 'How will that help? There's no Ian Hirst connected to any of these vehicles,

Cooper did a search. We can't find the man, so we're trying to find the van.'

'Did you search with the AA as the registered keeper?'

'Yep. No go. They must register the mechanic or driver as the registered keeper. The AA will be the owner, and there's no search parameter for that.'

Kate nodded. She hadn't expected that would work, as most companies listed the main user of a vehicle as the "keeper," unless the car was part of a pool.

'Okay. So, let's find out who's in charge of the AA fleet and find out what happens to their vans when they're no longer used. They might use a particular auction mart or reseller.'

Barratt was already on the phone, one step ahead as though he'd seen where her thought process was taking them.

'No luck,' he said a few minutes later. 'They put me through to the north-east manager, which is where the van would have been registered, but the fleet manager isn't there. He'll be back after the weekend.'

'Shit. Where's Hollis?' she asked, noticing the DC was conspicuous by his absence.

'Following up on Fowler, as per the DCI's instructions. O'Connor's still with Reese. Apparently, he's still claiming the booze and fags were for personal use.'

So, Raymond had gone over her head and sent Hollis out on what was, in her opinion, a wild goose chase. So much for having faith in her.

'Great. Right, let's get back to these records.'

She'd sent her team home at six and left the station herself less than an hour later. Hollis hadn't reappeared, and she suspected he'd be embarrassed at allowing Raymond to use him to get at her. Not that Kate blamed him. He couldn't resist the DCI's direct orders any more than she could – not if he wanted to keep his job. She'd caught up briefly with O'Connor. Reese was still, in the DS's words, "shut up tighter than a camel's arse in a sandstorm," but

O'Connor was convinced he could get him to talk. His phone records had been requested, and the network provider had been unusually helpful, promising them by the next morning. At least somebody was making progress.

As she drove back to her flat, Kate mulled over what she needed to ask her sister. On the surface, it seemed straightforward. Did she remember Ian Hirst? But the subject was fraught with difficulties. Getting Karen to talk about that period of her past was like trying to entice a stray dog to take a treat. Kate knew she'd have to be gentle and circumspect; Karen hated to talk about being at school during the strike and the bullying she'd faced – possibly at the hands of people Kate needed to find out about. It had got worse after the incident with Rob Loach and the note. Subtler, but more insidious. Her sister's attendance record was dreadful, and her list of fake illnesses had become increasingly imaginative.

The time difference between the UK and India didn't help either. India was five-and-a-half hours ahead, which meant when Kate pulled up outside her flat, Karen was probably already in bed. She could send a list of questions and hope Karen felt able to answer them in detail when she finally checked her messages.

Just as she closed the door behind her, Kate had another thought. Karen wasn't her only potential source of information. Drew Rigby said he'd been in the same year as her sister. He might remember Ian Hirst. She took her phone out of her pocket and scrolled through her text messages until she found the conversation she'd had with Rigby a few days ago. She typed quickly, keeping her question brief and to the point.

Do you remember an Ian Hirst in your year at school?

She hit send and threw the phone onto the sofa as she passed the door to the living room. Even if Rigby said no, she still had Karen.

She'd just opened a tin of soup when she heard her text alert sound. Dashing into the living room, she grabbed her phone hoping it was somebody, anybody, with a break in the case. It was Rigby.

Can't remember anybody by that name. Any more info?

Kate sighed. She hadn't really expected much, it was thirty years ago after all, but she'd hoped she might be able to spark Rigby's memory. She was just about to text back when her phone started ringing. It was Rigby.

'Hello?'

'Hi,' he said. 'Is this a bad time?'

'No, it's fine. What's up?'

'I was just wondering if you could tell me anything else about this Ian Hirst. Something that might jog my memory. There were over two hundred people in my year at school. The only person called Hirst I can think of was a Sheffield Wednesday footballer.'

Kate thought for a few seconds. She doubted Rigby would have any more information, and she got a sense he was just trying to insinuate himself into the case. But what if she was wrong? Could she afford to ignore a potential lead?

'Okay. There are a couple of things. Firstly—'

'Hang on,' Rigby interrupted. 'Are you in Donny?'

'Yes,' Kate said, unwilling to let him know she was at home.

'So am I. And I'm off duty. How about we do this over a pizza or a beer? We might get a chance to reminisce a bit as well. I'd love to know more about how your sister's doing.'

It didn't feel quite right; Rigby was a PCSO, and his suggestion felt a bit like a date. As though he could read her mind, he said, 'I know how that sounded, but I'm not asking you out or anything. You probably have plans anyway. I just thought if we could bat a few ideas about, something might jog my memory. You can pay for your own food and drink. In fact, you can pay for mine, if you want.'

Despite her misgivings, Kate smiled at his attempt at a joke. 'Okay. Do you know the Black Swan?'

'Just off the Market Place? I've been in a couple of times.'

'Let's meet there in half an hour. Okay?'

Rigby agreed, and Kate went back to the kitchen to pour her soup into a Tupperware tub and put it in the fridge. At least she might get a decent meal out of the meeting.

Kate decided to walk from her flat, taking advantage of the last hour or so of daylight, and she reached the town centre earlier than planned. The streets were fairly quiet, a few smokers outside pubs and a knot of teenagers outside the McDonald's near the Frenchgate Centre. The shopping centre had been a place of pilgrimage when she was a teenager – weekends spent wandering the "Arndale," as it had been, were a rite of passage. Now, the steel and glass curves bore little resemblance to the 1960s concrete-and-glass monstrosity of her childhood.

The Black Swan wasn't one of Kate's favourite pubs in Doncaster – she wasn't a big fan of chain establishments – but it had a reputation for decent, if generic, food, and it was fairly central. She pushed open the door and scanned the barn-like room to see if Rigby had already arrived. There was no sign of him, so Kate made her way over to the bar and ordered a small glass of red wine. She felt like she deserved a drink, but she didn't want to risk too much alcohol on an empty stomach.

'Hi, you're early,' a voice said from behind her just as she put the glass to her lips. She turned to see Rigby grinning at her. 'That'll save me the expense of buying you a drink.'

'I'll get you one,' Kate said. 'I'm the one who's dragged you here to see if you have any information.'

Rigby shrugged amenably and asked for a pint of bitter. They stood in silence, waiting for his drink to arrive, and Kate wondered what they would find to talk about, other than the case.

'So, two Thorpe Comp survivors,' Rigby began, taking a gulp of his lager. 'Shall we find a quiet corner and swap war stories?'

Kate followed him to a corner table flanked on one side by a wooden partition, creating an impression of privacy. She slid onto the bench seat, and Rigby pulled out a stool to perch opposite.

'Eating?' he asked, grabbing a menu from the pile on the table.

Kate nodded. 'I'm starved. I was about to eat when you rang.'

'Oh. What did I save you from? Can't imagine you have time for Cordon Bleu.'

'Tomato soup,' Kate admitted.

'I was going to order a pizza. Looks like we've rescued each other from poor culinary choices. What do you fancy?'

Kate skimmed the menu. It was mostly traditional pub fare with the addition of "homemade" burgers.

'Burger for me,' she announced. 'The works.'

Rigby nodded his agreement. 'I'll order. Okay if I run up a tab? We can split it later?'

Without waiting for her consent, he stalked over to the bar, allowing Kate time to study him from behind. And what a pleasant behind it was. He moved gracefully, like a dancer or a boxer, and his tight jeans and white T-shirt clung to his muscled body, showing off a toned back and legs.

'Stop it,' Kate whispered to herself. She was his superior; she shouldn't be looking at him that way. But there was something attractive about the contrast between his blue eyes and dark hair, and he certainly knew how to make the most of his assets.

'Fifteen minutes,' Rigby announced as he sat back down. He'd bought another round of drinks, even though Kate's first one was still nearly full and his pint glass still had a few mouthfuls left in it.

'I asked the barman what you were drinking. Shiraz?' He slid the glass over to stand next to the one she'd barely touched, and Kate knew she wouldn't be finishing both. There was something about Rigby's self-assurance that put her on edge, despite his good looks, and she didn't want to let her guard down around him.

'So, what's it like being back?' he asked. 'I hated it when I first got out of the army. Didn't want to be back. I did security for a big factory in Sheffield for a few years, but they went bust, so I applied to be a PCSO.'

He didn't seem to notice he'd not given her a chance to answer his question as he rambled on about his experiences in the army and what had brought him back "home." Which didn't seem to be very much. As Kate listened, she noticed Rigby was keen to slag off South Yorkshire, but he hadn't given a reason for his return.

'Why come back?' she interrupted. 'If you don't like it, why stay?'

He looked at her as though he'd never considered the answer to the question before, as though she'd just given him permission to leave and he was considering it.

'I don't really know,' he said. 'I think I just felt drawn to where I grew up. I couldn't go back to Thorpe, though. At least living in Donny gives me a bit of distance from that. Too many memories there. I suppose you feel the same.'

'Not really,' Kate lied. 'My memories aren't that bad. My mum died when I was little and that was rough, but I was mainly happy in Thorpe, until the strike. And then, we left.'

'When did you move?'

'July 1984,' Kate said. 'After I'd done my O-levels.'

'I wasn't far behind you, then. We moved to Adwick the year after.'

'How come?' Kate asked.

'Family stuff, you know how it was back then. Alliances formed, people fell out. My mum moved me away halfway through my O-levels. Bloody lucky to scrape a few passes.'

'Just your mum? Dad not around?'

Rigby shook his head. 'Useless piece of crap left us when I was seven. Mum met somebody else after we'd moved and started a new family. I think it was the best thing for both of us.'

'So, you survived four years of Thorpe Comp?' Kate said, changing the subject. Rigby seemed uncomfortable talking about his family, and she didn't want to get bogged down in his issues.

'Yep. What a shite hole, eh?'

Kate's non-committal answer got lost as a waitress arrived with cutlery and sauces.

'Do you remember Peg-Leg Pearson?' Rigby asked with a smile. 'Taught maths? He used to chuck the board rubber at us if we got a question wrong.'

Kate remembered the rumours about Mr Pearson, but she'd never witnessed one of his violent outbursts. She'd always found him fair and helpful if anybody was struggling.

'And that chemistry teacher, what was his name? Young bloke who wanted everybody to be his friend. I once sneaked into The Lion for an underage half, and he was there. Bought me and my mates a drink. Never get away with that these days.'

'Mr Davies,' Kate said.

'Aye, that was him,' Rigby was grinning, and his eyes lost focus as he lost himself in the past. He didn't seem like he was harbouring any resentment towards his former school, or his former home town; instead he seemed to be enjoying the nostalgia. Kate couldn't share the emotion. Her memories of secondary school had been soured by that last year and the bullying her sister had endured. And the awful notes from Robert Loach.

'You said you remembered my sister; did you know Rob Loach? He was in your year.'

Rigby's eyes drifted across to the bar as though he was trying to remember. 'I've tried. I know Jackie Reese is his sister, but I just can't place him. As I said, there were a couple of hundred kids in my year.'

Kate was just about to ask him again about Ian Hirst when their burgers arrived, and they busied themselves with cutlery and ketchup.

'Mmm, that's much better than I expected,' Kate mumbled around a huge bite of brioche and beef. 'I doubt I'll manage the chips, though.'

They ate in silence for a few minutes before Rigby asked, 'How's your Karen? You said she was abroad?'

Kate nodded, still working on her burger. 'India. She's been away for a couple of months. It's what she does. She'll take a job somewhere for a year or so, save up, and then, she takes off. She's been like it for about ten years. She trained as a teacher, and she does supply or temporary contracts to earn some money. She sometimes teaches while she's away to help fund her trip.'

Rigby raised his eyebrows. 'Sounds a bit unsettled to me. She not married?'

Kate shook her head. 'Came close a couple of times but no. I don't think she wants to be tied down.'

Rigby nodded thoughtfully. 'I thought I'd end up like that. I travelled a lot when I was in the army, couldn't imagine settling down, but here I am with a job and a house.'

'I don't suppose anybody's life turns out exactly like they expected,' Kate said. 'I know mine didn't.'

Rigby tilted his head to one side quizzically.

'I was going to be a psychiatrist. I did psychology and English at uni. Then, life took an unexpected turn, and here I am.'

'Unexpected how?'

Kate sighed, wondering how much to reveal. 'I got married. Had a son. Got divorced and ended up back in Doncaster. Oh, and I'm a copper. Not quite what I'd envisaged.'

'I always expected to be a miner, like every other lad in that school,' Rigby said. 'Thatcher probably did me a favour when she closed the pits.'

It wasn't a sentiment Kate had heard before, not from a Yorkshireman, and something about it didn't ring true. It sounded rehearsed.

'So, you were a fan?'

Rigby nearly spat out the mouthful of bitter he'd just taken to wash down the last bite of burger. 'Fuck, no! You couldn't grow up in Thorpe and be a fan of Thatcher. Is your boy in Doncaster with you?'

'No. He's nineteen now. He's at Sheffield University studying environmental science. Ironic that his grandfather earned a living from fossil fuels, and Ben'll probably save the world with renewables.'

Rigby smiled and nodded, but she could tell that he didn't think much of her observation.

Kate glanced at her watch. They'd been in the pub nearly an hour and hadn't got round to talking about the case. Time ságs

to move things along. She took a sip of her wine. 'So, you can't remember an Ian Hirst at school?'

Rigby shook his head.

'What about anybody else called Ian?'

The PCSO stared down at his empty plate. 'There was an Ian Jordan, or Jarvis, and an Ian Andrews in my form, but I can't remember any others.'

Kate picked up a beer mat and peeled one printed side off with her thumbnail to create a blank writing surface. 'Here,' she passed the beermat and a pen to Rigby. 'Write those names down. Were there any Hirsts in your year?'

'Not that I remember. Have you tried contacting the school?'

'One of my DCs tried, but it's the holidays. The office staff weren't very helpful.'

'You know the old school's been demolished?' Rigby said with a sudden grin, as though he'd done the job himself. 'It's a shiny new academy now. All that's left is the sports hall and the old boiler building. Still gives me the shivers when I see it. Some of my so-called friends locked me in there once for an afternoon. Said it was a joke, but it wasn't funny. When the caretaker let me out, I'd wet myself. Lucky for me it was only a couple of weeks before I left. Couldn't have coped with being called "Pisspants" for a year.'

Kate had heard about the demolition of the school. She could remember the boiler house with its squat chimney in a corner of the school site that was officially "out of bounds" but was unofficially a shortcut to the local chippy. She hadn't been near the school on any of her trips to Thorpe so far, and she had no intention of passing by out of a sense of nostalgia. Cooper had been informed the Thorpe Comp records "may" have been stored off-site somewhere, possibly with the county council, but she couldn't confirm until the head was back in school. A quick call to the county council had yielded nothing of use, but Cooper had the number of an archivist who "might be able to help" after the holidays.

Rigby drained his second pint. 'Another?' he asked, waving the glass at her.

Kate looked down at her half-drunk wine and shook her head. 'I need to get off. Things to do.' She stood up. 'I'll settle the bill.'

'Do you live locally?' Rigby asked. 'It's getting dark, and I don't mind walking home with you.'

Kate just smiled and went to the bar. She didn't need an escort, and she resented his suggestion she did. Unless he was angling for an invitation to her flat. She quickly paid the bill and turned back to the table, when an idea struck her, and she ordered another pint of bitter.

'Here you go,' she said, as she returned to the table. 'Have another one. And thanks for the chat. At least I've got a couple of names to try.' She shrugged on her jacket and left before Rigby could protest.

Kate poured herself a glass of wine and eased herself down on to the sofa. The Shiraz in the pub hadn't quite hit the spot, and she felt the need for another glass before bed. She flipped open her laptop and clicked on her personal email, deliberately avoiding the link to her work server. The case could wait until tomorrow. She needed to try to connect with her sister. She sat for a few minutes, trying to compose an email, something that would sound chatty but wouldn't mask the seriousness of the need for information.

Hi Karen,

I hope you're having a good time. I don't know when you're back from your trek, but I just thought I'd drop you a quick line on the off-chance.

You'll never guess where I'm spending all my time at the minute. Thorpe! I've been back every day for the last week or so. I've been back to Crosslands Estate. Nothing's changed, and everything's changed — does that make sense? I've just been to the pub with another Thorpe Comp survivor. He seemed to have had a better time there than either of us.

Ben's been in touch. He needs money, big surprise, but we had a decent chat. I think he might be thawing a bit. Garry still rings for a whinge every few days, but the answering machine seems able to cope.

I could use your help with something, if you don't mind. I know you don't like thinking about Thorpe Comp, but there's a connection between the school and a recent case. I'm trying to trace somebody who was in your year. His name's Ian Hirst, and he seems to have vanished off the face of the earth. Does the name ring any bells? His sister died in an accident in the quarry when we were little. Let me know if you remember him.

Are you okay for money? I'm paying Ben's rent, but if you need anything, I'll help if I can – just ask.

Look after yourself.

Love you.

Kx

Kate re-read it twice before hitting "send."

'Come on, sis,' she whispered. 'You're all I've got at the minute.'

CHAPTER 21

1984

Kathy knew something serious was happening as soon as she walked into the kitchen. Her father and sister were sitting at the table, their faces grave. Karen looked up as Kathy threw her school bag onto one of the chairs and sat on a stool to join them. Her first thought was somebody had died; the situation reminded her of the morning her father had sat the two of them down on Kathy's bed and explained that their mother had gone to heaven. But who could it be this time?

'What's going on?' she asked, looking from her sister to her dad and back again. Her dad looked old. Older than he did when she imagined him or tried to describe him to anybody. His receding hairline had exposed acres of lines on his forehead, and the crow's feet around his grey eyes were deeply etched.

'I need to talk to you both. I need to make a decision, and it affects all of us, so it's only right you two have a say.'

Karen looked frightened, and Kathy wondered if she, too, was reminded of the last serious conversation her dad had had with them both.

'I've been offered a new job,' her dad continued. 'It's better pay, and it might mean I can buy a house instead of renting. It would be something for the two of you when I'm not here anymore.'

'Could I have a dog?' Karen asked, her face breaking into a smile of relief that it wasn't news of another death in the family.

'I don't know about that. But it means we'd have to move to another county.'

Karen looked dubious. 'Would I have to change schools?'

Her dad nodded.

'Great. I hate Thorpe Comp.'

This was the first time Kathy had heard about her sister not liking school. Apart from her bouts of fake illness, she seemed to enjoy being with her friends, and she was good at some subjects.

'I thought you liked school?' Kathy said.

Her sister looked embarrassed; caught out in a lie. 'I used to,' she said. 'I had loads of friends when I first started, but I hate it now. Everybody picks on me because...' She glanced up at her dad. 'Because of dad's job. They say he's a scab because he's not on strike. I know you're not a scab, Dad, but they don't believe me, and they call me a liar. So now, a lot of my friends don't talk to me anymore, and the others don't seem to like me very much.'

Her lower lip trembled, and Kathy had a sudden urge to hug her. She hadn't realised her little sister had been going through the same hell that she had. She should have talked to her, or at least gotten Karen to talk. All the times she'd faked illness with a big smile; all the stories about what she'd done at school. Kathy had thought Karen had been okay, but she'd barely been coping. Seeing her finally give way to tears as the months of torment finally caught up with her was heart-breaking.

Their father never cried, not even at their mum's funeral, but he looked really upset as he explained again his job put him in a different union from the other men who worked down the pit, and his union wasn't on strike. He had to go to work, or he wouldn't get paid, and there was nothing he could do about it, no matter what he thought about what was happening. Kathy understood his situation, and she had explained it carefully to her sister, but it obviously didn't matter to the bullies at school; the ones who'd seen a chink of weakness and exploited it just as efficiently as miners exploiting natural weaknesses in the rock below ground. It didn't matter to those kids that there were different unions; different sets of rules.

It wasn't their dad's fault they were being singled out for torment, but Kathy could see his shoulders sagging under the weight of responsibility as he listened to Karen describe some of the bullying. None of it was as bad as the note that had been left in Kathy's locker, but to a fourteen-year old, it would have seemed insurmountable.

'So, where's the new job?' Kathy asked. 'Is it far?'

'Near Nottingham. There's a house we can rent, but, like I said, we might be able to buy one eventually.'

'What about school?' Karen wanted to know. It didn't matter quite so much to Kathy; she'd finished her exams and the results were due in a few weeks, and then, she'd be going to sixth form anyway, where it would all be new. Not many of her classmates were expected to get good enough grades, so she'd been seeing it as an escape. For Karen, it would be much more of an upheaval.

'There's a school in the town where we'd live,' her dad said. 'It's not as big as the one you go to now, but everybody says it's good. Their O-level results are usually excellent, and it's got a sixth form for you, Kathy. I think it might be the best thing for all of us. It's hard here while this strike's on, and I can't see an end to it. And even when it's over, nobody knows what'll be left in the way of jobs. I might have had to move anyway.'

Kathy could see he wasn't being completely truthful. It wouldn't be the best thing for him. This was his home; this was where his friends were, where his family were from. It was where he belonged. A sudden flash of understanding jolted through her like electricity. This was for her and Karen. It was because of the note.

'I think it sounds great, Dad,' she said, standing up so she could put her arms around him. She knew she'd long grown out of hugging him, and Karen was the same, but she needed to show him she understood exactly what he'd done for the two of them.

'Thanks, Daddy,' she whispered as he put his arms around her shoulders and pulled her close.

'Just look after your sister,' he whispered back. 'It'll be hard on her at first.'

Less than six weeks later, Kathy stood at the gate of her new school, daring herself to walk in. Karen had already made friends on the estate and had gone in with them, but Kathy had kept herself to herself over the holidays. She'd been helping to get the house organised and making sure she was ready for school. She'd been given a reading list for her English A-level course and another for history and had decided to spend as much time as possible trawling the library for textbooks and novels she would be reading over the next two years. She didn't want to be a know-it-all, but she needed to make the most of this opportunity. It might be her ticket to university and beyond, and she didn't want to mess it up.

And then, there was her dad. He'd started his new job, but he didn't seem to be very happy, and Kathy knew he felt like her about the move away from their old house. The new house was great, it had a big garden, her bedroom was huge, and it was handy for the shops, but it had no memories, and that was hard for them all. The old house had bits of her mum woven into the wallpaper and curtains and paintwork. The kitchen walls still showed the brush marks where she'd tried to paint over the mural her dad had sketched out for a joke. The wallpaper in Kathy's bedroom hung crookedly around the door where her mum and dad had argued over the right way to paper around the corner, and the curtains in the sitting room were ones Mum had chosen and altered to fit. There was nothing of her mum in the new house, except a few framed photographs.

She glanced across at the students pouring in through the double front doors of the school, a building so completely different from the late Victorian brick monstrosity she had attended for the last five years. This school was barely three years old, and it was all windows and right angles. There was a crest in a concrete panel above the main entrance and a Latin motto Kathy couldn't read from where she was standing, but which she knew was *non scholae sed vitae discimus* and translated as something to do with learning for life. The Latin intimidated her when she'd been to visit with her dad. She'd expected the school to be stuffy like an old grammar, but the head of sixth form had been all smiles, and there hadn't been a black gown in sight.

It had been the start of the summer holidays, and Kathy and her father had been with a group of other families new to the area. The parents all seemed eager to please, but the students had seemed like a surly bunch, and Kathy had been the only one impressed with the library and the sports centre, complete with a full-size swimming pool. The tour also took in the shiny science labs and the fully carpeted classrooms in the sixth-form wing. It was nothing at all like her old school.

So, now, here she was, first day and she felt like she was a first year again. She shrugged her bag higher up her shoulder and marched down the flagstone path to the door. Most students seemed to have already dispersed to their various form rooms, and the corridor was deserted apart from a group of three stragglers gathered around an open locker. Kathy approached, heart hammering in her chest, to ask her way to G14, her form room for the year.

The three girls gave her the once over, eyes assessing her from top to toe, before the one in the middle of the group answered. 'It's just down there, second left.' She turned and pointed. 'I'm Diane. Are you in Miss Gilchrist's form?'

Kathy nodded, trying to weigh up the girls. Diane seemed to be the leader of the group. She was wearing turned-up jeans and a baggy T-shirt with the name of a band that Kathy didn't recognise emblazoned across the front. Her friends were dressed in a similar manner, but one had a bright red T-shirt with black numbers randomly scattered across the front and the other wore a plain white shirt tied at her midriff. All three sported shaggy haircuts, two blonde and one darker. Kathy thought they might pass for Bananarama's younger sisters.

'I'll walk with you, if you like,' said one of the blonde girls. 'I'm Faye. I'm in Miss Gilchrist's form as well. She's okay, really. She seems a bit strict, at first. I had her for English last year, but she sometimes lets it slip a bit and talks to us like we're adults.'

She grabbed Kathy's arm, before she could introduce herself, and began to steer her down the corridor chatting about teachers and subjects and university options without pausing for breath.

Miss Gilchrist was already at the teacher's desk when Kathy and Faye entered the room. She scowled at the two girls from beneath a severe fringe of greying hair. 'Good afternoon, can I help you?'

'Sorry we're late, Miss. I was helping a new girl. She was lost.'

Miss Gilchrist stared at them both for a few seconds, as though considering whether beheading might be too severe a punishment, and then, her face cracked into a smile, which despite the deep wrinkles it produced, seemed to shave a decade from her.

'Okay, find a seat. I'll get your timetables in a second. You I know, Faye Whitton. Who's your friend?'

Kathy looked at Faye and then at the teacher. Here was her chance to reinvent herself; to cut the ties to her former life and to start to forge a new life, a new identity. She took a deep breath and said the line she'd been practising in front of the mirror for the last few days.

'I'm Kate,' she said. 'Kate Siddons.'

CHAPTER 22

2015

The autopsy report on Callum Goodwin was sitting in her inbox when Kate arrived at her desk the next morning. It made grim reading. Callum had similar neck injuries to Aleah Reese, indicating he'd also been strangled, and Kailisa put the time of death as soon after his abduction. Kate hoped it was the latter. He must have been kept somewhere for a night, and then, his body dumped over the bridge like a bag of rubbish. Kate couldn't imagine how somebody could just dispose of a child like that – it was as though their killer had no respect for the child or his family, and Callum was just pawn in his game.

The area around the outdoor centre had been searched extensively, but there was no sign of the boy's scooter. Whoever had taken him must have either dumped it elsewhere or kept it as a trophy. There was no unexpected DNA, but Callum's body held much more trace evidence than Aleah's had, possibly due to the locations of the two bodies. The pond Aleah had been found in would have helped to eradicate anything left behind by the killer, but Callum's body had obviously been in two different locations. Kate had a quick scan through the findings and the photographs and prepared to brief her team.

She was interrupted from her reading by a loud 'Yes!' from O'Connor's desk. He'd arrived early and had been poring through what looked like a list of phone numbers for the last half hour.

'Something good, O'Connor?'

He grinned and made his way over to her desk. 'Something very good. I've been looking through Craig Reese's phone records, and I've found a number Reese has been ringing almost daily – including on the evening of the day Aleah went missing and the day after. I've just cross-referenced the unknown number with the murder investigation, and I've got a match.'

'Good work,' Kate said. 'Anybody we know?'

'Oh yes. Craig Reese was ringing your mate, Ken Fowler. Barratt had Fowler's contact details in his notes. It's the same number. We had to let Reese go yesterday, but I'm having him now. And Fowler.'

'You're sure it's the same number?' Kate's mind was spinning as she tried to make sense of the connection. 'Why would Reese ring Fowler the day after Aleah went missing?'

O'Connor shrugged. 'If it was me and I had our lot sniffing around, I'd be keen to get rid of thousands of quid's worth of fags that were sitting under my shed. Maybe give them back where they came from?'

It made sense. If Fowler was Reese's supplier, then Reese would go to him for help. So much for them just bumping into each other that night.

'Bring Fowler in,' she said. 'I'll see Raymond about a warrant to search his house and any other properties he owns. I knew that smug bastard was holding something back.'

By eight o'clock, Kate's team were assembled and eager to hear the latest. Barratt had arrived first, quickly followed by Cooper and Hollis. O'Connor had rolled up a few minutes later, still looking pleased with himself. They all looked much fresher than when Kate had last seen them, but she knew this was going to be another tough day.

'Before we go back to Callum Goodwin,' Kate said. 'O'Connor has an update on his illegal cigarettes and booze gang. And, Barratt, you'll love this.'

O'Connor quickly gave them the broad strokes of his findings and ended with Kate's suggestion Fowler be brought in for questioning and his house searched. Barratt looked like a kid that had been promised ice cream and then given sprouts. Kate knew he'd been sure Fowler was hiding something, and he was probably gutted he'd not been the one to find out his secret. She decided to make sure he was involved in the arrest and questioning in some way. It wasn't much in the way of compensation, but it would be some reward for the hard work he'd put in with the suspect.

'Right,' she said, using the remote to turn on the projector. 'There's nothing concrete to link Fowler to the two abductions and murders, but I'm sure once we've got him here, O'Connor will pursue this angle.' She glanced at the DS who nodded vigorously.

'Okay. We've got Callum Goodwin's PM results this morning, and there's quite a bit to think about. First, he was killed in the same manner as Aleah Reese.'

'Same killer?' Cooper asked.

'Too early to be sure, but my gut says it's the same man. And I'm convinced it is a man. Secondly, we have a large amount of trace on the body. Carpet fibres.'

She tapped her keyboard and a magnified image slid on to the whiteboard.

'Kailisa thinks commercial vehicle rather than domestic, but they've been sent away for further analysis. And then, there's this.'

Another tap and she revealed the image that had both confused and energised her when she'd seen it on the email. It showed an area of Callum's back with a lividity mark clearly imprinted in the skin. A ruler next to it showed it to be approximately twenty-five centimetres in length, and the ridged pattern was very different from the marks on Aleah Reese's body.

'What's that?' Barratt wanted to know, squinting at the image.

'I can't say for sure, but it looks like the spiral binding of some kind of notebook.'

Cooper nodded in agreement.

'It does,' she said. 'But it's too big to be a notepad. The wire binding in those is only about half that length.'

'So what else could it be?'

'Artist's pad?' Hollis suggested. 'One of those A4-size ones.'

Kate made a note of his suggestion.

'The lines are quite widely spaced,' Barratt said. 'It looks like quite a thick spiral. Could it be a road atlas?'

Kate made another note.

'That would fit with the carpet fibres,' Cooper said, her face alight with enthusiasm. 'Callum could have been placed in the back of a car, and he ended up lying on a road map on the back seat.'

It was a good suggestion, and it made sense, apart from one thing.

'So, how did he snatch Callum, subdue him, and manage to get him somewhere he could kill the boy without being seen?' Kate asked. 'The estate was crawling with police cars. It's a hell of a risky snatch at the best of times, but at the minute, it's crazy.'

'Maybe he didn't have the car with him. He parked it somewhere quiet, got Callum to go with him, and then killed him when they got to the car.' Cooper wasn't letting her idea go easily.

'But nobody saw him walking along the street with the kid. It doesn't make sense,' Hollis interjected.

'We know that people see what they want to see,' Kate said. 'Is it possible he just carried Callum off in plain sight, but he did so in such a way as to make his presence seem normal? As though what he was doing wasn't out of the ordinary.

'How could he do that?' O'Connor asked. 'Somebody would have seen him.'

'Yes, but what if, whoever he is, had a valid reason for being there? Somebody who lives nearby? A family friend? The bloody ice cream man?'

'But none of the statements we've got so far mention anybody like that.'

'So, we get more statements. Get the uniforms out there and expand the door-to-door. Somebody must have seen something,' Kate said, and it sounded almost convincing to her own ears.

'What about Ian Hirst?' Cooper asked. 'He doesn't live locally or he'd have been on the electoral register. Could it have been him?'

Kate sighed. 'I just don't know. We're missing something. Raymond doesn't think there's a link between the two families.

His feeling is these killings are either random and opportunistic, or they're linked with the illegal cigarettes and booze.'

'What about Craig Reese? Could Aleah have found his stash so he had to keep her quiet? Then, he took Callum to make it seem like it was part of a pattern and nothing to do with him?'

Kate turned to Barratt, and he shrugged apologetically. He knew she wasn't convinced Reese had anything to do with either murder, but he wouldn't let it go, and Kate had to admire his tenacity.

'Reese is alibied for the whole day, apart from a few very small gaps. I just can't see him having had the opportunity. And where would he get a car from?'

Dead ends. Lots of them.

'Right, actions, folks. What do we need to do?'

'Go back through the statements collected during the initial door-to-door the day before yesterday,' Barratt suggested. 'And we need to keep on with the yellow van.'

'Right,' Kate said. 'That's you and Cooper for the day. And Cooper?'

The DC tilted her head, anticipating the next instruction.

'Find Ian bloody Hirst.'

She nodded and turned back to her computer.

'Barratt, Hollis, I need you to organise a fresh door-to-door. Do some knocking yourselves, if you need to. And go back a bit. Start from the weekend before Aleah went missing. I'm not convinced these killings are opportunistic. I think he's got a plan, and he would have needed to recce the area. Somebody must've seen something. Let me know the minute you find anything that might be useful.'

Kate spent the morning reviewing the Callum Goodwin case notes and trying to find any connection with Aleah Reese. Cooper had produced pages of background on Craig Reese and Trevor Goodwin and then gone back a generation. The only link Kate could see was the murdered children both had grandfathers who had worked at

Thorpe Main. But most of the kids on the estate could probably claim that. Kate's father's father had worked at the pit, and *his* father had moved from Staffordshire to Mexborough to work at Denaby Main. It was in the blood of everybody in the area.

She grabbed a sheet of paper from the printer and began to sketch out a timeline, going back beyond the one on the incident room whiteboard. It was more like a family tree for both families based on Cooper's notes. Nothing jumped out at her, so she went back to her notes on Ian Hirst. This time, the timeline had been deliberately organised like a family tree to show Tracy's parents, Ian's mother and Ian.

'What the hell happened?' she said to herself, circling Tracy's name. She needed more information about the sister's death. Somebody must remember it. She thought about the Loaches or Jud Reese. They would have been in Thorpe at the time, but she couldn't imagine them being interested in her casual enquiries. There would be people in the village who remembered the incident well, if only she could find them.

There was *somebody* who might be willing to help, somebody who didn't live on the Crosslands Estate but would be keen to find whoever had killed the two children. Kate checked the relevant statement for a number and picked up the phone.

It was early afternoon when Kate pulled her Mini up outside Aileen Porter's house on Jubilee Terrace. The houses still seemed to watch as she rapped the door knocker and waited for Mrs Porter to answer.

'Hello again,' Mrs Porter said as she opened the door with a smile that made Kate feel like a long-lost friend. 'Come in, the kettle's on.'

She led the way into the kitchen which smelled faintly of smoked fish.

'Sorry about the smell,' the older woman said. 'I've had a bit of Finnan haddock for my dinner. I've opened all the windows, but it takes ages to clear. Cup of tea?'

Kate accepted and took a seat at the kitchen table watching as Mrs Porter bustled around the small kitchen preparing the teapot and finding mugs and spoons.

'Here we go,' she said, putting the pot and mugs on the table. 'Just let it mash for a minute. So, what did you want to ask me about?'

'How's Dave?'

The older woman's face turned grim, her mouth settling into a straight line as she was reminded of the recent tragedy. 'He's all right, I suppose. He was in Sheffield, you know, not on the rig. Got himself a fancy woman and didn't want me to know.'

Kate nodded.

'He'll be over for the funeral.' She glanced at Kate, suddenly hopeful. 'Is that why you're here. Have they got a date?'

'Not yet,' Kate admitted. 'It's still too early. There might be other tests to be done on the…on Aleah. I'm sure somebody will be in touch with your son when there's a date.'

Mrs Porter poured two mugs of tea as she nodded her understanding. 'So, why *are* you here? I don't believe it's just to ask about our Dave.'

Kate found herself warming to the woman's directness – it was somehow refreshing after ploughing through newspaper reports and labyrinthine witness statements. She knew she'd made the right call. If Mrs Porter remembered anything about the death of Tracy Moore, she wouldn't dramatize it or exaggerate the facts.

'I want to ask you about something that happened forty years ago. A young girl was found dead in the quarry. I've read all the newspaper reports, but I thought you might remember what happened and what people were saying about it.'

The woman took a slurp of her tea and studied Kate over the rim of the mug. 'Why ask me?'

Kate sighed. 'To be honest, a lot of the people I've been in contact with on this case would be reluctant to give me the time of day, let alone talk about a long-dead child. The police aren't very popular around here.'

'And what makes you think I'll tell you owt?'

'Because I think you want to know what happened to your granddaughter, and that's your priority. I think you'll help me in any way that you can, if I promise you it might help me find out who killed Aleah.'

They both sipped their tea, Kate hoping she'd said the right thing.

'Her name was Tracy Moore. I was at school with her mother. They lived up Crosslands.'

Kate nodded.

'They found her in them tunnels, air shafts, I think they were. The kids used to play over there all the time before it was filled in. Surprised there weren't more accidents, to be honest.' She pursed her lips and shook her head in disapproval at the thought any parent who would have let their child play in such a dangerous environment.

'I've read the reports,' Kate said. 'But what I can't seem to find out is what she was doing over there on her own. Why would she just wander off and decide to crawl through a tunnel?'

'Well, there was a lot of talk about her being bullied by a couple of other girls. She wanted to hang around with them, but they didn't really want her. I heard they tormented her quite badly, hit her, and pushed her around to toughen her up so she could be in their gang. A woman I know on the estate told me Tracy was over there with some other kiddies, and they made her go down the tunnel, then they ran off and left her. Another tale is she was hiding from the same gang. I don't know what the truth is behind it all, but there were other kids involved, and I don't think it was as accidental as the newspapers made out.'

Kate took out her notebook and jotted down the important details. She scribbled *bullying?* and circled it twice with her pencil. 'Who were these other children, Mrs Porter? Do you know?'

'Not for definite, but there was a lot of talk about who was in the gang. There were a couple of girls who lived on the estate and another two from just up the road here. I don't know who the ones on the estate were, but the other two were Joanne and Carla Reese, Craig Reese's sisters, twins. They're both a lot older than him. Always thought he must've been an accident when his mam thought she was past all that.'

Kate jotted down the names, trying to conceal the trembling in her hand. This was it. This was the link. 'Does the name Ian Hirst mean anything to you?' she asked.

Mrs Porter thought for a few seconds. 'Tracy's mother, Barbara, married a Hirst, Paul or Peter I think his name was, and I think they had a little lad. Can't remember his name, though, could've been Ian, I suppose.'

'You've been very helpful,' Kate said, snapping her notebook closed. 'And I *will* let you know when we find out anything about Aleah's funeral. I'm sure somebody will let your son know, but I'll make it a priority to have somebody contact *you*.'

Mrs Porter nodded her thanks and stood up to show Kate to the front door. 'I hope you catch him,' she said as she ushered Kate back out onto the street. 'And when you do, lock him up and throw the key away.'

CHAPTER 23

2015

As soon as Mrs Porter's door had closed, Kate took out her phone and rang Sam Cooper. 'Got another job for you,' she said. 'Find out anything you can about Joanne and Carla Reese, Craig Reese's sisters. They might have been involved in the death of Tracy Moore. And if they were, they might be in danger.'

She hung up and checked her email, desperate for a response from Karen. Nothing.

'Shit,' she breathed, trying to work out her next move. A text pinged in as she was trying to decide whether to join the door-to-door or go back to Doncaster and help with the data trawl.

Call me. Got a new lead.

It was Hollis. He must've tried to ring while she'd been on the phone and sent a text when he couldn't get through.

He answered after the first ring.

'What've you got?' she asked.

'You know you wanted us to go back to the weekend, instead of just concentrating on the day Aleah went missing? Well, I've just spoken to somebody who claims to have seen something "suspicious" the day before Aleah was taken.'

'Suspicious how?'

She heard Hollis take a deep breath.

'He saw a white car, says it was one of those little Fiats, the retro ones, parked at the top of the Reeses' street.'

'So? They're not uncommon.'

'No. But he swears there was somebody sitting in the front with a camera. A woman. He didn't recognise her, and she wasn't there when he came back from doing his shopping, but he noticed the camera because he thought it looked professional, and he wondered if she was a reporter. He was a bit confused about the timing at first and thought it was after Aleah went missing, but then, he remembered it was a Monday because he met a friend for a pint and he always does that when he goes shopping on a Monday. He can't remember much about her, other than the camera and that she was blonde and pretty.'

'Sara Evans. Must've been. What the hell was she doing there, and where was Dave Porter? He was with her in Sheffield that week. Was he in the car?'

'No idea, but I've got Cooper trying to confirm whether Sara Evans drives a white Fiat 500. My guess is yes.'

'I think we need to get back over there and find out what she was doing in Thorpe the day before her boyfriend's daughter went missing. You up for a trip to Sheffield?'

'Always,' Hollis joked. 'Where are you?'

Kate explained what she'd been doing and arranged for Hollis to pick her up at the retail park outside Rotherham; she could leave her car there for a couple of hours.

Traffic was heavy as they left the Parkway and drove into Sheffield. Rush hour was just starting, and all the roads seemed to be backed up.

'Might as well catch a tram,' Hollis muttered as yet another set of lights turned red to allow two trams to cross in front of them.

'What's the rush?' Kate asked. 'She might not be at home.'

'But she might, and I don't want to miss the look on her face when she finds out that we know she was lurking on Crosslands Estate before Aleah was taken. What the hell was she doing there?'

Kate had no easy answer to that. Had Sara somehow befriended Aleah and then lured her away from Main Street with promises of a visit with her real father? Or had Porter taken her, and it had gone wrong when Aleah asked to be allowed home? But none of her thoughts linked with the information she'd gleaned from Dave Porter's mother. How could Sara Evans be linked with the elusive Ian Hirst?

'Finally,' Hollis sighed as the lights changed again, and the road ahead cleared. 'We might get there before tea time. He took a different route from their previous visit, driving up through the university to Broomhill and then cutting down towards Endcliffe Park. Kate studied the students who were milling round the campus, despite it being the holidays. She wondered if Ben was amongst them somewhere, or he might have been on one of the trams that halted their progress earlier, heading back to his shared house in Upperthorpe. She was glad he'd been in touch, glad the first few planks of a bridge had been laid between them.

'Right, how do we play this?' Hollis asked as they pulled up on the narrow street. He'd parked a little way down the road from Sara Evans's house in one of the few available spaces.

'I think we just confront her with what we know. If we try to trap her in a lie before we tell her we know she was in Thorpe, she might just get defensive and clam up. Have you heard from Cooper?'

Hollis checked his phone. 'Yep. Sara Evans is the registered keeper of a cream Fiat 500. Cooper's checking CCTV for the date in question to see if we can spot her in the area.'

Kate scanned the street and was pleased to see the small car tucked into a parking space a few doors past Sara's house. They hadn't noticed it before, but they hadn't known to look. The joys of hindsight.

'Excellent. Let's go.'

Kate followed Hollis down the alley between the houses and stood back to allow him to knock at the back door. Sara Evans opened it almost instantly, face flushed, drying her hands on a tea towel.

'Yes? Oh, it's you.' Her curious, open expression turned to one of suspicion as she regarded the two police officers. 'What do you want?'

'Can we come in?' Hollis asked, one of his feet already on the bottom of the two steps which led up to the door.

'Dave's not here. He's gone into town to do some shopping.'

'It's not Mr Porter we want to talk to,' Hollis said. 'It's you.'

'Well…I…' She seemed to be desperately trying to think of an excuse not to let them in, her eyes flitting from Kate to Hollis and back again.

'It would be better if we came inside,' Kate said. 'Some information has come to light, and I'd rather we didn't discuss it on your doorstep where anybody could overhear.'

Sara opened the door wider and allowed them inside. The kitchen was warm, and Kate noticed the oven was on and the sink was full of used baking paraphernalia.

'I was just making Dave a cake. It's our five-month anniversary.'

Kate just nodded. 'Sara. Why were you in Thorpe the day before Aleah went missing?'

'What? I wasn't.'

'We have a witness who says that a woman matching your description was sitting in her car a few doors up from the Reeses' house. You do drive a cream Fiat 500?'

'Yes. But so do a lot of people. They're very popular cars.'

'They are. That's yours outside, I assume, a few doors up?'

Sara nodded warily.

'We have your registration number, and while we're conducting this interview, one of our colleagues is checking all the available CCTV around Thorpe to see if your car shows up. We have an approximate time from our witness, so that should narrow it down. At the moment, I don't mind telling you, you're our number one person of interest because you lied, and you're still lying.'

Sara's face paled, and she collapsed onto one of the chairs scattered around the kitchen table. Her eyes flickered wildly left and right as she tried frantically to think up an excuse, a reason for being where she said she hadn't.

'Okay,' she admitted. 'I was there. On Monday, though, not on the day Aleah was taken. You can check CCTV for that, right? You'll only see my car on Monday.'

'Oh, we'll check,' Hollis said. 'What about other vehicles? Is the Fiat the only car that you drive?'

Sara nodded eagerly. 'It's my only car. I'm sure you can check that as well.'

'So why were you there? Our witness said you had a camera with you. What were you taking photographs of? It's a bit of a change from your usual subjects.'

Sara reddened, and she looked down at the table. 'I was trying to get some photos of Aleah, for Dave. His mum told him her stepfather wasn't very reliable, and I was hoping to get some evidence Dave could use.'

'Use how?'

'In court. To get access to his daughter.'

'Court?' Kate couldn't get her head around what she was being told. Everything so far suggested Dave Porter had given up on his daughter a long time ago. He'd said himself he thought his relationship with her might be re-kindled, but not until she was old enough to make her own decisions.

'And Mr Porter knew about this, did he?' Hollis asked.

'No. Not really. We'd discussed Aleah's situation, but he didn't know I was trying to help. He was out that morning catching up with a friend. He doesn't know I was there.'

'What were you hoping to achieve?'

Sara sighed and shook her head. 'I don't know. I thought if I could get some photos of Reese being rough with her, or of her looking neglected. Anything really that might help Dave. I didn't even see her, though.'

'And you didn't go back?'

'No.'

'Did you take any photographs at all?'

Sara nodded. 'A few. Of the house and the street.'

'We'll need copies of those,' Kate said. 'In fact, we'll take the camera you used and the memory card. If it checks out, you should have it back in a few days.'

Another resigned nod. Kate raised her eyebrows at Sara, indicating she meant what she said. She wanted that camera. Now.

Hollis went to the car to get an evidence bag while Sara went upstairs to retrieve her camera, leaving Kate alone to speculate about Sara's motives for going to Thorpe. They seemed plausible, if a bit misguided, but she found it hard to believe Porter hadn't given his blessing. Then, she remembered the looks that had passed between the two of them during the previous visit. The longing, loving looks that spoke of sex and infatuation. Perhaps Sara had wanted to surprise her boyfriend, or at least convince him he didn't have to stay away from his daughter.

'Here,' Sara said, returning to the kitchen and thrusting the camera towards Kate. 'Be careful, it was expensive.'

Kate dug in her pocket and donned a pair of nitrile gloves before handling the item. It was a Canon EOS, and it looked top of the range. 'Is the memory card with the pictures still in the camera?'

Sara nodded.

'And have you downloaded the photographs to any computer or other device?'

'No. I was going to delete them, but I just forgot. Have a look, if you like.'

Kate switched the camera on and then passed it back to Sara. 'It's a bit complicated for me. Can you get them to display?'

Two taps of the arrow key, and Sara passed the camera back. Kate was looking at a shot of the Reeses' house taken from further up the road. The front door was in focus, but the windows and walls were blurred. The next two had zoomed in on the window of the living room; others were shots of the street.

'Is there any way to store these photographs on the device, or are they just on the memory card?' Kate asked.

'They're just on the card. You could just take that and leave me the camera. I need it for a job next week.'

Kate nodded. It made sense, and she didn't want an expensive piece of equipment going missing. 'Okay, take the card out.'

She'd just opened the side of the camera when Hollis returned with an assortment of evidence bags.

'We're just taking the card,' Kate informed him, and he passed her the smallest bag. She placed the memory card inside, sealed, dated, and numbered it and gave it to Hollis.

'We'll have a look at it back at base. See what Cooper makes of the pictures.' She stood up to leave. 'We'll be in touch Ms Evans.'

Sara didn't show them out.

Cooper and Barratt were still deep in their data mining when Kate and Hollis got back to the incident room. Barratt was working his way through a page of DVLA information, and Cooper was focussed on her computer screen, scanning what looked like traffic camera footage.

'Any luck with Sara Evans's car?' Kate asked, pulling up a chair and looking over Cooper's shoulder.

The DC nodded. 'Yep. Found it pretty quickly once we'd got the reg. No sign of it on the day Aleah was taken, though. I'm looking for the yellow van at the minute, but the feed's black-and-white so it's not easy.'

'Where is this?'

'Main road through Thorpe. Crosslands is to the north, and the rest of the town is to the south. Anybody heading onto the Crosslands Estate would show up on one of two cameras.'

'But he probably didn't take the van onto the estate. It was parked at the bottom of the hill in the square.'

'It'd still show up. Unless he came in from the south. The only camera that would cover that is on Rotherham Road.'

'Hollis,' Kate shouted at the DC who had just crossed the office to pour himself a coffee. 'CCTV scanning. We need all the eyes we can get. Cooper. Get the feed from the Rotherham Road camera. Let's find this bastard!'

Half an hour later, Hollis took a sharp intake of breath. 'I think I've got him.'

The other three leapt from their seats and gathered around Hollis's screen.

'Look. A light-coloured Transit van. Index number NE55 NNK. He came into Thorpe off Rotherham Road.

'Gotcha!' Kate punched the air. Cooper was already back at her desk, entering the registration number into the PNC.

'Who is he?' Kate asked.

Cooper stared at the screen, waiting for a name. 'Anthony Malloy. Took ownership of the van in February 2012. Registered address 45 Fitzroy Gardens, Rotherham.'

'Google Maps, where the fuck is Fitzroy Gardens?'

Cooper's fingers clicked across the keyboard and a photograph filled the screen. 'It's in Thorpe Hesley. Just off the main road. Hang on. Here we go. No. No. That's not right.'

Kate peered over her shoulder as she panned down the street which ended in patch of wasteland.

'The numbers stop at thirty-two. There is no forty-five.'

Kate shook her head. 'That can't be right, have another look.'

Cooper zoomed in to show Kate the numbers on the house doors. There was nothing after thirty-two.

'Hang on,' Kate said. 'Look there.'

She pointed to the waste ground where a tumble of red bricks was just visible through the long grass.

'Demolition rubble. Some of the houses were knocked down. We need to know when.'

'Give me a few minutes,' Cooper said and started to type.

Kate sat back at her own desk. What the hell was going on? They were looking for Ian Hirst, and they'd found Anthony Malloy. Was he their killer? And if so, who the hell was he?

'Two years ago,' Cooper said. 'Before that the occupants of forty-five were a Mrs Barbara Malloy and a Mr Anthony Malloy.'

'Barbara is Ian Hirst's mother's name! It's too much of a coincidence. Find them, Cooper. They might be able to tell us where her son is.'

Kate was buzzing. This was what she loved about the job, the thrill of getting close to the final piece in a puzzle. They were closing in on the killer, Kate could feel it. He thought he'd been so bloody clever, but he wasn't clever enough. It had taken a while, but they'd found him in the end.

'They're dead,' Cooper said. 'Barbara died last year, and her husband followed her in February this year. They'd moved to sheltered housing in Rotherham; Bellingham Court.'

'Shit! Suspicious?'

'Lung cancer and a stroke.'

'Shit, shit, shit! Okay. Hirst must be using a different name; that's why he's not showing up on any of the databases. Try Ian Malloy. Barratt, Hollis ring Craig Reese's sisters, see if they can shed any light on who this fucker is.'

Kate slammed out of the office and took the stairs up to the canteen two at a time. This felt personal. Hirst was messing her around, and she didn't like it one bit. It felt like he was always one step ahead of the investigation, always just around the corner while Kate was running frantically down the street to catch up with him. They'd got a name, they'd got a vehicle, they'd even got the beginnings of a motive, but they still couldn't quite put it all together and find the man.

Two hours later, they were no further forward. Cooper had managed to track down one of the Reese sisters – Joanne – but she'd never heard of Ian Hirst. She claimed to vaguely remember the name Tracy Moore but couldn't be sure. She'd been curt and uncooperative during the phone call, revealing her sister lived in Australia but little else, so Kate made her the subject of an action for the following day, hoping a visit from a detective might jog her memory.

She glanced at the clock in the corner of her computer screen. Half past six.

'Guys, I think we should call it a day. I'll fill Raymond in, but you lot should get off and have a kip. Tomorrow, we'll trawl more CCTV, try to ring Carla Reese and interview her sister. We also need to go through the product of the latest door-to-door. It's already turned up one lead; there might be all sorts in there.'

'Kate, I might've got something,' Cooper said. She'd been examining the photographs from Sara Evans's memory card. 'Look at this.' She was pointing to a wide-angle shot of the street with the Reeses' house in the middle.

'There's a vehicle there, at the bottom of the road. All I've got is the rear light unit and a bit of bumper, but if I enlarge it…'

She pressed a key twice, and the photograph zoomed to the area she was talking about. A sliver of red and orange plastic came into focus and part of the paintwork of the vehicle.

'It's yellow,' Kate breathed. 'He was there.'

'It's not a van,' Cooper said. 'The light unit's wrong. And it's not just yellow, look.' She pointed to a smudge beneath the reversing light. 'There's a bit of orange.'

'Weird. A car like that would stand out a mile.'

Hollis joined them trying to make sense of the enlarged pixels. He tilted his head to each side then laughed. 'It's one of ours,' he said. 'It's the back of a patrol car. There's a yellow-and-orange diagonal stripe. The backs of the cars have yellow-and-orange stripes. It's a police car.'

'The day before Aleah went missing? Wonder what it's doing there?'

'We could check the duty logs, see if there's anything mentioned,' Cooper suggested.

'Do it,' Kate said, and they all leaned over Cooper's shoulder as she typed in the date and location.

'Nothing,' Kate said.

'Could have been a routine drive through the estate,' Barratt suggested.

'Yes, because Crosslands is such a crime hot spot, and we have the money for that,' Kate said sarcastically. A niggling thought was developing in the back of her mind, and she didn't like the feel of it. 'Is there any way we can find out who it was?'

'Not really. We can find out who was on duty at the time, but if there's no log of a visit to the estate, it could be anybody. We could check who was busy at the exact time, but that will take a while. And it could be an officer who was about to go on or off duty; they might still have had the car. Without an index number, it's like trying to find a needle in a haystack.'

'Well, that's what we need to do. Action it for tomorrow. I want to know who was in that car and what he or she was doing there. Right. Home, the lot of you. Back at seven to do some serious digging.'

CHAPTER 24

2015

S oup microwaved and beer opened, Kate settled down on her sofa and logged on to her laptop. Raymond had been unimpressed with her lack of progress, and she could tell he wasn't really convinced by her theory about Ian Hirst. He was still looking at Craig Reese, despite his alibi, and urged her to do the same. He seemed convinced Reese could have had time during the day to abduct Callum Goodwin, and this was all connected to the illegal cigarettes and alcohol.

O'Connor was in his good books because he'd organised a search of Ken Fowler's house, and the team had turned up thousands of pounds worth of illegally imported cigarettes and bottles of high-end spirits in the cabinets and drawers of his garage. He was still being questioned, but O'Connor was convinced Fowler was the one with the logistical know-how to organise such an operation.

Craig Reese had buckled and admitted his own role. It was, as O'Connor suspected, small-time. Reese had also implicated the bookmaker Bob Allan, leaving Kate wondering if there was more to the altercation on the day Aleah went missing than Reese had told them. She was happy to let O'Connor untangle it all.

She almost scalded herself when she saw an email from Karen, spilling her soup as she leaned forward to open it.

'Shit!' she cursed, trying to wipe the red mark from the front of her top. She put the spoon and bowl down so she could focus. Her hand was trembling as she scrolled to the message title and hit "enter."

Hi Kath,

I thought I'd get back to you straight away as your last email seemed quite important. I'm in Leh now, back from the trek, so I have plenty of internet access – not that I want to be reminded of what's going on in the world. I survived nearly two weeks in a tent – that must be a record for me. I think the cook and horsemen made life that bit more bearable – I've never had "bed tea" in my sleeping bag before. The scenery's spectacular, and the monasteries are fascinating. I'll send some pics when I have a bit more time.

I had a good think about what you said about Ian Hirst. I do remember a lad in my year at school whose sister was killed in some sort of accident. He was a little shit and probably behind a lot of the bullying in the months before we left. He once did a presentation in English that really sticks in my mind. We all had to give a talk about something that we'll never forget. He spoke about his sister going missing, and the police finding her in one of the tunnels in the quarry. He cried when he told us. The girls were really sympathetic, but some of the lads teased him about it. I think he got into a couple of fights because of it.

I've been wracking my brains and really don't think that his name was Ian, but I think his surname might have been Hirst. He said that his sister had had a different name, and he was glad because it stopped people from asking him about what had happened to her.

I don't know if this helps, but I'm fairly sure that he was called Andy. There was three Andrews in my class, and I think he might have been one of them. They all called themselves Andy. It used to really bug the teachers – there were three Lees as well. Bloody unimaginative lot in Thorpe!

I hope this helps.

I'll send pix soon.

Stay safe.

Love, Karen. X

Andy. He was using his middle name. How the hell had she managed to miss that? They'd been looking for the wrong man. Energised, Kate did a quick 192.com search for Andrew Hirst. There were dozens. Six lived in South Yorkshire. That's where she planned to start.

Kate finished her soup, stacked the pan and bowl in the dishwasher, and settled down with a second beer. She turned on the television and flicked to the BBC News channel, hoping to catch up with at least some of what was going on in the world. Her mobile rang just as she was sighing through yet another report on how the new government was planning to fund the NHS. She glanced at the screen. Garry. She considered letting it go to voicemail, but she knew he wouldn't use her mobile number unless it was important.

'What?' she snapped, in no mood to listen to more of her ex's whining.

'Kate? Have I caught you at a bad time?'

'Depends what you want.'

'Have you spoken to Ben today?'

'No. I've offered to pay his rent for a year, so I don't expect to hear from him for the next twelve months.' She knew she sounded bitter, and that it wasn't fair on her son. She'd been pleased to hear from him and glad he'd accepted her offer of help. She just didn't feel like indulging Garry.

'He was supposed to meet me earlier. I'm in Sheffield on a course for work, and we'd planned to meet up. I waited at the station, but he didn't turn up.'

'He probably found something better to do. Have you tried his mobile?'

'Of course. He's not answering. I rang the house landline, spoke to one of his friends, but he hadn't seen him.

'How long did you wait?'

'An hour and a bit. He'd have texted if he was going to be late. I'm worried, Kate.'

'Look, he's probably in a pub somewhere, and he's forgotten all about meeting you.'

'Should I contact the police?'

'No point,' Kate said. 'He's only been missing a few hours, and he's not in an "at-risk" category. He'll probably turn up tomorrow hungover and apologetic.'

'I suppose,' Garry conceded. 'I'll let you know if I hear anything.'

Kate hung up. Her son was an adult; he could look after himself. Half an hour later, worry was tormenting her like an out-of-reach insect bite. She thought about calling somebody in Sheffield, maybe asking for a favour. But what she'd told Garry had been true. Nobody would be interested for at least another eighteen hours.

Her feeling of disquiet hadn't abated when she woke up the next morning. She showered, dressed, gulped down a bowl of cereal and a mug of coffee, and was at her desk just after seven. The rest of her team straggled in and were waiting for their actions by seven-thirty. Kate was vaguely aware of Raymond staring at the small group through the glass of his office door, and she knew she'd need to get him up to speed before he came looking for her.

'Right. Big day today and a change of plan,' she said. 'The Reese sisters can wait, because we're going to find this bastard now I know his name. He's not Ian Hirst; he's Andrew. He's been using his middle name since he was a kid. My sister was in his class at school, and she remembers him talking about the death of his half-sister. I've done a PNC search and looked on the electoral roll and now have seven Andrew Hirsts in South Yorkshire. I've ruled two out due to their age, but I can't get a DOB for the others. One of them might well be the one we're looking for.' She handed out a sheet of A4 to each member of the team. It contained the addresses of all the local Andrew Hirsts.

'Barratt, take the first two, they're fairly close together, Mexborough and Wath and they're both close to Thorpe. I've sent uniforms out to the two in Sheffield. Our man is forty-five and local. If you find anything, anything at all, I want to know immediately. Cooper, I want you to find out who was in that patrol car in Sara Evans's picture. Get yourself a coffee, because I think you're in for a long trawl. Hollis, with me.'

She allowed the rest of the team to leave before speaking to Hollis. 'My son, Ben, has gone missing. I don't think it's anything to worry about, he's a student on his summer break, but I want you to know, in case I need to shift focus for a few hours.'

Hollis nodded his understanding.

'We're going to the last known address of Barbara and Anthony Malloy, and we're going to knock on the door of everybody in Bellingham Court until we find somebody who remembers Andrew Hirst.'

The sheltered housing turned out to be a new development of bungalows close to Rotherham town centre. Hollis pulled up the car at the entrance to the cul-de-sac and glanced round.

'Nice place. Wouldn't mind living somewhere like this myself when I retire.'

The bungalows were all red-brick which glowed in the morning sunlight, and each was surrounded by a small grass border. Some had flower beds at the front, and one or two had small areas of block paving occupied by mobility scooters.

'Come on, no time for daydreaming,' Kate said. 'Otherwise you might find yourself "retired" a bit sooner than you'd planned.'

Hollis laughed and got out of the car.

'Right. The Malloys lived at number eight, so let's start with ten and six and work out from there.'

The first door they knocked on was opened by a woman in a healthcare provider's uniform who was clearly too young to be the resident. She told them Mr Carrington had only been living there for six weeks, so he couldn't have known the Malloys.

Kate made a quick note of the conversation and then knocked on the door of number six. No answer. She noticed a doorbell on the door jamb and pressed it twice. A minute passed with no response.

'Next,' she said to Hollis, turning back to the street.

'Can I help you?' The door had opened, and a tiny woman stood on the threshold, held up by a walking frame. 'I'm sorry it took me so long to get to the door, but, well, you can see.' She nodded at her feet which were twisted into unnatural angles in her slippers. 'Arthritis. Can't get around like I used to.'

Kate smiled sympathetically, offered her warrant card and introduced herself and Hollis. The old woman took her time scrutinising Kate's ID.

'What do you want with me?' she asked.

'Could we come in for a few minutes and ask you a couple of questions. It won't take long.'

The woman nodded and stepped aside. 'First door on the left. I'll follow you in. It might take me a little while.'

The house was immaculate. The hall floor was dark laminate that gleamed in the sunlight and the paintwork was a brilliant white gloss, unscuffed and uniformly applied. Kate led the way into the sitting room which was pleasantly spacious, the chair and sofa were plain beige, and the coffee table was dust-free and devoid of clutter.

'Nice place,' Kate said. 'Mrs…?'

'Frith,' the woman said. 'I had the home-help in yesterday. She always does a lovely job. Can I get you a drink?'

Kate considered the amount of time it would take for Mrs Frith to get to the kitchen, make tea, and get back. Too long.

'No, thanks,' she said, with a glare at Hollis, who looked like he was about to say yes. 'We won't keep you long. I just want to know if you remember the Malloys who used to live next door?'

'Of course,' the old woman said with a smile. 'Lovely couple. So sad they died within a few months of each other.'

Kate nodded. 'Did you know them well?'

'As well as you'd expect really. We were neighbours for about eighteen months before Barbara died. Tony used to come in, every now and then, and do little jobs for me. He was good with his hands.'

'Did you know Barbara's son?'

Mrs Frith smiled. 'I only met him once, but Barbara used to talk about him a lot. Ever so proud of him, she was. Don't you know him?'

Kate sat up in surprise. 'Why should I know him? Is he famous or something?'

The old lady laughed. 'No, he's not famous. He's one of your lot. He's in the police force.'

Kate removed her notebook with a trembling hand, pieces of the puzzle clunking into place as she underlined the last section of notes and wrote the date.

'Can you describe him?'

Mrs Frith looked at her blankly for a minute.

'I suppose so. He's tall. Dark hair, looked like he'd had it cut recently when I saw him, but he might have grown it by now. Quite muscly-looking, probably goes to one of those posh gyms. He was around here a fair bit before his mam died. I always knew it was him because of his van. Bloody bright yellow. Tony gave it him. He was turning it into one of them campervans.'

'What did his mum call him when she spoke about him? Was he Ian, or Andrew, Andy?'

'He was Andrew. Never heard her call him Ian. Barbara always called him Andrew, but he introduced himself to me as Drew.'

At that moment, Kate's phone began to vibrate in her pocket.

CHAPTER 25

2015

'Cooper, what have you got?' Kate turned away from Mrs Firth, hoping the woman couldn't hear the rising panic in her tone.

'I've been through the duty logs. Our most likely candidate for the patrol car driver is PCSO Drew Rigby. He'd been in Mexborough earlier and logged the car back in about forty-five minutes after the photograph was taken. Rigby would have been on his way back to base.'

'But he wasn't responding to a call-out? There wasn't anything on the estate at that time?'

'Nope, and nobody seems to have been anywhere near the estate apart from Rigby.'

Kate stood up and went into the hallway of the bungalow. 'Cooper, listen. Is Rigby on duty today?'

'No, I checked. He rang in sick.'

'Right. Get his home address.'

She heard the tapping of a keyboard, then Cooper gave her an address in Wheatley Hills just east of Doncaster town centre.

Kate stuck her head around the door of the living room and gestured to Hollis who quickly made their excuses to Mrs Frith and followed her to the door.

'Cooper, get somebody around to Rigby's house now. If he's there, bring him in. He's Ian Andrew Hirst! He's the fucker we've been looking for.'

She waited for Hollis to unlock the car and pulled open the door.

'We've got him!' she said, banging the dashboard. 'He's a clever sod, but we've got him!'

'Who is he?' Hollis asked. 'And where are we going?'

'Back to Doncaster. He's our killer. He's Tracy Moore's brother. I don't know why he calls himself Rigby, but it might be his mother remarried, and Rigby took his stepfather's name. He's been pissing up my back and telling me it's raining, and now, I'm going to have him.'

'And he's one of us?'

'He's a PCSO. I met him at the quarry the morning Aleah's body was found. He did the initial search of the house. He was at the second search, after you got the statement about the van. He's everywhere. I even had a drink with him the night before last to see if he could remember anything about Ian Hirst. He must've thought that was hilarious.'

Her phone rang again. Garry.

'Has he turned up?' she asked before her ex-husband could say anything.

'No. Kate, I'm worried. I finally managed to get hold of another one of his housemates. Ben left the house just before lunchtime yesterday. A police officer called at the house and told him you'd been in an accident. Ben left with him.'

Despite the stuffiness of the car, Kate went cold.

'Kate?'

'I'm still here. Are you absolutely sure about this?'

'That's what his friend said. I'm assuming it's a lie, and that you're fine?'

'Yes. Did the friend give you a description of the police officer?'

'No. I didn't ask. Why would I?'

'Okay. Text me the number of Ben's housemate. I'll talk to him.'

Kate hung up and looked up the contact number for Sheffield University. Somebody had given Rigby Ben's home address, and she wanted to know who and why. She got through to the main switchboard, who transferred her to admin, who put her on hold. She tried to take deep breaths, desperate to remain calm until finally a human voice cut through the music, and Kate explained what she wanted to know.

'I'm sorry, but we can't give out student details over the telephone,' the man at the other end of the phone told her. Kate almost growled in frustration.

'I don't need his details. He's my son. I'm a Detective Inspector with South Yorkshire police, and I need to know if my son's details were given to one of our officers yesterday.'

'I'm sorry, but how do I know that you're with the police?'

Kate took another deep breath. 'I'll give you the number of Doncaster Central police station. You can confirm I work there, and then, you can ring me back. I'm Detective Inspector Kate Fletcher, mother of Ben Fletcher. My son is missing, and I need information. If you continue to refuse to help me, I will arrest you for obstruction. Now, ring this number.'

She gave the switchboard number for Doncaster Central and hung up.

'What's going on?' Hollis asked, glancing from the road to Kate and back again.

'I think Rigby's got my son,' she said, and as soon as she actually managed to vocalise her fears, she felt tears building behind her eyelids. She saw Aleah Reese floating face down in a pond and Callum Goodwin's abandoned body in the bushes under a bridge. What would he do with Ben?

'Why would he take your son?'

It was a good question.

'For the same reason he took Aleah and Callum. He wants revenge on people who have hurt him in the past. Aleah was the niece of two girls he holds responsible for killing his sister.'

'But she wasn't. She's Reese's stepdaughter.'

'I'm not sure he knew that when he took her, and there might be a link with Jackie's family. He obviously blames Callum Goodwin's family for the suicide of his father, for some reason.'

'But what about you. What did your family do to him?'

Kate shrugged. 'I don't know. We left after the first few months of the strike. It didn't affect us because Dad was a pit deputy. Different union. My sister was in the same class as Rigby at school, but she doesn't really remember him that well.'

'You left,' Hollis said. 'Could that be it? We think his dad was a scab, yours was working, but he probably didn't get the abuse Hirst did, and then, you left and got on with your life. Now, you're back, big boss, and he's not even a proper copper. Could that be it?'

Kate replayed the conversation she'd had with Rigby in the pub. He'd seemed dissatisfied with his life. He wasn't happy being back in South Yorkshire, and he wasn't happy in his job. He'd already told Kate he'd like to be a detective. Was it pure jealousy? Or was it because she'd not allowed him to walk her home. Had he felt rejected, and this was his revenge?

'I honestly don't know. He's twisted. I wouldn't let him walk me home from the pub – maybe I bruised his ego. To be honest, I don't give a toss what his motivation is. I just want to get my son back before…'

Her phone rang again. 'Fletcher.'

'DI Fletcher. It's Conrad James from Sheffield University. I've verified your identity, and I can now give you the information that you asked for.'

'And?' Kate prompted, wanting to scream at him to hurry up.

'One of our team has confirmed a police officer came to the admin building looking for a way to contact your son. He was in uniform, had appropriate ID, and she had no reason to doubt him.'

Kate thanked him and hung up. That's how he'd done it. He'd used his uniform and his position. He could easily have told Aleah her mum was in trouble, and that she had to go with him to see her. The kid would have trusted him, because he was a policeman. And he would have been able to drive around the estate unnoticed, before he snatched Callum. The police presence had been stepped up; nobody would have thought twice about a patrol car being parked near the Goodwins' house.

The route back to Doncaster blurred past the car windows as Hollis drove as fast as he dared. They hit the main drag to Warmsworth doing over eighty miles an hour, and Kate watched as the roadsides grew increasingly urban as they approached Doncaster.

Just as they got stuck at their third set of red lights, her phone rang again. 'Cooper?'

'We've just had a report back from the officer that we sent to Rigby's house. There's no sign of him, and no vehicle in the driveway. The officer checked doors and windows, says there might be signs of a scuffle in the kitchen, overturned table, smashed crockery that sort of thing.'

'Enough to force entry?'

'He's not sure. He's a PC. Needs confirmation from somebody higher up.'

'Okay. Cooper, listen to me. I'm fairly certain that Rigby's got my son, Ben. If he has taken him, then that could be what the scuffle was about. Ben might be in the house. That gives us reasonable cause to enter. Get somebody over there now with the big key and get inside that house. I'm heading over there now.'

She gave Hollis the address, and he did a quick lane change. Ten minutes later, they pulled up on a street of well-kept semis a mile away from Doncaster town centre. Two patrol cars were parked outside the address Kate had been given, and a line of police tape was strung across the driveway, flapping lazily in the light breeze. Kate flashed her ID and ran up to the front door where a PCSO was standing guard.

'Around the back, ma'am,' he said, pointing to a side gate. She ran to the backdoor to where Barratt was standing in deep discussion with two uniformed officers.

'Fletcher,' he said, the relief obvious in his eyes. He'd clearly not wanted to give the order to break into the house. 'The kitchen's a bit of a mess, but there's no sign of any other disturbance. He could have just left in a hurry and knocked the table over. I'm not sure we can go in without a warrant.'

Kate sighed. Barratt was right. She cupped her hands to her eyes and pressed against the window. The table was on its side in the middle of the kitchen floor, and a broken plate and cup lay next to the fridge. A mobile phone lay face up next to an expensive-looking stainless steel bin. Why would he go out and leave his phone?

'Hang on,' Kate said. 'Barratt, keep your eye on that phone. If it lights up, let me know.'

She stepped back from the window, leaving Barratt with his face pressed against it and dialled Ben's number.

'It's ringing.'

'Okay. Once more to be sure.'

She rang Ben again.

'Definitely ringing. Whose phone is it?'

'It belongs to my son. I think Rigby's taken him to get back at me. He could be in the house.' She looked over to the small huddle next to the backdoor.

'We're going in.'

Ten minutes later, Kate was sitting on the back step with her head in her hands. She'd been so hopeful when she'd seen the phone, but the house was clearly empty. There was no sign Ben had been kept there, apart from the phone. Barratt had called the SOCOs, and they'd do a full DNA search, but the result would take a few days, and she wasn't sure her son had that long. Rigby had killed Aleah and Callum almost as soon as he'd taken them. Why would he have kept Ben alive? Except that Ben wasn't a child, he was practically a grown man, and to subdue him and kill him would have taken more force and planning than strangling a kid. She still couldn't understand why Rigby had taken him. It made no sense to her that she could have had anything to do with Rigby's messed-up childhood. She hadn't known the family, and she had no memory of him as a boy.

'Empty,' Barratt said from behind her. 'And there's nothing to tell us where he's gone.'

Kate struggled to her feet. She'd been trying to treat this like any other case, to dissociate herself from the victim, who just happened to be her son, but it wasn't working. Her phone rang, and her heart jumped with the hope it would be good news, or any news. At least knowing what had happened would be better than this awful uncertainty. She glanced at the screen. Raymond.

'Hello?'

'Fletcher, I want you back here ASAP. You've just been removed from this case. You can't be involved now your son is a victim, you know that. Get yourself back to HQ and let the others do their jobs. I've got every able body on duty looking for Rigby. We'll find him.'

She didn't respond.

'Fletcher, Kate, that's not a request or a suggestion, it's an order. You know it's for your own good.'

She almost smiled at his uncomfortable use of her first name. He was right. She shouldn't be here, it could compromise any investigation into Ben's kidnapping.

She nodded to Hollis, and they made their way back to the car.

CHAPTER 26

2015

Garry rang again just as they were trying to find a space in the police HQ car park, and Kate almost dropped the phone in her rush to answer. 'Any news?'

'I was about to ask you that. You're the police officer. Nobody's telling me anything.'

She gave him a brief account of their findings at Rigby's house and promised to ring back if she heard anything, but she was unable to keep the panic out of her voice.

'Kate, I'm coming over there. I know there's nothing I can do, but at least we'll be able to support each other. Are you at the police station?'

'For now,' Kate admitted. 'I think my DCI might send me home, though.'

'Well, I'll come with you, if that happens. I want to know about this bastard who's taken Ben, but I don't think we should talk over the phone. I'll get a train and see you later.'

'I don't know what to do,' she admitted to Hollis as she stuffed the phone back into her jacket pocket. 'I can't sit around and wait, but I've no idea what Rigby's thinking. Where could he have taken him?'

'Okay,' Hollis said. 'If we're going to do this, let's be logical.' He pulled into a parking space and turned to face her. 'He left Aleah where his sister had died. He left Callum where his father killed himself. Both these places were important to him, symbolic. He'll have taken Ben somewhere equally symbolic.'

Kate shook her head. 'But where? We don't know of any other deaths in his family, and anything could have happened to him in his childhood that we know nothing about.'

She looked out of the window at the row of liveried cars in front of them. She couldn't make sense of any of this. She'd never done anything to Drew Rigby, so why did he feel the need to punish her?

'I can't go back in there,' she said, glancing up at the windows of their office. 'I can't just sit at my desk and wait.'

'Shall I take you home?' Hollis offered.

Kate shook her head.

'What did he say to you, Rigby, when you met him for a drink? Did he give you any clues at all?'

'We talked a bit about the case, and he gave me a couple of names that were probably fake. We reminisced a bit about school days, and some of the teachers we remembered. He asked about my sister. That's about it. Shit! I wish I'd known. I felt there was something a bit off about him, but I just thought he might fancy me. Stupid, really.'

'There's no way you could have known who he really was,' Hollis said. 'He's obviously been planning this for ages, and he wouldn't have taken any risks with you. I'm going to ring upstairs and see if they've found anything.'

Kate shut her eyes, reliving the conversation with Rigby as Hollis had a hushed conversation with somebody on their team. It wasn't Raymond, she could tell by the tone, but she wasn't quite sure who Hollis had contacted.

'Right,' he said. 'That was Cooper. I've told her to tell Raymond you've decided to go home, and I'm driving you.'

'I don't want to go home, though.'

'I know, I was just trying to buy us some time. Sam says she's been trawling CCTV for Rigby's van. She's been using the traffic cameras tracing forward from his house. He was on Thorne Road at five o'clock this morning, then she picked him up near Balby fifteen minutes later. Warmsworth after that, but she hasn't got any further yet. O'Connor's helping, and they're working as fast as they can.'

'He's going back to Thorpe.' As soon as she said it, Kate knew she was right. Everything bad that had happened to Rigby had happened in Thorpe. Where else would he go?

'Did she say if they could see a passenger in the van?'

Hollis shook his head.

'That doesn't mean anything, though. He could have Ben tied up in the back.'

'Where else is there? The quarry, the pit, and where? He could be anywhere; a park where somebody called him a name, his mum's old house. He could be anywhere, Hollis!' She heard the tremble in her voice, but she was powerless to control her panic; she was used to being in charge, in control, but she needed somebody else to take charge. As though he could read her mind, Hollis kept pushing.

'I know. Think. What did he tell you? He's arrogant. He thinks he's going to get away with this. He might have made an off-the-cuff remark that was actually a hint, but he would never have expected you to work it out. He thinks he's cleverer than you. Where is he?'

Kate ran through the conversation again. Wine, Karen, Ben, school, Thatcher.

'Pisspants,' she said, realisation dawning. 'That's where he is. They called him Pisspants, and he blames me, somehow. But I wasn't even there. We'd moved.'

Hollis just looked at her.

'He got locked in the old boiler house at the school and wet himself. Some of the other kids started calling him Pisspants.'

'What's this got to do with you?'

'Not a clue. But it's all I've got. It's worth a try. We need to go to Thorpe Comp.'

'Okay, but it's the holidays. It'll be closed.'

'We don't need to get into the buildings; the boiler house is off to one side. Rigby told me it wasn't knocked down when they rebuilt the school. All we need to do is get onto the site.'

Hollis started the car.

'I hope you're right about this, because we could get into some deep shit with Raymond.'

'I don't care. I just want my son back. I'll let Garry know there's been a change of plan. If I tell him where the boiler house is, he might be able to meet us there.'

Hollis nodded and pulled out of the car park.

The school had changed dramatically. Kate remembered an open gate and a huge car park with a path down one side leading to the front entrance of the school. Now, it was much smaller. Part of the Tarmac she remembered had been buried under a two-storey building that had a huge sign over the door proclaiming it the "Warren Horsley Building." She had no idea who he was, but doubted an ex-pupil would have ever wanted to donate money for school buildings. The Victorian main school building had been replaced by a modern and, no doubt, state-of-the art construction of pale brick and red painted steel. This was all Kate could see through the bars of the locked gate, but it reminded her of an open prison.

'Plan B?' Hollis asked.

Kate led him away from the gate, back along the main approach road to the school. The corner shop was exactly where she remembered it, but it was now a cheap off-licence – probably still frequented by pupils during their lunch break – and the road down the side of the school was as quiet as she'd hoped. A yellow van was parked on the corner.

'It's his,' she said to Hollis, pointing at the number plate. He peered through the side window and shook his head.

'Looks like I might be right,' Kate said.

After the first house, a gap led to a back alley which ran down the side of the school site. It had high walls on one side where the tiny yards of the terraced houses ended and on the school side was a low brick wall topped with a fence of red metal bars. They were much too close together to squeeze through, but Kate hadn't given up. In her day, the fence had been green, but that was the only difference. If the students of 2015 were like those of thirty years ago, they wouldn't let a fence keep them from a shortcut.

About ten yards down, she found what she was looking for. Two of the bars were slightly off perpendicular. She pushed one, and it slumped to one side.

'Yes,' she said. 'Some things don't change.'

She pushed through the gap and held the bars apart to allow Hollis to follow her, wondering how Rigby could have got Ben through the gap without anybody seeing. Cooper had said it was early when he left home. He could already have been here for hours. If Ben was drugged or tied up, Rigby could have forced him through onto the school grounds without much fuss. Or, if he was dead…Kate shook her head. She wouldn't allow herself to go there.

'Where's the boiler house?' Hollis asked.

Kate pointed to a low brick building with a squat chimney at one corner. 'The door's around the other side.'

'We need to call this in. We can't do this on our own.' He started to dig in his pocket for his phone.

'No,' Kate said. 'If we have a load of cars up here with blues and twos, he might panic and lose control. If Ben's still alive,' she paused, choking back tears, 'If Ben's still alive, then we don't want Rigby scared into doing something stupid. Let's have a look.'

She skirted the side of the building, treading gently on the gravel in the hope that her footsteps wouldn't be audible inside. The door was on the side that faced the main part of the school. It was made of steel with a huge bolt across the middle and a hasp for a padlock about two-thirds of the way up. The padlock lay at her feet, the shank cut in half, and the bolt was undone. She pointed them out to Hollis before pressing one ear to the door to see if she could hear anything inside. Nothing.

Hand trembling, she pushed the door open an inch. The room beyond was in darkness. Kate stepped inside, wincing as her shoes crunched on broken glass. If Rigby was in here, he knew she was coming.

'Rigby. It's Kate Fletcher. I know you're in there.'

'So, come in, then,' a voice said. 'Let's see you.'

She pushed the door again and stepped inside leaving it open to allow as much light as possible to illuminate the interior. The inside of the boiler house was a single low room with benches along one side and a huge iron construction at one end Kate assumed was the boiler. Long disused, it was rusting, and the pipe that led up to the chimney had come loose from the wall and hung at an awkward angle. Two windows had been boarded up, the small gaps around the sides of the wood allowing tiny cracks of light through.

'Where's Ben?' she asked.

Rigby reached down and dragged a body from under the bench. 'Here he is. Nice lad. Shame I've had to knock him about a bit.'

Kate studied her son in the light from the open door. His hands were secured behind his back, and his head hung down on his chest. Rigby was holding him half upright by his collar, and from his limp posture, it was clear he couldn't stand. His eyes were closed, and his dark fringe was matted above one eye. That side of his face was black with dried blood. Kate couldn't tell if he was alive.

'Invite the other one in,' Rigby said.

Kate looked at him, making her expression blank.

'You wouldn't come here on your own, and anyway, I watched you come through the fence.' He suddenly grabbed a knife and held it next to Ben's neck. 'Get him in here. Now!'

Hollis had obviously been listening as he stepped into the rectangle of light, his shadow momentarily obscuring Kate's view of her son. The knife told her one thing. Ben was alive. Rigby was using him like a bargaining chip, and he couldn't do that if he'd already killed him. As if in response to Kate's thoughts, Ben moaned and moved his head, but he was too weak to do much more than try hopelessly to drag his feet underneath him in a pathetic attempt to stand up.

Rigby shifted position, grabbing Ben with one arm from behind, keeping the knife at his neck and his eyes on Kate. 'Phone,' he barked. 'On the floor. You too, pretty boy.'

Hollis took his phone out of his pocket and placed it carefully in front of Rigby. Kate copied his movements.

'Right. How long have we got?'

'What?'

'Before the cavalry arrive. You have called for back-up?'

Hollis looked at his watch. 'They'll be here any minute.'

'Doubt it,' Rigby said. He nodded to an object hidden in the gloom on the bench. 'You don't think I'd leave home without my radio. There's been no traffic in the last twenty minutes. Well, nothing of interest. Nobody knows you're here. I was just seeing if you'd lie. That makes life a bit easier for me. Plenty of time, then.'

He grinned at them both, as though he was welcoming them to a party, and hoisted Ben higher so he could get a better grip on his neck.

'Let him go,' Kate said. 'Whatever your problem is, it's not with him, it's with me. Let Ben go.'

'Ooh, didn't have you down as the maternal type,' Rigby mocked. 'But no. Not yet. I want him to hear what a bitch his mother really is, and why he's had to suffer.'

'I've never done anything to you, Drew. I don't even remember you. Or is your ego so fragile that this is about me turning you down the other night?'

Rigby laughed. 'You. Pretty boy. On the floor, over there.' He pointed with his knife to where he wanted Hollis to sit, away from the door against the brick wall. Hollis stood his ground.

'Now!' Rigby yelled, jabbing the knife into Ben's neck.

Hollis took two steps and sat.

'Better. Easier to keep an eye on you.' He relaxed his knife hand, and Ben slumped against his chest.

'Okay, Detective Inspector *Kathy* Fletcher. Let me tell you a little story.' He shifted position until he was resting against the bench, using it to support his own weight and that of her unconscious son.

'You remember the strike, right? When the miners downed tools and the government crucified them for it? Well, some people couldn't afford not to work, some people didn't get any money from the miners' relief funds, and so, they got bussed to other parts of the country where people didn't know them. When the strikers found out, they called them scabs and chased them out of their homes. Sound familiar? My dad *had* to go back to work. My mum was in pieces after our Tracy died, and she'd been seeing an expensive psychiatrist. We even had a car so Dad could drive her to her appointments. She could barely go out of the house without him.'

Kate shrugged, unsure of where he was going.

'Some people were in a different union, like your daddy, and they kept working. They didn't suffer at all. Some people tried to say that they were scabs, but they didn't care. They were all right. Only it didn't seem very fair, did it? So, I tried to even the score a bit. Do you remember the notes, Kathy? The ones telling you to die. That was me, sweetheart. I didn't want people to find out about my dad, so I diverted attention on to you.'

'So?' Kate said. 'That was years ago.'

'Long memory, me,' Rigby said with a grin. 'Little Kathy couldn't keep quiet about it, though. Had to go to the teachers and tell tales. Only she didn't know who wrote the notes, and the wrong lad got expelled.'

'Rob Loach.'

'The one and only. When Rob found out that it was me, and I'd let him get kicked out for it, he got some of his mates to lock me in here for a day. And Pisspants was born. They made my life hell for those last two months, the names, the punches. If my mum hadn't got married again and moved us away, I think I'd have probably ended up like my dad. It was torture. Just like the torture you're feeling now, because you don't know what I'm going to do to little Benjy.'

'So,' Kate said, trying to stall him. 'Aleah's aunties bullied your sister into getting stuck in the tunnel, so you killed their niece.

That's a bit of a tenuous link; they're not even blood relatives. Not the greatest plan. Why not go after *their* kids?'

Rigby laughed. 'I thought about that. Carla lives abroad, and Joanne doesn't have kids. Then, I found out who Aleah's grandad was. It was perfect. He was another one of the bastards who killed my dad. Jumped him twice and got others to have a go as well.'

'And Callum Goodwin's grandfather refused to help your dad when he was on strike?'

'That Goodwin bastard told him if he could afford to run a car, he wasn't getting a penny from the union.'

'Which forced him back to work, only he couldn't live with the shame. Jesus, this is really fucked up.' She laughed. 'Who's next? The children of those kids who laughed at you for crying in class when you told them the story about your sister? There were plenty of them, weren't there, *Andy*?'

Rigby scowled at her. 'You don't know what you're talking about.'

Kate saw her son's mouth twitch. He was aware of what was going on. He was awake, and he was trying to stand up. His feet were firmly on the floor, and she could see the strain in his face as he tried to ease himself upright. She needed to get Rigby to focus on her, to goad him into making a move and letting her son go.

'Don't I?' she said. 'Poor little Andy, telling his sad story, and all the boys laughed at him. I know all about it. Karen remembers you, and what a little wimp you were. Jesus, there's no wonder your dad killed himself, having a little spineless little shit like you for a son. And you're no better now, are you. Killing kids. Must take guts that.'

'You fucking bitch!' Rigby dropped Ben and lunged at her.

'Get Ben!' she yelled at Hollis, who leapt up and grabbed the boy by the collar of his T-shirt. He stumbled through the door, virtually dragging Ben after him. Kate turned to check they'd got out and felt the knife slice through the forearm she'd thrown up to defend herself.

'Shit!' she hissed, grabbing the wound with her other hand. Rigby was staring at her like a trapped animal. She was between him and the door, but she needed to stall him to give Hollis time to get Ben away and call for help.

'You know you're done, don't you, Drew? You can't walk away from this mess.'

His eyes darkened. 'I don't care. I never expected to walk away. I just wanted it done. I wanted other people to suffer like I did. I never meant to kill Aleah. I was just going to keep her for a bit, to torment the family. But she struggled, and I had to get rid of her. And then, you turned up. Kathy Siddons. It was like an omen. You even told me all about your son. I knew I had to keep on, to get revenge on the lot of you. After I killed Aleah, then the other one was easy. I'd have done your boy as well. Made you watch.'

'So now what? Slit your own throat. Take the coward's way out, like your dad?'

She was taunting him, hoping he'd lose control again and make a mistake, something she could use to get herself out of this mess.

'Don't talk about him. You're not fit to even mention his name.'

'What about you? You didn't keep his name. Who was Rigby? A stepdad? Or just a random name so that you could hide who you are?'

He shook his head and actually grinned at her. 'You're a fine one to talk. What's with Kate? I'm not the only one who wanted a fresh start and a new name, am I? You stuck-up cow. So much better than the rest of us. Detective fucking Inspector Fletcher. Who did you have to sleep with to get that job?'

'Not you. And for that, I'm eternally grateful. Give it up, Drew. Drop the knife and let's get out of here.'

'Shut up, bitch!' His eyes fixed on hers, and she could see he was considering his options. *There is no way out*, Kate thought, *he must be able to see that*. He could kill her, but he'd be caught, or he could kill himself, but all he had was a knife.

'I need you to get out of the way. I've got somewhere I can go.'

'No. Put the knife down.'

The radio crackled into life. Hollis must have found somebody to ring for help. The dispatcher gave their location and a summary of the situation. Rigby grinned when he heard himself described as "armed and dangerous."

'Hear that?' Kate asked. 'They're coming for you. Give me the knife and make it easy on yourself.'

Rigby shook his head. 'I told you to get out of my way!' he yelled.

'No. You'll have to go *through* me.'

He stared at her, his face contorted with fury. 'Right. Have it your own way, you bitch!'

He lunged forward trying to shock her into moving, but Kate stood her ground, still blocking his exit. She didn't feel the knife at first; she thought he'd just hit her in the side. Then, she saw the blood. As though the red somehow triggered her pain receptors, a stab of hot agony pierced her abdomen, and she doubled over, grasping at the wound with both hands. Rigby pushed past her, out into the sunlight. He was getting away, and there was absolutely nothing she could do about it.

The cool brick wall was somehow comforting as she allowed herself to slide down into the darkness. She could hear noises from outside, but they seemed far away as though she was underwater. Voices. Shouting. Somebody yelling her name.

She shifted to her uninjured side and started to drag herself through the door. It took all the strength she had to just get her head outside so that she could see what was going on. Two figures were locked together on the gravel in front of the boiler house. One was clearly Rigby, and he was in pain. The other, sitting on Rigby's back, pinning him face down, was Garry. For a second, Kate thought she might be hallucinating until her ex-husband turned to her.

'Are you okay?'

Kate shook her head and raised a bloody hand.

'Shit, Kate. What do I do?'

'Hold him there until somebody with some handcuffs arrives. Then, ambulance for me. Is Ben...?'

He's fine,' Garry said, tightening his grip on Rigby's upper arms. 'I could kill this bastard.'

'No. Police. They're on the radio.' She knew she wasn't making sense. She just hoped Garry understood.

The last thing she heard before she closed her eyes was sirens coming closer.

EPILOGUE

It was a terrible day for a funeral; muggy and grey with the ever-present threat of a thunder storm. The mourners gathered around the grave were wilting in their sombre black, and the minister was breathing heavily as he said a final prayer.

Kate scanned the faces that were peering into the small hole in the ground. Family, friends, and a few representatives from the police force. Tatton was standing discreetly behind Jackie Reese, and Hollis was somewhere on the periphery. She had no way to understand the pain these parents were feeling. Her son was fine. He'd recovered quickly and was looking forward to a holiday in France with his father before the new term at university. She had thought she *might* lose him, but, in her heart, she'd never believed he was gone. Even when she'd seen him limp and lifeless in Rigby's grip, she hadn't truly believed he was dead.

She shifted her weight to her other leg and winced as her stitches caught on the dressing under her blouse. Still a few days before she could have them removed. She'd been told she'd been lucky; another inch either way and the knife would have completely penetrated one of her major organs. A slight nick to her colon was nothing much to worry about.

Movement in the main group caught her eye. Jackie and Craig were throwing soil into the grave. Dave Porter stepped forward and took a handful of earth. He stood on the edge of the grave, hesitated, and then mumbled something Kate didn't hear. Jackie turned and smiled sadly at him as he threw the soil in a damp clump. His mother grasped his hand and pulled him back into the crowd. As she stepped back, she looked up and caught Kate's eye.

'Thank you,' she mouthed, with a nod.

Kate nodded back, then she turned and walked towards her car. Overhead, thunder cracked, and the first spots of rain fell on the grey cement driveway of the cemetery, turning it black as they seeped into the dry surface. The summer was ending with another downpour.

ACKNOWLEDGEMENTS

I'd like to thank the team at Bloodhound Books for continuing to have faith in my writing and especially Betsy for her patience with me during the cover design process. I'd also like to thank the other Bloodhound authors for encouragement, sound advice and quite a few much-needed laughs.

I'm grateful to Clare Law, my editor, for her helpful suggestions and for her patience with my terrible habit of comma splicing. I'm an English teacher so I should know better.

My brother Graeme was a big help in confirming or correcting some of my memories of "Thorpe." It's strange to write about a place I know so well and still find that some of the things I remember are actually not quite accurate.

I'd also like to say a big thank you to everybody who has bought, read or reviewed either of my previous novels. The support is much appreciated.

And finally, as always, thanks to Viv.

Printed in Great Britain
by Amazon